No Place for Peace

Pillars of Peace: Book II

By Tom Dumbrell

ISBN: 9798497880595

"The battleline between good and evil runs through the heart of every man."

—Aleksandr Solzhenitsyn

Characters of the Quadripartite

Easthaven

Prince Cyrus – A daydreaming storyteller who grew up in the farming communities of the Low Country with his adoptive sister Francine. Cyrus saved Francine as a child when their village was attacked, and they grew up with their adoptive father, Osbert, and his son, Edgar, in Corhollow. Prince Cyrus later learned that he was the twin brother of King Augustus and the son of the late King Anselm and his dowager queen, Adaline. When his brother was presumed dead, Cyrus stepped in to impersonate the young king at the behest of Thaddeus and Garrett.

Wendell – Easthaven's own Master of Coin. Wendell is a traitor, hidden in plain view among the royal family in Eldred's Keep. Wendell conspired with the Verderans to assassinate King Anselm and is set to deliver the king's son, Augustus, a similar fate.

Francine – The adoptive sister of Prince Cyrus, Fran also grew up in the Low Country before her parents were killed and Cyrus saw her to safety. Fran is wise beyond her years, strong-willed, and a vital source of support to her brother, Cyrus.

King Augustus – The newly crowned king of Easthaven. Augustus is a hot-headed young man who is the son of the late King Anselm and dowager queen Adaline. He is Prince Cyrus's twin brother.

Marcia – A young maid in Eldred's Keep. Marcia caught Cyrus's attention during the prince's time in the city, at which time Cyrus was impersonating Augustus. Even though Cyrus deceived Marcia about his true identity for a time, their bond developed through a mutual love of storytelling.

Adaline – The dowager queen. Adaline was married to King Anselm for many years. Together, they had their children, Augustus and Cyrus, though Cyrus did not grow up in the castle with them. Part of the treaty with King Simeon's kingdom said that any second-born son of Easthaven must be ceded to Auldhaven (and vice versa), so Adaline and Anselm secreted Cyrus away to the Low Country rather than hand him over to Simeon.

Thaddeus – An ally for the ages. Thaddeus is a wise old man who mentors King Augustus as he did for the king's father, Anselm, before him. Thaddeus can always be relied upon for sage words of logic and advice. He and Garrett also mentored Cyrus when he was standing in for Augustus to help him fill his twin brother's shoes.

Broderick – The man charged with coordinating the armies of Easthaven. General Broderick has a booming voice and a short temper. His plate armour clinks with every step, and a vein on his forehead pulses when his hackles are up.

Cornelius – The Master of Prayer. Residing in Easthaven's basilica, Cornelius is an old, bearded man whose face is often pressed to the pages of religious text.

Seth – Chosen shield to King Augustus. Responsible for the king's wellbeing, Seth previously helped free Prince Cyrus when he was captured by Simeon's men and was central in reuniting Cyrus with his adoptive sister Francine.

⚜ ⚜ ⚜

Auldhaven

King Simeon – King of Auldhaven. Simeon recently returned to his home country after an unsuccessful attempt to invade Easthaven. Simeon received a stab wound to his leg from Prince Cyrus after conspiring with Cyrus's own brother, Augustus, to see the prince killed. The king is known for his cunning. Cyrus made a pact with Simeon to give himself up to Auldhaven after he saw things settled in his own country.

General Lambert – A general and a sycophant. Lambert exists to serve and protect his king, Simeon. He and Cyrus (disguised as Augustus) took an instant dislike to each other.

Cornesse

Queen Mathilde – The warrior queen. Mathilde is fearsome with a blade and clever. Her army's intervention helped spare Easthaven from defeat and inevitable invasion during the recent conflict with King Simeon. She had a brief notion of pursuing a romantic relationship with Cyrus, who did not have those sorts of feelings for the queen. Augustus, however, was keen on the fearless Cornessian.

Lucien – A giant of a man. Lucien is tasked with ensuring Queen Mathilde's safety. He and Cyrus once went sword-to-sword in a contest meant to prove Cyrus's worth to Mathilde. While Lucien is definitely the more impressive warrior, Cyrus was able to use his cunning to win the challenge, and Mathilde pledged her troops to Cyrus, which was a key point in their joint defeat of Simeon.

Verdera

King Ferdinand – The old king of Verdera. King Ferdinand was responsible for signing the Treaty of Eriwald with King Anselm, King Simeon, and Queen Mathilde's father, Maxim, eight years ago. King Ferdinand is said to be extremely unwell and was not available to see Prince Cyrus during his recent visit to the Verderan capital, Casarossa. Instead, Cyrus met with his sons, the Verderan princes Rafael and Alonso.

Prince Rafael & Prince Alonso – The twin sons of King Ferdinand. In their father's absence, Rafael and Alonso played host to Prince Cyrus during his visit to Casarossa. The young men have tempers that are dwarfed only by their ambitions. They are known to have conspired with Wendell to assassinate King Anselm, and they have threatened to bring an army to Easthaven's shores in order to see King Augustus from his throne

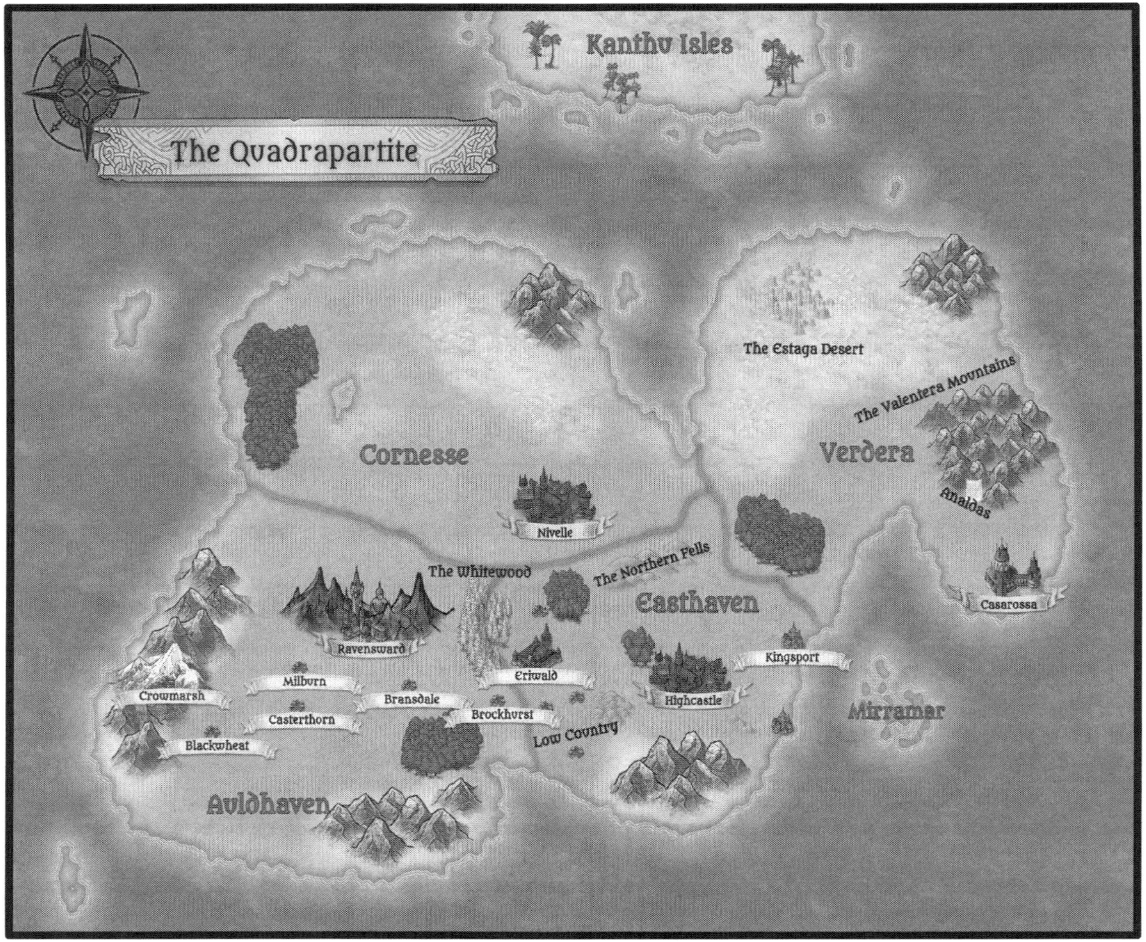
The Quadrapartite
Kanthv Isles
The Estaga Desert
The Valentera Mountains
Cornesse
Verdera
Analdas
Nivelle
The Northern Fells
The Whitewood
Easthaven
Casarossa
Ravenswurd
Kingsport
Eriwald
Milburn
Crowmarsh
Bransdale
Highcastle
Brockhurst
Casterthorn
Mirramar
Low Country
Blackwheat
Auldhaven

For Breana…

Behind every ~~great~~ good man, is a woman waiting to correct him.

Dearest Marcia,

I'm writing to you from Eriwald. I'm sorry I have not written sooner, but it has been a busy time. It's wonderful to see the people return to their homes after Simeon's occupation, but the city is bigger than you could possibly imagine and in need of some leadership. There were several who courted the position of Magistrate, but there was only ever one candidate in my mind. You might remember Merrill from his visit to Eldred's Keep a couple of months ago? He's the warden of Ironwell who travelled to the capital to plead for food and aid on behalf of his people. I can't say I am always the best judge of character, but Merrill is honest and loyal, and I think that makes him more qualified than most.

Despite keeping busy, I still spend a lot of time wondering when this will start feeling real. As a child, I dreamt of a life lived amongst kings and queens, but this feels closer to a nightmare. A large part of me wishes things would go back to the way they were before. It wasn't so long ago that I was just a normal boy, living a normal life in a normal village with my normal family, and well, I'm sure you get the picture…

I'm not sure I have enough parchment to record all of my regrets, and the truth is that it wouldn't change anything anyway. Garrett always told me to embrace my fate and make the best of the situation. I miss his company every day, but I still hear his voice, and I know that I will be a better man for it.

I need you to know that I never meant to mislead you and that our time together was perhaps the only time I felt like myself: Cyrus. Not a king, or even a prince, but an awkward boy from the Low Country who fell for a beautiful girl and would do anything to try and make things right. This letter is the last that I will write before leaving for Simeon's castle in Ravensward, and it may be the last that you will hear from me. But you know how the stories go, so I'm still hoping against hope that the boy might get the girl in the end.

I don't know if you will be able to forgive me for concealing my true identity from you, but the thought gives me hope and much needed comfort for whatever lies ahead. I have written to my mother and to Fran as well, and I would only ask that you continue to care for them as you did for me. Perhaps one day, we will all look back and laugh about this crazy situation. Maybe I'll even bring you to Eriwald and show you this magnificent city or sail you to the port of Casarossa, where colourful birds would greet us from the branches of exotic trees while the sun glistened on the water. I know Mathilde would gladly welcome us in Nivelle, and we could spend our days drinking wine and…there goes my imagination again.

Stay well, Marcia, and know that I will be thinking of you, wherever I go.

Cyrus

Cyrus folded the page carefully before stamping it closed with the royal seal, red wax cooling to form the shape of a blazing sun. This was the last of the letters he had needed to write before he set out on his onward journey, and he slumped in his chair as a wave of despair washed over him. Two weeks had passed since his departure from Eldred's Keep, and though the thought had crossed his mind many times before, he found himself wondering once again if he was doing the right thing. After a lifetime of running, he had finally defeated Simeon. Fran was safe within the castle walls, and he held position—that of a prince, of all things! Truth be told, Simeon had shown little honour when they had last met, but as Thaddeus's wisdom rang in his ears, Cyrus knew that his actions alone would determine his worth. He let his head drop with the realisation that he had to go to Ravensward as he had promised Simeon that he would. The same thought process, as always, a never-ending circle in his mind. The same outcome, as always.

His eyes lifted as he slid the parchment across the rich wooden desk to join the other letters, waiting only to be sent on to Highcastle. His attention was drawn to the window that looked out from his chambers onto the vastness of the city. Daylight beamed into the room, accentuating an ornate fireplace and a sturdy bedframe that stood draped with a colourful array of shimmering fabrics.

"Your horse stands ready in the courtyard, your grace," came a voice, and Cyrus smiled as Merrill marched into the room, drawing to an awkward halt as the sombre nature of the situation seemed to catch up with him.

"Are you sure you must go?" he asked after a brief pause, his voice tinged with sadness. "I don't mean to seem ungrateful, but are you sure there wasn't a better candidate for the position of Magistrate? I only hope that I can repay your faith in me, your grace."

Cyrus sat up in his chair as Merrill removed his tricorn hat and fumbled with it, the man's eyes now fixed on the floor. His demeanour reminded Cyrus, as it had during their very first meeting in Eldred's Keep, of his adoptive father, Osbert. At this thought, Cyrus breathed with deep satisfaction at his choice to appoint Merrill as Magistrate of Eriwald.

"I'm sure, Merrill. You were the very best of the bunch," he said in reassurance, his own concerns momentarily pushed to one side. "I remember that day you visited me in Highcastle. I must have seen a hundred people that day, yet you were the only man who stood before me in the interest of others, not your own. Your actions provided food for your townsfolk and those in other towns and villages throughout the Low Country. I only ask that you steward these people in the same way. I don't know that anyone is ever ready for this type of thing, but surround yourself with good people and learn from your mistakes, and I think you'll be just fine. If things ever get too out of hand, remember that we have good friends in Nivelle. Queen Mathilde is no stranger to my family's complicated history, and she will always be a friend of Easthaven."

"But your safety, my lord," came Merrill's response, head raised, his hat now gripped tightly at his side. "I should come with you to Simeon's kingdom, to Ravensward. I'm not much use with a sword, but I would gladly give my life to protect you."

"A kind offer, well received," said Cyrus with affection, still slightly awed that he had inspired such loyalty from someone. "But this is something that I must do alone. Too many lives have already been lost." He rose from the chair and crossed the room to place a consoling hand on Merrill's shoulder. "Besides," he continued, "you're not a lot of good to the people of Eriwald in Simeon's dungeons, are you? No, I need you here. I need someone that I can trust."

Merrill's concern broke, and he bowed his head in appreciation as Cyrus patted him on the back.

"Could you please see that those letters are dispatched for the capital?" Cyrus finished, gesturing back toward the desk. "Now, where is that horse of mine, before I change my mind?"

"Oh, there's no changing your mind when it's set on something," said Merrill, shaking his head as he made for the exit.

Though Cyrus began to follow, the magistrate's voice grew distant as Cyrus turned back for one last look at his chambers. The room was more than he could have ever dreamt of in his life before, yet it was modest when compared with the opulence of the palace in Casarossa or the grandeur of Eldred's Keep. A smile reappeared on his face as he recalled his previous adventures, but like his time in Eriwald, the moment was fleeting, and a sickening sense of inevitability descended upon him once more as he motioned a silent goodbye to yet another place he had briefly called home.

⚜ ⚜ ⚜

There had been a period of fine weather in the Low Country, and the bright white stones of the courtyard dazzled Cyrus as he emerged from the castle, causing him to shield his eyes.

"Merrill!" he called, opening his eyes with some hesitation as spots of lights danced before him. Yet when his vision cleared, he found that he was alone.

"Caspar!" he added in a similarly unsuccessful attempt to summon his stable hand. "Anyone?" he uttered weakly, but the only response was a faint echo of his voice reverberating against the courtyard's surrounding walls. It was a moment of perfect quiet, and Cyrus closed his eyes once more as a gentle breeze rustled the branches of a nearby cherry blossom, its sweet scent hanging in the air with familiarity that transported him back to his first time in the city and his meeting with Simeon in the shadow of the Pillars of Peace. Cyrus wondered briefly now how things might have played out differently. Sure, they'd been able to save many of Eriwald's citizens as a result of that meeting, but what if he had been able to find the words to prevent Simeon from waging war? Could he have done more to negotiate peace, and if so, would Garrett still be alive?

"Your father was a great man," sounded a voice from behind him, and while Cyrus was startled, there was no need to turn. He knew the voice belonged to Garrett. It was as though Cyrus's thoughts had summoned the man to him.

"He had a vision," Cyrus responded eventually, eyes drawn toward the four colourful pillars and the cherry blossom within. He pondered what the pillars represented, what Anselm had intended.

"I won't return until it has been realised. I'm ready to accept my fate, just like you told me I should."

"When was it that I told you this?" came Garrett's response.

Cyrus smiled at the older man's forgetful nature. "You remember," he said, trying to jog Garrett's memory. "On the beaches of Mirramar, just after you'd told me your life story." He laughed to himself briefly and turned to catch the reaction on Garrett's face, but it was his own expression that dropped.

"Mirramar?" said Merrill, his face now scrunched in confusion. "I've never even been in a boat. Are you okay, my lord? It's a very hot day. Perhaps you need some water?"

Cyrus rubbed at his eyes, though he knew it had been a trick of the mind. It wasn't the first time this had happened, he reflected with his stomach dropping. "Yes, sorry, water would be good. Excuse my babbling, just a hot day as you say, and—"

"This bloody horse!" shouted Caspar, interrupting the awkward moment and dragging Cyrus's mare into the courtyard. "The slowest, laziest beast I have ever known, but the minute you put her saddle on, the very suggestion of some actual work, and she's off like her life depends on it. If she weren't Prince Cyrus's horse, I'd have her turned into meat and sold to the Cornessians!"

It was Caspar's turn to halt suddenly as he noticed Cyrus, eyebrows raised, staring back at him. "I'm so sorry, my lord," he continued with a nervous tremble that Cyrus indulged out of amusement. "I have never known a horse with so much, er, character. I only took my eyes from her for one moment, and she bolted down the main thoroughfare!"

He paused to scratch at the roots of his sweat-drenched brown hair. "It wouldn't be so much of a problem, but it's market day, as you know, and the traders from Nivelle are demanding compensation for damages." He grimaced, as though awaiting some horrible sentence to befall him.

But Cyrus could contain himself no longer. "Well, there you go then, Merrill," he said between bouts of laughter. "Your first official task as Magistrate. I did tell you that it wouldn't all be glamour!"

He stepped forward to take the reins from Caspar, scratching his horse's nose before reaching to straighten the saddlebag upon her back. "The *beast* has a name, as you well know," he added, glancing sidelong at Caspar.

Caspar dropped to his knee at Cyrus's signal, and the prince put his foot into the stirrups. "Her name is Adagio," Cyrus said, throwing his leg over his mare, "and it seems that she will never fail to put a smile on my face."

"Be safe, my lord," said Merrill, and though his expression conveyed a smile, sad eyes belied worry that was all too familiar to Cyrus, for he felt it in himself.

"Same to you," he replied, shoulders back and chin raised in an attempt at confidence. He wondered if he should have added something more insightful or inspiring, but that was always Garrett's thing, or perhaps even Thaddeus's. In the end, Cyrus only managed an approving nod in Merrill's direction before Adagio's impatience had them hurtling through the city, away from the new Magistrate and toward…whatever would be next. Cyrus swallowed hard and then set his face, chastising himself for his own trepidation.

It was only a short ride to the city gates, but a blur of faces lined the streets as the wind whipped through Cyrus's blonde hair. Adagio never slowed as they burst out across the stone bridge and into the open countryside, and Cyrus never looked back. The thought occurred to him that he was finally free, but as always, he wondered just how long that freedom would last.

"Urgh," grumbled Cyrus, and though his voice carried on the breeze, he was somewhat relieved that no one was there to see him. One foot stuck in the mud, the other dangling helplessly over a submerged boot—this was not how he had envisaged the beginning of his supposedly heroic journey.

It had only been a day since his departure from Eriwald, and things had at least started out well. The sun had been high in the sky as Adagio broke out onto the meadowlands west of the Eriwald, a sea of green turned yellow by the sun. And it had seemed as though Cyrus could hear the crunch of every blade of grass underfoot as they continued toward the border.

In many ways, it was a feeling of great relief, a feeling of inevitability and of freedom. Cyrus had imagined all of the possible outcomes and had come to accept them. Put simply, his fate as he saw it was to be either life imprisonment or death, a decision which rested solely with King Simeon, a man not known for his mercy or aptitude for forgiveness. In either case, though, Cyrus's decision to follow through with his word to Simeon would mean safety for those back in the castle, for his mother, his sister, and all those who had helped him thus far. Better people had already made similar sacrifices, and what made Cyrus any different? It was a small gesture all told, but as Cyrus recalled the fabled heroes of old, he reflected that sacrifice seemed to be far easier in the telling than in the doing.

There must be another way, he thought for what felt like the thousandth time. His stomach turned with the grim reality of his situation. If there was one, he still hadn't discovered it.

It was Cyrus's first time travelling this far west, and after seeking advice from those in the castle, he had decided to take the most direct route: a day's ride across a gentle prairie before tackling the veritable no-man's-land that was the Marshes of Carrowmore. Though the wetland stretched only a handful of miles, the marshes would have been impassable during winter, but traders had suggested that the recent drought would make conditions suitable for passage. It was a stretch to call it a foolproof plan, but it was preferable in Cyrus's mind to a detour into the Whitewood, a woodland famed for its white-barked trees and feared for its maze-like composition. The Whitewood was perhaps best known for contributing much of the border between Auldhaven and Easthaven and was rumoured to be something of a lawless frontier that ensured perilous transit for even the boldest traders. It was, in the end, a fairly straightforward decision for Cyrus. The marshland was both shorter and safer, but Cyrus had already come to realise that things so rarely go to plan. His bootless foot was testament to that.

"Steady, girl," he muttered to Adagio, while inwardly cursing himself. It had seemed a smart choice at the time to dismount. Adagio was not built for speed, but Cyrus hoped her broad frame would provide all the balance he needed to overcome the bogginess of the marshes. So, they had walked together, and it had worked for a time. It was a slow, careful trudge, but they had been making fine progress until an unfortunate misstep left Cyrus's boot stuck in the mud.

He took her reins in his left hand and lowered his foot back toward the boot cautiously, hoping that she would remain still. Despite the sea of sludge around them, Adagio stood nonchalantly upon an island of dry earth. She was no match for Allegro, of course—who was back in Highcastle with Cyrus's twin brother, King Augustus—but it was this very fact that made Cyrus appreciate her all the more. In many ways, Cyrus and Adagio were alike, reluctant adventurers cast into an unwanted journey with an uncertain outcome. He couldn't have hoped for better company, all things considered, and as his foot sank back into his sodden boot, he claimed a small victory for their combined efforts, wriggling free to join Adagio upon dry land.

On reflection, he thought, the Whitewood might have been the smarter choice after all. While conditions had indeed been dry in the marshes, Cyrus had failed to consider the impact that ten thousand pairs of boots can have on such a delicate landscape. Evidence of Simeon's retreat was all around them. Pieces of discarded armour sat glistening in the sun, while birds devoured scraps of food and rats swarmed upon the bodies of those left behind. They no longer travelled in mud but through a relentless bog that seemed capable of swallowing Simeon's army whole. Every step felt like a mile, and Cyrus had forsaken his saddle to alleviate the burden on his increasingly disillusioned mount.

"Argh!" he yelled in frustration, swatting away yet another fly as it landed on his forearm. Was there no end to their appetite, to their persistence? An insatiable swarm seemed to follow them without reprieve, and Cyrus found he was starting to enjoy the journey even less than the idea of his destination. Adagio grunted her own frustration as she tried to shake the flies' attention away, and Cyrus waved his arms wildly to help her cause. They were a team, after all.

"Come on, girl," he added, gently tugging at her reins.

It had been slow-going, but dry land was in sight, and it occurred to Cyrus that, for all her shortcomings, Adagio had an uncanny knack of finding the right path. Patches of green were beginning to reappear among the quagmire, and Cyrus put his faith in his companion as she slowly but surely led the way.

⚜ ⚜ ⚜

A setting sun told Cyrus it had taken nearly a day to cross the marshes, and he exhaled a thankful breath of relief as his mud-drenched boot embraced dry land once more.

"We made it, old girl," he said, patting Adagio's muzzle as they dragged themselves toward the sanctuary of the dirt road ahead. He imagined what they must have looked like and realised that he was talking to a horse more than any sane person would, but she was all the company he'd had since leaving Eriwald. They had made it, though, and it was only a short stretch now to

Brockhurst, the border town that would signify the beginning of the end on his journey toward Simeon.

Though relieved by the sight of the road, Cyrus immediately noticed how quiet his surroundings had become. He could hear his every step, his every breath, and the eerie atmosphere made him feel nostalgic for the buzzing cacophony that had accompanied them across the wetlands. The dirt path they were on now was untamed at first, but as it wound ever westward, trees began to line the road, and Cyrus became more uncomfortable still with the silence. Adagio's eyes seemed to shift suspiciously, worried-sounding huffs coming from her nose, and a constant suggestion of movement in the thicket hinted that they were not alone.

Then suddenly, voices sounded from the direction in which Cyrus was heading.

"Come now, Farley, you know how this works!"

Cyrus could hear the distant sound of water, and a large stone bridge came into view as he rounded the corner. Two men in armour with green trim—Simeon's men, he suspected, though their backs were turned to him—stood with another man before them. Cyrus presumed this man, who was facing him and therefore the first to register Cyrus's presence, must be Farley.

"We don't need your sort this side of the bridge," continued one of the soldiers to Farley with more than a hint of contempt in his voice, "and we certainly cannot allow you to hunt on our lands. Hand them over!"

Cyrus edged ever closer and noticed that Farley was holding two lifeless rabbits in his hands. He seemed to be around Cyrus's age, but Farley was much larger in build, a full head taller and with dark hair in a mushroom cut. His dirty white tunic barely covered his upper body, while his too-short trousers seemed to have been fashioned from a canvas sack, kept in place by a length of old rope.

"You can't do this," said Farley, and the corners of Cyrus's lips quirked at the familiarity of the man's Low Country accent. When the soldiers raised their blades and moved forward menacingly, however, Cyrus's smile slid off of his face.

"We won't ask you again," said the other soldier, and Cyrus was seized by a feeling that he hadn't truly experienced since the attack on Simeon's tent: the need to act.

"Come on, fat boy, it's not as though you'll waste away!" said the first soldier with a laugh.

Farley's face reddened as he backed away, yelling, "No!" His eyes widened, and Cyrus was transported back to Coldwynne and the final expressions on Fran's parents' faces before their lives were snuffed out by their attackers. He couldn't let that happen again, not even to a stranger, but as Cyrus made to speak, Farley disappeared from sight, a loud thud sounded, and cruel laughter suddenly filled the air.

"Stop!" Cyrus shouted instinctively.

As the two soldiers turned, they parted to show Farley in a heap on the floor.

"That's enough!" Cyrus shouted, feeling cold with dread at Farley's form. His voice didn't come off as heroic as he had hoped, but it certainly caused a distraction, and to his relief, Farley sat up to show that it had been little more than an awkward fall that had taken him down.

"Leave him alone?" asked the more vocal of the two soldiers, a stringy man with a patchy beard and shoulder-length brown hair. "Well, since you asked so nicely!" He bowed in mockery before lifting his head to reveal a sadistic smile. "We don't take orders here, boy. We make them. Why don't you take that horse of yours and head back the way you came before this really becomes your problem?"

Cyrus took a backward step as the shorter of the two men began in his direction, sword raised while his free hand shifted greasy blonde hair from his eyes. "You want me to cut him, Colton?" asked Cyrus's aggressor, creeping forward with his teeth bared.

"No, no, no," said the other soldier, Colton, in mock disapproval. "Always so keen to cut things, Flynn. We are men of peace, remember?" He turned back to Farley, nudging him with a boot. "I'm sure he gets the picture."

"I've asked you to stop," said Cyrus, halting to stand his ground. He was no more than ten feet from greasy-haired Flynn, and he was struggling to maintain his composure. Farley was on his knees dusting himself down, and Cyrus realised that while he had taken their attention away from Farley, this meant that he himself had become the new focus of Simeon's men's attention.

"Yes, we heard you," answered Colton, breaking the silent tension, "but we don't take orders from mud-covered peasants, especially those from east of the border."

"And I heard you," came Cyrus's instinctive response, "but I wonder if you'd say the same thing to a prince?" His chest puffed slightly, but the response, of course, was laughter.

Cyrus had been expecting that, and it was scarcely different from his visit to Casarossa, where Captain Lorenzo and his men had boarded Roscoe's ship with similar incredulity.

"A prince, you say?" scoffed Colton. "What an excellent development. You'll be showing me your—"

"Royal seal, but of course," interjected Cyrus with confidence that would have made Garrett proud. He felt as though he were once again impersonating Augustus as he had done for so long while the king had been missing. "I'm sure you'll find it all in order," he continued, pulling the parchment from his saddle bag. "Signed and sealed by my brother, King Augustus, only a few weeks ago."

All traces of laughter seemed to seep from the soldiers' faces, and Flynn arrived to snatch the parchment, turning it in his hands as he squinted at the page in an attempt to refute his obvious illiteracy.

"It checks out, Colton," he shouted back to his companion, running his fingers over the king's insignia. "No doubt Simeon will pay handsomely for this prize!"

"Oh, I'm sure he will," said Colton, his eyes narrowed in thought, "but I doubt the young prince is here through coincidence, nor does he seem lost. So, what brings you to my bridge, Prince…?" He raised his eyebrows as his sentence trailed off.

"Cyrus. My name is Cyrus." He could sense that Colton was the more considered of the two. "Your king is expecting me. I gave him my word that I would come."

"An audience with King Simeon?" sneered Flynn, close enough that Cyrus could feel his rancid breath hot upon his face. "Surely you aren't buying this, Colton?"

The light was beginning to fade, but Farley was now on his feet with a mixture of panic and confusion upon his face.

"Run, Prince!" Farley shouted at Cyrus, but Colton raised a hand to silence him.

"Now, let's all calm down, shall we?" Colton began, turning to brush dirt from Farley's shoulder. "The war is over, and we are all friends here."

Flynn lowered his blade as Colton moved to whisper in his ear, his words loud enough that Cyrus could hear. "This is our opportunity, Flynn. Think about it, our ticket to the castle. We should take the prince to Simeon and let the king decide what to do with him." He paused to flash a smile at Cyrus as Flynn considered Colton's wisdom with blank eyes.

"You sure this isn't just a chance to see that old friend of yours?" Flynn asked Colton finally, chewing at the nails on his right hand. His tone carried more than a hint of scepticism, and for the first time, Cyrus sensed a hint of tension between them as he felt his own curiosity pique at Colton's friend in Simeon's castle. "We're border guards, Colton, damn good ones. Let's do what we do best and guard our borders. There's no need to go chasing dreams. Besides, it's getting dark. We'll never make it to Ravensward before nightfall."

"He's right," interjected Farley, his voice shrill and unexpected, causing Colton to startle. "It's too dangerous. You can stay at mine, your Highness. My house is nearby. Somewhere safe to spend the night."

Cyrus didn't know what to think, his brain beginning to feel befuddled by his own tiredness. "We *have* had a long day of travel," he said, turning to Adagio, who stood with quiet impatience. "A hot meal wouldn't hurt either."

"Wouldn't hurt at all," Colton added with a smile. He turned to Flynn, "What do you think? Judd and Wybert will be here to watch the bridge any minute. Seems like good timing if you ask me."

Flynn nodded, and his lips curled. "I've nowhere better to be," he said, and he raised an eyebrow at Cyrus, who wondered if life was ever easy.

He steadied himself. "What do you say, Farley? Perhaps we can share your catch with our friends here? All in the interest of peace."

"Of course, your Highness," said Farley, dropping to one knee. He seemed a gentle—if simple—sort, and Cyrus was pleased to have navigated the situation away from danger, both for his own sake and for Farley's.

"Tell me, where is your house?" he asked in expectation.

"The edges of the Whitewood," answered all three men in unison.

Cyrus's head slumped at their answer. Perhaps they weren't as safe from danger as Cyrus had hoped.

⚜ ⚜ ⚜

Rabbit stew bubbled in a pot as Farley added yet another dash of salt for flavour. Cyrus had survived his journey from Eriwald with what little bread and cheese he held in his saddlebag, and his mouth watered at the prospect of a hot meal. Farley's ramshackle wooden house had a thatched roof full of holes, so their group had elected to build a fire in a nearby clearing where the white bark of the surrounding trees seemed to glisten with a translucent quality that reminded Cyrus of Allegro's gleaming coat.

"Who knew you were such a chef?" said Colton, inhaling deeply, his expectant face lit up by the firelight.

"Look at the size of him," said Flynn with a snort, pointing in Farley's direction. "He's had plenty of practice!"

The corner of Colton's mouth turned up, but Flynn was left to a solitary bout of laughter before clearing his throat to compose himself once more, glancing around the fire to see that no one else had joined in his taunting of Farley.

Adagio whinnied as Cyrus fed her a carrot, and Cyrus took a deep breath before attempting to move the conversation along. "So, who's the old friend?" he asked Colton, curious as to the subject of Flynn's earlier accusation. "The one at Simeon's castle?"

It took Colton a moment to recall the exchange, and he scratched at his straggly beard as he answered, "Just an old acquaintance. We grew up together, trained in the king's guard together. Thought we were going to conquer the world together…" He paused, biting his lip, the group silent but for the spit and crackle of the fire. "But," Colton continued, "it seems he was destined for bigger things, and here I am minding a pointless bridge in the middle of nowhere with only an idiot for company."

Cyrus coughed up some of his ale with unexpected laughter, the joke momentarily quelling his curiosity.

"Hey!" Flynn called, "Don't get at me because things didn't work out for you in the capital!" He snorted deeply before spitting into the fire. "You always get like this after a drink or two, all regretful. It doesn't suit you."

He paused as Farley ladled thick stew into wooden bowls before handing a serving to each of them.

"You think we have it bad?" Flynn continued through loud chewing as he managed to get as much broth on the front of his tunic as in his mouth. "I've heard rumours of rebellion to the west.

You might find that the heroes in the castle won't have it so good when the uprising begins."

"Uprising?" asked Cyrus, but Flynn ignored his question, and Cyrus was left to consider what this might mean for Simeon. What it might mean for him.

The silence among their group was a testament to Farley's cooking. The atmosphere was much improved, but Cyrus could sense their host's unease, his eyes twitching between the two guards as he ate, any small sound causing him to shift uncomfortably on the overturned log where he sat.

"The food is excellent, Farley. Thank you," said Cyrus eventually, in an effort to reignite the conversation.

"Aye," agreed Colton, "and perhaps we were a little harsh on you before, lad." He stepped up from his own perch to pass an empty bowl in Farley's direction. "Good ale, good food…all we're missing is music."

"Pah," spat Flynn, food all over his chin as he licked the bowl clean before dropping it at his feet. "The boy is a simple idiot. We've had what we came for, we've got the prince, so let's kill him now and be done with it."

Farley's eyes widened as Flynn unsheathed his sword and stumbled to his feet, the effects of the ale seeming to take a turn for the worst.

"That's enough," yelled Colton, and Cyrus stepped in front of Farley as Flynn moved to stand toe-to-toe with his countryman.

"Oh, I'm sorry," Flynn continued, feigning politeness with his hand over his heart, "I didn't realise that you held such affection for our enemies." An unexpected hiccup stalled his tirade momentarily, and Colton's hand hovered over his sword, still sheathed. "Maybe

Farley can be the one to suffer all the stories about your time in Ravensward, your efforts to get into the King's Guard, and how you managed to mess it all—"

The pommel of Colton's sword thudded sickeningly as it connected with Flynn's nose, sending drops of blood flying through the air. Flynn's arms fell loose for a moment, and his sword fell to the dirt. He shook his head to restore some semblance of clarity and responded with a punch of his own, the two soldiers wrestling each other to the ground.

"Stop!" called Cyrus, rushing over to the two men. He tried to pull them apart, but their grips were tight, their anger fierce. Farley remained on his stump, and Cyrus saw with a shock that the man's eyes were rolled upward, his body shaking wildly. Cyrus threw his arms into the air, frustrated at his own helplessness and entirely unsure how to help any of them or whom he should even be attempting to help first.

Flynn and Colton had drawn knives, and though Cyrus yelled, "No!" he knew there was no safe way to put himself between the two men. He'd done all he could, and the thought of trying to save them seemed hopeless now. Instead, he turned his attention back to Farley, thinking he might be able to help sort him out. The young man's eyes were now closed, and as Flynn and Colton's fighting continued before him, Farley began to sing, the soul-piercing voice of an angel bursting forth, catching Cyrus off-guard.

"Long, long ago, the sun high in the sky,
Brave old King Isidore led his men to fight.
His enemy, King Edmund, with the sun in his eye,
Never saw them coming and watched his men die.

Freedom for the East, defeat for the West,
An end to the oppression, he laid it to rest.
First king of Easthaven, he stood to the test.
On the open plains of Freyburn, he defeated their best."

Cyrus stood, open-mouthed and frozen in place, hardly noticing that silence had fallen over the whole group, including the two who had been seconds away from killing each other. Cyrus looked to Colton and Flynn, still tangled on the ground, their expressions mirroring his own. The fighting had stopped, and Farley shook his head as though emerging from a trance, shifting his eyes toward the ground as though too embarrassed to meet anyone else's gaze.

"Where did you learn to sing like that?" asked Colton, pushing Flynn down as he climbed to his feet.

"What does it matter?" asked Flynn, propped up on his elbows. "Or are you one of them now?" He gestured accusatorially to Cyrus and Farley, who remained wordless.

"You know, you really are an idiot," said Colton, and he sheathed his knife as he walked back toward the fire. He picked a thick, woollen blanket from a leather sack and huddled into it, pulling the blanket up to his chin. "I think that's enough for one day," he told Flynn before turning to Cyrus. "We'll keep watch on the house overnight. Get some rest. We depart for the capital at first light."

Cyrus threw the last of his ale onto the fire and followed Farley back toward the house, his host seeming to avoid eye contact at all costs. Adagio remained tethered at the fireside, and there was time for Cyrus to give her a final word of reassurance before Flynn's curses grew quieter in his wake. Cyrus wondered vaguely whether both Flynn and Colton would survive the night in each other's presence, but there was little that he could do about it, and he was too tired to think about it for long.

The heavy wooden door screeched open when they arrived at the house. "Home sweet home, your Highness," said Farley, speaking at last as he gestured into the darkness.

Cyrus only smiled before encouraging his host ahead of him.

"We'll have this place well-lit in no time," Farley continued, fumbling around and knocking what sounded like a cooking pot onto the floor. "A house fit for a king…or a prince!" he laughed nervously before an orange light flickered as candlelight filled the room.

"Most kind," said Cyrus, his gratitude interrupted by a yawn, "I'm very grateful for your hospitality, but it has been a long day. We should get some rest."

"Of course, your Highness," agreed Farley, rushing back into the darkness. There was another clatter of pots and pans before he appeared at Cyrus's side once more, startling him with a ring of heavy-looking metal keys that would have been more appropriate in the hands of a jailer. "I've just the place!" he said, his voice falsely cheery, giving Cyrus the impression that Farley wanted him to forget the singing incident altogether.

They walked together through the house, the weak candlelight providing Cyrus with an occasional glimpse at his surroundings. Bookshelves lined the hallway with ancient-looking tomes, leatherbound and covered in cobwebs, as well as glass jars containing who-knew-what. The wooden floorboards creaked underfoot. Cyrus tried not to focus on how eery it all felt.

"I'm sorry for singing, your Highness," said Farley unexpectedly, apparently unable to put it behind him. "My mother taught me when I was small."

Cyrus's eyebrows raised at the thought that his host had ever been described as small.

"I struggle to express myself with my own words," Farley said, "but mother taught me that there are few problems that can't be solved with song." He stopped in front of a door and took a moment to find an ornate key, which he eventually plunged into the door in front of them.

"This is my mother's room," he said, stepping forward to light a candlestick upon a table. Light spilled into the room to reveal a small bed covered in patchwork blankets, a rickety desk with the wood chipped away at each corner, and a mirror stained with black spots.

"And this is my mother!" Farley said, causing Cyrus to jump as the man appeared suddenly beside him. He was surprisingly graceful for someone of his size, and Cyrus's heart raced as he followed Farley's extended arm to an unnerving portrait of a large woman in a black gown with a small boy, presumably Farley, at her side. Both of their faces were stern, their mouths drawn into hard lines, but it was the woman's eyes that left Cyrus the most unsettled. Her irises were as black as the night they had just left outside, and her gaze seemed to follow Cyrus's every move.

He wondered where Farley's mother was and why her painting was placed here, but tiredness got the better of him. "It's lovely," he said with a grateful smile, tearing his eyes from the odd portrait. "Thank you, Farley, but I really should rest."

"Of course, your Highness," he said, bowing once more as he headed to the door. "Sleep well, my prince, and do not fear. I won't let anyone hurt you." His eyes trailed to the window, and Cyrus knew he was thinking of Flynn.

Farley closed the door, and Cyrus sat on the bed. Both Farley and his house seemed quite unusual, but it was going to take more than a few strange words to keep him from sleep at this point.

⚜ ⚜ ⚜

Sunlight flooded the room, and Cyrus stretched out, yawning contentedly as he embraced the warm, fuzzy feeling that follows a good night of sleep. In truth, he had been exhausted, and with the daunting prospect of Simeon's dungeons ahead of him, he was keen to indulge every last moment of comfort, stretching his arms out like a child making angels in the snow.

Outside the window, birds were singing in the trees, and the sound of voices told Cyrus that the others had awoken before him. He thought of Farley's stew from the night before, and his stomach rumbled. Perhaps they were making breakfast. He stretched out once more, remembering the strange events of the previous evening, and relaxed with some satisfaction at Colton's changing attitude toward Farley. Minor though it was, the evening's proceedings had only served to reinforce Cyrus's hopes for amity. Even the greatest of enemies can find friendship in the right circumstances, and he was hopeful that this would be the start of more positive relations between Easthaven and their neighbours, though a truce between Flynn and Colton was his most pressing concern.

There are few problems that can't be solved with song. Farley was an odd sort, but he hadn't been wrong. Cyrus dropped his legs over the side of the bed and gave his best effort at replicating Farley's performance from the previous evening, the melody still bouncing around his head, the lyrics somehow already ingrained in his brain. He shuffled the patchwork quilt into something that passed for order and walked over to the portrait on the wall, where he smiled at Farley's mother before continuing toward the door, his singing voice tuneless but carefree as it echoed about the house.

He took one last look at the room before leaving. Cyrus wondered when, or indeed if, he would ever sleep in a bed again. After all, he had no idea what awaited him when he arrived at Simeon's castle. He gave a sad smile as the song ended, the lack of his own voice bringing silence into the air. He reached for the door handle, but as he tried to turn it, he found that the door was locked.

Farley, you fool, Cyrus thought. He appreciated vigilance as much as anyone, but locked doors had always given him a feeling of claustrophobia, and he was hit with the sudden urge to relieve himself, yesterday's ale returning to haunt him as it so often did.

"Farley!" he shouted cupping his hands around his mouth to project the sound. "Let me out!"

He was already shifting uncomfortably, and when Farley's mother's portrait caught his eye once more, he was strangely annoyed at the lack of concern on her face. Shouldn't she care about Cyrus's imminent problem?

"Farley, I'm serious!" he tried again. He could still hear voices at the front of the house, and his frustration was developing as rapidly as his anxiety. "Farley!" A final attempt. Again, no answer, and it occurred to Cyrus that something wasn't right.

He placed his ear to the door, and the jumbled sound of Farley's voice became clearer than before.

"No!" Farley called with desperation in his voice. "I won't let you do this!"

The sounds of struggle rang in the air, and Cyrus could hear Colton grunting with exertion, though his words were nonsensical.

Fearful for Farley's wellbeing, Cyrus rushed to check the window and found that the glass panels were fixed in place by solid metal bars. It would have to be the door, then. Cyrus braced himself as he slammed a shoulder into the door's heavy wood with Farley's mother looking on, her expression as stern as ever.

The door itself was solid, inches thick, and heavy. It took a couple of attempts, but the lock started to break away, and the doorframe eventually splintered so that Cyrus practically fell into the hallway. The previous evening had been dark, but he followed the corridor that he remembered before emerging into a living area with a small kitchen whose shelves were full of glass jars. A selection of large knives was arranged on the kitchen surface, but Cyrus's eyes were inexplicably drawn to the colourful liquids, assorted herbs and spices, and other substances that decorated the inside of the jars.

Outside, the struggle continued, but as Cyrus peered nervously around the room, he noticed a collection of lifeless animals returning his stare, rodents and birds no longer living but preserved and arranged to create an uncanny impression of life. His stomach flipped uncomfortably. What was this place? The hair on his neck stood at attention as a chill went down his spine. He breathed frantically, and he realised that he had to get out.

"You won't hurt him!" came a muffled voice that Cyrus assumed was Farley. He had to save him, and the selection of knives before him were no longer threatening so much as inviting. He grabbed a razor-sharp carving knife and rushed to the front door, ignoring the madness around him. This door was unlocked, and Cyrus wasted no time before pushing through and out into the warm morning air. He knew death and violence like an old friend, but nothing could have prepared him for the scene that he found.

"Cyrus, help!" Colton called, choking on his words as Farley slammed him onto the ground with his hands at his throat.

A length of rope was tied around Colton's neck, and as Cyrus followed the rope with his eyes, he noticed that it was connected to a thick white branch with a jagged end, which suggested that it had broken away from one of the trees by force. A creaking noise caught Cyrus's attention among the mayhem, and movement drew his attention to a similar branch on a nearby tree, where Flynn's lifeless body was hanging. His legs were dangling limp, and his feet were pointing downward with a look of surprise forever fixed upon his face.

The knife fell from Cyrus's hand in shock. "Farley, what are you doing?"

Colton's face was bright red, and there were angry lacerations around his throat as he continued trying to force his attacker away.

Cyrus noticed that Farley was shaking, and he recalled the trance that their host had fallen into the night before, breaking into song around the campfire. Cyrus had thought Farley odd, but he knew now that he was dangerous. He could see the life draining from Colton's bloodshot eyes, so Cyrus rushed to pull Farley away from his victim knowing that time was of the essence.

Colton gurgled with relief as Cyrus tackled Farley to the ground. He had the larger man pinned, but Farley had a maniacal look on his face, and his eyes were rolled upward as he clubbed Cyrus effortlessly away with a meaty hand. The connection was like being hit with a rock, and Cyrus was thrown face down, his head spinning as he tried clumsily to climb to his feet.

"I won't let them take you!" cried Farley, sweat pouring down his maddened face, his arms lashing out like a trapped animal as Colton staggered to his feet to draw a blade. "They killed my mother, and they are going to try and kill you!"

Colton scoffed, his sword extended even as he folded to rest his spare hand on a knee. "He put something in the stew!" he said dismissively. "He must have added something to make us sleep, and Flynn… he killed Flynn. He's crazy!"

How had it come to this? Cyrus raised his palms in an effort to calm the mood and shuffled slowly toward his discarded knife.

"It's okay, Farley," he said gently, as though speaking to a spooked horse. "I'm safe. Nobody needs to get hurt."

He knelt slowly to pick up his knife without ever losing eye contact with Farley. The atmosphere was finely balanced, and as Cyrus thought to Farley's bowing and scraping, he wondered if this reverence could be used to his advantage. "You've done a very bad thing, Farley," he said tentatively. "I would never have asked you to do this, you know, but I understand why you did it, and perhaps if we can all just calm down, I might be able to forgive you."

The panic on Farley's face faded slightly as a smile of relief emerged. "I just wanted to keep you safe, your Highness. They killed my mother. They called her a witch and—"

Colton appeared and smashed the pommel of his sword into the back of Farley's head, knocking Farley to his knees, shocked and disorientated. It had been some time since Cyrus had heard a man cry, but the sound was hysterical as Farley finally raised his head and felt the blade of Colton's sword resting upon his neck.

"Just say the word," said Colton, with some of the colour having returned to his otherwise emotionless face. But Cyrus, who had had his fill of bloodshed, shook his head wordlessly, and Colton cursed to himself as he pushed Farley down into the dirt with a heavy boot before making his way to stand at Cyrus's side.

All was silent but for Farley's bubbling cries. The man was broken, a face full of mud and tears pooling on the ground as Flynn's body swayed silently in the breeze.

"We're done here," said Cyrus sadly, unable to look at Farley. He walked to ready Adagio. "I think we've overstayed our welcome."

The journey away from the Whitewood was mercifully uneventful. Cyrus and Colton walked pensively at Adagio's side as Cyrus led his mount back toward the bridge where they had met the previous day.

When they arrived at the bridge, they saw that two new soldiers stood there, where Colton and Flynn had been only the previous day. Their unenthusiastic mutterings were the only welcome as Adagio passed between them, and hooves clip-clopped against the stonework as Cyrus tried to steady her, knowing that she was fearful of the water below. With the river at their backs, Cyrus took his first steps on Auldhaven soil. In the end, Cyrus reflected, feeling slightly deflated, that it was little more than a few bricks that separated the two countries. The ground felt the same, the air smelled the same, and Cyrus wondered why war even existed and how he had ever imagined it to be justified or glorious.

Neither of them spoke of Flynn, though Cyrus sensed a suggestion of relief in Colton, whose mood swelled with talk of the capital. "It has to be seen to be believed, you know?" he said, walking alongside Adagio and trying to keep up. "To my mind, Ravensward is the greatest city in the world. I don't know why I ever left."

"Life outside of a city isn't so bad," said Cyrus, thinking to the freedom of his own childhood in the Low Country. "Perhaps you were just made for country living?"

"Perhaps I was just too lazy, more like!" Colton laughed before recent events seemed to catch up with him. He sobered. "I always wanted to be in the King's Guard, but I just didn't want to work for it. I walked away from the training as a young man, and there was good money on offer for border guards because of the conflict with Easthaven."

"Some things just happen for a reason."

"You're not wrong," Colton agreed, smiling sadly. "I didn't think I'd ever return to the castle, but then you showed up and...well, here we are. I'll get you there safely," he added, putting Cyrus's mind at ease. "I still know people in the castle. Who knows, maybe there is hope for me yet?"

Cyrus nodded as Adagio continued forward slowly. Hope was not a word that he'd come to associate with Simeon's castle, but he understood the sentiment and was grateful for Colton's company. "Getting there safely is one thing," he said eventually, "but getting there quickly is another. You need a horse," he added, stroking Adagio behind the ear. "A horse, and we need supplies for our journey."

"You're too kind," said Colton, "and my feet will thank you. There's not much to it, but we'll find all we need in Brockhurst."

"Perfect," said Cyrus, and Colton smiled before breaking into a sprint to move ahead of Cyrus and Adagio.

"Are you coming or what?" he called back breathlessly, colour rising in his face. "You never know, we might even find time for a drink!"

⚜ ⚜ ⚜

Small and hotchpotch, Brockhurst was one of those places that people visited but never stayed. A number of rickety carts lined the small town square, and there were no houses, only shops for food, a small inn for travellers, and a tavern, which sounded with the only true sign of life. A doorbell chimed as Cyrus and Colton entered a bakery, and the shopkeeper rushed to take his place behind the counter with a look of surprise that suggested it had been some time since he sold his last loaf. They bought bread and sweet buns for the journey, before the lure of activity drew them toward the tavern. They made the short walk back across the town square toward the source of the noise, Adagio watching them appraisingly from her tether.

A few drinks later, Cyrus found that he was actually beginning to enjoy the company. He hadn't realised how much he had been missing Garrett, and talk of Ravensward meant that he and his companion were not short of conversation. They could have stayed there for days in the end, but a nagging feeling pulled Cyrus ever onward. Delay as he might, he knew that he couldn't run forever. That's why he was here, after all.

It was late afternoon when Colton struck up a conversation with a passing trader who the barmaid had said sometimes sold horses. The man had long grey hair and a straggly beard stained yellow, either from pipe smoke or the ale that had missed his mouth. After Colton enquired, the man led them outside to see the horse in question.

"He's my very best, bred from a family of champions," said the old man, running his hands over the black stallion, whose obsidian coat shimmered.

"And the price for such a beast?" asked Colton.

"No less than ten marks."

"Five."

"Eight," said the man, his eyes narrowed.

Colton turned to Cyrus. "I don't know. It's your money."

Cyrus walked to inspect the stallion, with Adagio still fastened nearby and watching the scene intently. Though the setting was very different, Cyrus found memories of the market in Casarossa flooding back to him. He thought of the mirror he had bargained for that day, and a nostalgic smile appeared on his face. It was a silly little gift, really, but it was something for his sister to remember him by.

"So, what do you say?" asked the trader expectantly.

Cyrus's smile faded, and he reached to retrieve his money pouch. "Eight is fine. You have yourself a deal." He doubted very much that he'd be needing money where he was going in any case.

⚜ ⚜ ⚜

The road from Brockhurst was to be a simple one, a straight shot to the capital with a smattering of small towns and villages along the way. The road was flat, and the horses rode well, though Cyrus couldn't help noticing that Adagio was somewhat taken by Colton's stallion, and it took an occasional tug of the reins to ensure that they remained on track. She was, like all the other women in Cyrus's life, something of a mystery to him. But watching the two horses flirt with one another was a welcome distraction, and their safe passage through Auldhaven's countryside provided an ideal remedy to their run-in with Farley.

After a few hours of hard riding, they stopped at a river to allow the horses to rest. Graceful willow trees lined the riverbank, their branches swaying in the gentle breeze. The reflection of each tree seemed to dance on the water as swans drifted slowly by. Despite how much he was dreading his destination, the peacefulness of this setting washed over Cyrus.

"I think I'll call him, Morven," said Colton, leading his stallion down toward the water's edge.

Cyrus took his eyes away from the swans and looked toward Colton. "A fine name for a fine horse."

"A regal name," Colton added hastily, and Cyrus feigned ignorance despite being familiar with the historical figure from whom the name was derived. He could tell Colton wanted to tell the story.

"King Morven was Simeon's grandfather," Colton continued, as Cyrus inwardly recalled some of the many tales of King Morven that Cyrus himself had told. "He established the finest cavalry that the world had ever seen and was known as the 'Horse Lord' after historic victories against the Cornessians. Above all, Morven was known for being powerful and headstrong. I think the name will suit him perfectly." Colton moved to run his hand through the horse's mane. "I've been meaning to ask, have you met King Simeon?"

Cyrus sensed that the question had been coming, and he crouched to cup his hands and splash cold water onto his face as he considered the answer.

"Once or twice," he said eventually, before standing to stretch his back out.

"And how did that go?"

"Not great."

"It can't have been that bad."

Cyrus blew out his cheeks. "It's a long story."

"Well, tell me about your last meeting," said Colton, his words formed around a mouthful of half-chewed bread.

"I stabbed him in the leg," Cyrus answered baldly. There really wasn't any other way to put it.

Colton's face turned to a grimace. "Ah."

The weather was fine, the landscape was green, and as they continued their journey, the sight of every friendly face and waving child helped to distract Cyrus from the dangers ahead, as well as those he'd left behind. It was all so very familiar: farming communities with animals working the fields, spirals of smoke rising from small stonework chimneys. Good, honest people just going about their lives while the faceless nobility sat in distant castles making decisions with far-reaching consequences. Cyrus grimaced at his part in it but took some comfort in knowing that his actions might bring an end to the conflict. Every stride of Adagio's legs took Cyrus a step closer to his fate, whatever that might be.

❧ ❧ ❧

The afternoon of the second day gave Cyrus his first glimpse of Ravensward. The city was built into a deep valley surrounded by mountains on three sides. Huge, jagged rock formations seemed to envelop the city from above, snatching the sunlight and casting a cool shadow over the capital.

"I guess we made it," said Cyrus, rolling his sleeves back down to the wrist. It was a statement more than a question, and as the two of them sat silently upon a hill, eyes following the path to the city, Cyrus found that he was awestruck by the scale of what lay before them. It was known as the City of Spires, and while not as uniform as Eriwald nor as jumbled as Highcastle, Ravensward had an imposing quality with its myriad buildings rising from the earth to form elaborate peaks. Was this man's attempt to compete with the majesty of nature, Cyrus wondered, or perhaps an effort to mirror the natural splendour that surrounded the city? Whatever the answer, Colton's attempts to describe the city had fallen a long way short of the spectacular reality.

Cyrus ushered Adagio forward, and the two riders continued onward, descending into the valley below. Before them, buildings became taller with every step, and Cyrus began to feel smaller and smaller, dwarfed by the city and the fate it might hold. This wasn't the first time he had doubted his decision, and Fran's voice echoed in his mind. *Just stay here with me, and Gus, and Adaline. We're alive, and we're safe. Please don't do this.*

Colton must have sensed Cyrus's reservations as Adagio paused just ahead of the city limits. "Nearly there now," he said with a warm smile. "The castle isn't far, but stay at my side. The city is a labyrinth to outsiders."

Cyrus returned the smile with one of his own before following Colton into the dark streets of the capital. His stomach was in knots, and he wondered if Colton's encouragement was the only thing that kept him moving forward. The first thing that hit him when they entered the city was the smell: a damp stench stinging at his nostrils with an overwhelming aroma of sewage, far worse than he had known in even the poorest corners of Highcastle. Dirty faces peered up at them from all around. Children younger than Fran, their clothes stained, hair matted, teeth yellowed or absent. A large man in an apron emerged from a shop to discard a bucket of waste into a gulley trickling with brown water at the side of the road. Poultry stripped to the carcass, the softened remains of browned-off fruit. Cyrus grimaced, wondering where the waste would go, but he needn't have bothered. Stirred to life by the banquet before them, small hands reached in desperation to snatch as much as they could hold before descending into the darkened backstreets.

"They call them Shadows," said Colton, his eyes now lowered. "They live in darkness. Children with no family, no friends, and no names."

"That's terrible," said Cyrus, stating the obvious. "But why?"

"Money," answered Colton. "Money and food."

Colton stepped down from his horse and broke bread into small pieces that he offered to those still trawling the sludge for remains.

"It hasn't always been this way," he said, "but winters have been harsh in recent times, and it's a struggle to provide for everyone." He turned back to Cyrus empty-handed as the last of the children scuttled away. "Simeon sends wagons to poorer areas of the city with food, but it has been in short supply of late, and the bigger Shadows," Colton cleared his throat, "I mean, the bigger *children* take food from those who are smaller and weaker. They live in communities around the city, in abandoned buildings, sometimes underground, and they have their own hierarchy. It is a life we can never truly understand."

"Why?" asked Cyrus, shaking his head as he surveyed their sorry surroundings.

"Because few of them ever learn to form words. There are rumours of children going missing recently, but they don't have anyone to speak up for them, so who can say?"

Cyrus felt his stomach drop. Forget Shadows, these children were living like animals, and in the capital of all places. He snarled at the neglect and instinctively blamed Simeon in his mind before the memory of their meeting in Eriwald halted his rising temper. *I will need the green pastures of the Low Country to feed my people,* Simeon had said. This is what it was all about. This is why Simeon had crossed the border. But if they needed more food, why didn't he just ask? And could Cyrus have done more to help and to avoid the conflict that followed? He let his head fall at the thought that he was in some way responsible for their suffering.

"We should go," said Colton, and Cyrus found himself grateful for the intervention, as his own thoughts had started to spiral into despair. "We need to make it to the castle before nightfall, or I'll have to protect you for another day, and I'm not paid to mind royalty!"

They hadn't met in the best of circumstances, but Cyrus believed Colton to be a good man. He gave a brief nod of agreement as Colton climbed onto Morven's back, and they continued along the main road, where the turrets and spires of the citadel loomed above all others as they drew nearer to the castle. The stone was as dark as the shadows it cast, and the appearance of armed men atop crenelated walls told Cyrus that they had arrived at their destination.

He turned to look back at the city. Might this be his last memory of freedom? Cobbled streets lined with narrow buildings. Rooftops pointed jauntily skyward. The capital bustled with activity, and yet it was all so quiet, so cold, and so dark. It was somehow awe-inspiring and hopeless in equal measure—perhaps it awed him how hopeless it felt—and a large part of Cyrus was relieved to break free of its shadowy grip as he edged toward the castle gates, the sound of Adagio's hooves echoing against the stonework. Colton announced himself to the guards on the parapet, and the portcullis creaked into motion before a group of Simeon's men appeared at the entrance to meet them.

"Well, well, look who it is," a familiar voice called before Cyrus could discern the faces before him. "I didn't think we'd be seeing you again!" The mocking tone finally registered, transporting Cyrus back to his first time in Eriwald—his meeting with Simeon, and the loathsome general that had accompanied him.

"Lambert, you old dog!" said Colton slipping from his horse to embrace the general warmly.

"What an unexpected surprise, Colton. I see you've brought us quite the gift!"

Cyrus's skin prickled under the general's gaze. Lambert's skin carried the same healthy colour as it had during their previous meeting, yet his wispy beard had thickened as if hinting at the rugged experience of war. Funny really, thought Cyrus, since the general had done little more than escort Simeon's defeated army home.

"Ah yes, the prince," said Colton, turning to gesture Cyrus forward. "We've had quite the journey."

"It certainly appears so," said Lambert, wrinkling his nose at Cyrus's ragged, mud-spattered appearance.

"The prince travels of his own accord," Colton continued. "He says he is here to see the king."

Cyrus swung down from Adagio's back, ushering her forward toward the men. He noticed that Lambert's retinue were armed but sensed a closeness between Colton and the general that gave him some reassurance.

"So, this is your friend?" he asked Colton, inclining his head toward Lambert.

"Friend?" said Colton, lips upturned in a warm smile. "Something like that!" He pushed Lambert away playfully before turning back to Cyrus. "We grew up in the city together and trained in the King's Guard. Like I told you, Lambert here got all the luck, and well, you know what happened to me."

"You got what you deserved," answered Lambert in jest. "And here you are trying to bring a dangerous man into my castle!"

"Your castle these days, is it?" asked Colton with eyebrows raised. "Well, I'll be sure to run that by the king when we see him."

Laughter broke out between them before Lambert placed an arm around Colton's shoulders. "It's good to see you, old friend," he said warmly. "Now, let's get the prince to Simeon and get this over with. I'm dying to hear about this bridge of yours!"

⚜ ⚜ ⚜

Cyrus breathed deeply as the doors swung open. He straightened his back, steadied his nerves, and walked between the armoured guards with his chin high. It was all for show, of course, and though Cyrus knew that the effort wouldn't be lost on Simeon, he wondered if it was as much for himself as anything else.

Inside, the throne room was every bit as imposing as he had expected. Shrouded in yet more shadow, it reminded Cyrus in many ways of the throne room in Eldred's Keep. Weapons perched upon the walls, the faces of Simeon's forebears staring down at him. Squinting at the ceiling, Cyrus noticed grotesque faces etched into the beams above, their expressions fixed somewhere between pain and fear, while rich tapestries lined the walls displaying colourful illustrations of Auldhaven's many military conquests. An armoured boot thumped down behind him, and Cyrus realised that he had stopped still to observe his surroundings. He made to move but stumbled forward as the guard nudged him toward the throne.

"Well, this is a surprise," came Simeon's voice, his appearance obscured by the dim light. "I thought I'd never see you again, despite what you might have said the last time we met."

Cyrus continued forward as his eyes adjusted to the light. "We are men of honour, are we not?" he asked with the extent of his composure, his voice echoing in the vast room. Simeon was not a man of great physical stature, but he had a presence that Cyrus remembered from their previous meetings, and this time was no different. "There were rumours that you had died, but I knew better than to believe them." He forced himself to smile, bracing for a repeat of the verbal sparring that he had experienced in Eriwald.

"Show some respect, scum," snapped Lambert, appearing at the king's side to draw his sword in Cyrus's direction. "Did you really think that your sneaky little assassination attempt could end a great king like Simeon? You crept into an enemy's camp on the eve of battle and think to lecture us on honour?" He stepped forward, and Cyrus noticed that Colton was holding Lambert's arm to halt his advance, Lambert's face a picture of fury. "You have only delayed the inevitable, and King Simeon will—"

"Yes, thank you, Lambert," said Simeon, and Cyrus noticed that the king's voice lacked some of the spirit it had had during their last meeting, but, Cyrus reflected, it still carried as much authority as ever. Simeon continued, "It is for me to decide what Simeon and indeed Auldhaven will do."

Cyrus turned his attention back to the king, and on closer inspection, he found a very different Simeon upon the throne. The man's face was pale and gaunt, and grey strands of hair were plastered to his forehead with sweat. Despite his best efforts, Cyrus's eyes widened.

"Yes, that would probably have been my reaction too," said Simeon, taking in Cyrus's reaction to his appearance. "I may not be dead, but it seems that it may only be a matter of time." He chuckled to himself before breaking into a painful cough.

Cyrus wasn't sure where to look but found his interest drawn to a wooden walking cane rested against the throne.

"And it was *my* sneaky ploy that led us to this position, Lambert," Simeon corrected with a sad glint in his eyes. He seemed a shadow of the fearsome adversary that Cyrus had encountered only weeks before, and this unpredictable turn had Cyrus feeling relieved and uneasy all at the same time.

"Say what you will of Prince Cyrus, but he is certainly a man of his word," Simeon said, inclining his head in Cyrus's direction. "I am tired for now, but please see him to the guest chambers. I would dine with the prince this evening. There is much that I wish to discuss."

"But, your Majesty," said Lambert incredulously, kneeling at his king's side, "he is our enemy and a crafty one at that."

"There's no denying it," answered Simeon, his lips upturned in a smile, "but the prince seeks peace, and I think we can all agree that I am in no condition for war."

He raised himself slowly from his throne, and Cyrus noticed Simeon's right leg shaking involuntarily as Lambert offered an arm for support. "Excuse me, Prince Cyrus, but I see that you carry the effects of your journey. Please bathe, rest if you must, and I will see you for dinner."

"Am I your prisoner then, Simeon?" asked Cyrus, eyes narrowed.

"My prisoner? Whyever would you say that?" asked the king, turning as he hobbled by. "No, Prince Cyrus, you are my guest."

Cyrus used the prongs of his fork to push food around the plate. It was a decadent dish of suckling pig in a rich plum sauce, and it took a well-timed cough to mask the sound of his stomach's grumbling. He pulled the sleeve of an extravagant silk shirt to look at the bracelet that Fran had given him, and though this had been intended as a distraction, the memory of home only added to his growing nerves.

"Something wrong with your meal?" asked Simeon from the opposite end of the ornate, oblong dinner table. "I know some people prefer pork with apple, but the chef insists on plum. Something about tartness, though I couldn't tell you what exactly."

"It's lovely," answered Cyrus solemnly, without ever lifting his gaze from his plate. Luxurious guest quarters, rose baths, lavish clothes, and now this. He'd expected fury from Simeon, maybe even spite, but he should have known better; mind games had always been the king's gift, and despite his diminished stature, Cyrus had never been so uncomfortable.

"And your quarters?" Simeon continued softly, his voice and presence like that of a kindly uncle. "I trust that you were suitably comfortable?"

Cyrus found the polite façade to be torturous, and he was uneasy with the feeling that Simeon was able to read his every thought. He found himself wishing that Simeon would simply cut to the chase instead of playing the part of the generous host. Cyrus's accommodation was equal to anything in Eldred's Keep and furnished with the very finest materials, while the wardrobes were stocked with the latest fashions from tailors across the land. He had expected to meet his end in Ravensward, but Simeon seemed intent on toying with him first. It was a strange feeling to embrace, but Cyrus acknowledged that he had travelled to the capital to give his life, and with this in mind, he really had nothing more to fear. He didn't have to indulge this murderous fool, and he was tired of playing the old man's games.

"You know, the roses were grown in my own gardens," said Simeon with a brief chuckle. "It's a funny story, really, because—"

Cyrus's chair screeched on the stone floor as he kicked it back, and his hand slammed down on the table. "What is it that you want, Simeon?" he snarled in the king's direction, and though he had done so in anger, the sight of Simeon's withered person left him with an immediate feeling of guilt. "Either put me in your prison or end this," he added, picking up a carving knife from the table and offering it to Simeon, his voice lowered to plead with his enemy who only raised a shaky hand to steady his glass of wine.

"Kill you?" asked Simeon, eyes narrowed in a look of confusion. "And why would I want to do that?"

"Your leg!" snapped Cyrus, pointing with the knife. "I stabbed you and ended your attack on Easthaven. Surely you want revenge?" It seemed like the most obvious thing in the world, but Simeon only laughed before breaking into another sad smile.

"All true," said the king eventually, clearing his throat, "but circumstances change, and I'm not the man that you met before." Simeon raised himself slowly from his chair and declined the attention of two nearby maids and gestured them out of the room so that only he and Cyrus remained.

The king moved slowly in his approach, and Cyrus noticed a putrid smell in the air as Simeon claimed the knife from his hand. His skin was pale, his brow glistened with sweat as it had earlier in the day, and his eyes were bloodshot as he placed the knife on the table and perched beside it with his wounded leg outstretched.

"I'm dying, Cyrus," he said quietly. "The irony is that you never meant to kill me, and yet here we are. The surgeon tells me that the wound is too infected to be healed and that every day is a bonus now."

Cyrus's heart pounded. He had, on many occasions, dreamt of Simeon's demise. He had wanted to be the man behind the blade, the man who brought evil to its knees, and in a roundabout way he had been. Here he was, alone with the man responsible for the death of so many of his loved ones, yet his only feeling was an unexpected twinge of guilt. The man beside him was, after all, just a man, one with his own ambitions and his own people for which to provide. Cyrus had hoped to end the cycle of death, but in the end, he had only contributed to it.

"I'm sorry," he started feebly with a tremble in his voice, "I only meant—"

"It's all right," said Simeon, interjecting to spare Cyrus's apology. "You did what you had to do, and I got what I deserved." He winced as he manoeuvred the injured leg to try and find comfort. "You promised that you would come to me, and you have made good on your word. You are a man of honour and will be treated accordingly."

"So, what will it be then?" asked Cyrus with a lingering sense of dread despite Simeon's words. "If not death, then what? A lifetime in your prisons? Perhaps something worse? There is still time to make things right, Simeon. We can work together and forge a bright future for both nations. Think of your legacy."

At this, Simeon's face produced a more familiar grin.

"You are a good man, Cyrus, a prince to be proud of. One that I would be proud to call my own. You'll know, of course, that I have no heir. My wife was taken from me years ago, and there are no children to show for our time together."

Cyrus nodded as Simeon spoke, and though puzzled by the king's words, he tried to ensure that this didn't show in his expression.

"I loved the queen very much, but there is great pressure for a king to produce an heir, and I am not without my weaknesses." He reached into his trouser pocket and produced a silver locket on a chain, which he passed to Cyrus.

"Open it," he gestured, prompting Cyrus to unhook the small clasp and reveal the presence of two small portraits, one of a beautiful young woman with dark brown hair, the other of a small child no more than a couple of years old, a boy by the look of it.

"It's a fine ornament," said Cyrus, a little lost. He sensed that Simeon was building to something and felt some relief at the realisation that the king meant him no immediate harm, but he couldn't figure out where he was supposed to fit in all of this.

"Indeed, it is," said Simeon, reaching to take the locket back. He rested it gently in his hands and shifted his attention from Cyrus with a wistful stare. "Evelyn," he began, brushing his index finger over the portrait of the woman. "She was our maid. A common girl born to serve, and yet you never saw her without a smile on her face. She had a presence that could light up a room."

Simeon laughed to himself, and Cyrus was reminded of the first time he had met Marcia, the way she floated around his chambers like an angel. He'd been king at the time—or at least pretending to be—but she had always been in control, leaving Cyrus in her wake, captivated by her spell.

"She was never from my side," Simeon continued, head still buried in the locket, interrupting Cyrus from his revery. "Things with the queen weren't always easy, but in Evelyn I found comfort. You know as well as any the burden of being a king…"

Cyrus muttered words of agreement as he returned to his seat, marvelling internally at the turn of events. Simeon no longer commanded his fear but rather his pity. He wasn't the cold-hearted murderer that Cyrus had so often envisaged, but a man at the end of the road, looking back upon the paths that he might have taken.

"So, what happened?" asked Cyrus, feeling both moved to indulge his host and swept up once again in a good story, just as he had been back in Corhollow in what felt like another life completely.

"One thing led to another, and Evelyn fell pregnant," said Simeon. "I had not thought it possible after so many years trying with the queen, but pregnant she was, and when the queen learned of Evelyn's condition, there was no doubt as to my part in it." He looked down at his hands, which he had clasped in his lap, and Cyrus was struck to see that Simeon looked somewhat embarrassed, like a young boy caught in wrongdoing.

"And the child?" ventured Cyrus, suddenly concerned by the unknown infant's plight. He wasn't sure whether to ask but felt some connection with his own unusual upbringing and sensed that there was more to the story than Simeon had offered so far. In his mind's eye, Cyrus pictured the little boy from the locket.

"Taken," Simeon answered abruptly. "The queen ordered Evelyn from the castle and banished her back to her homeland in the west. I was forbidden from travelling to see her and heard nothing from them until this locket was delivered to the castle years later."

"Delivered?"

"Yes, Evelyn's brother, Robin, brought it in person." A heavy teardrop splashed down onto Simeon's sleeve.

Cyrus almost felt embarrassed enough to look away from the crying king, but the story had him transfixed.

"He said that Evelyn had died from a terrible sickness but that the boy's name was Brandon and that his true identity as my son would be kept from him. I had never known such pain and have only felt it once since, when the queen died. I sent Robin back with a gold ring inlaid with emerald, the only gift I would ever be able to give my son."

"And you've not seen them since?" asked Cyrus, now entirely unconcerned by his surroundings or the threat held by Simeon. "Not Robin or Brandon?"

"Not once," came the king's solemn reply. "I was taken by my grief for the queen; besides, the boy was a bastard with no legitimate claim to the throne. I couldn't…"

Simeon trailed off, and Cyrus felt strangely compelled to place a hand of reassurance on the king's shoulder until the older man raised himself to his feet and walked back toward his seat at the dinner table.

"I was never able to make things right with Evelyn, nor did I attain the queen's forgiveness. I thought perhaps I might someday take another wife, might still have time to father a legitimate heir, but I could never move past the loss of the queen, and so here I am, without anyone to take my place when my time comes. I've spent my life fighting for the betterment of Auldhaven, and yet I find myself at death's door with nothing but regrets to show for it all."

Simeon turned around more sharply than Cyrus had thought possible considering his injured leg, and their eyes met properly for the first time. A shadow of sadness hung over the room, but Simeon had a look of steely determination about him once more, along with a characteristic twinkle of mischief in his stare.

"I will die soon, Prince Cyrus, of that there can be no doubt. However, I believe that you are correct in what you say. Perhaps there is still time to make things right. You have shown me that an upbringing outside of the castle can indeed bring wisdom, and in you, I see hope for Brandon as my successor."

Cyrus swallowed hard as the pieces of Simeon's plan fell into place. The king's leg continued to shake, but he stood straighter than before, his presence demanding Cyrus's attention once more as he spoke.

"Why are you telling me this?" Cyrus asked eventually, pretending as though he did not have his suspicions and halfway hoping he was wrong in his assumptions about Simeon's plans.

"Because I know you want peace," answered Simeon with an assured tone, "and I want my son. These are, I believe, very fine foundations on which to negotiate."

"Negotiate?" asked Cyrus, face scrunched as he scratched thoughtfully at his scalp.

"Yes," said Simeon, smile now fully formed. "I cannot risk the discovery of Brandon's identity before he reaches the safety of the castle. The nobility has a frightening appetite for power, and our recent foray into eastern lands has left me somewhat…vulnerable."

He paused to take an apple from a plate of fresh fruit before crunching into it the same way he had during their first meeting in Eriwald.

"Do this thing for me, Prince Cyrus. Find my son and bring him home, and I will give you all that you desire."

Cyrus's head spun with the task before him. "Peace?"

"Oh, I can give you even more than that," answered Simeon, lowering into his seat with a look of deep satisfaction. "For this, I'm prepared to offer you freedom."

Wendell hated looking in the mirror.

What he found there was too brutal, too honest. But it hadn't always been this way.

He squinted as though it would help to reverse the years, as though he might be able to once again see a young nobleman with a spring in his step and a song in his heart. Heads would turn, and girls would flutter their eyelids as he came into view. A handsome man with a sword in his hand and the world at his feet.

He reached to scratch an insufferable itch on top of his bald scalp. An egg with eyes and a web of blue veins at each temple for decoration—this is what he had become. He missed his hair, his long, dark, wavy hair and that ridiculous little flick that would leave his admirers swooning. But good things so rarely last, Wendell had learned, and as his hair had thinned, receded, and disappeared, so had the admirers.

It was hard to believe that he was even the same man. His body was so soft and puffy these days, like an overgrown baby but with none of the redeeming innocence. He could barely recognise his face under all the extra skin. Jowls had appeared from nowhere, as had a wattle at his neck that seemed to worsen every day. He was a pragmatic sort, but there was no reversing the effects of time. The hair wouldn't simply grow back, and he would never be that man again.

He raised his right hand in front of his face, his reflection peering back at him through the absence of two fingers, a daily reminder of the unforgivable injustice that had befallen him. Life as it should have been hadn't simply passed him by; Anselm had taken it from him with a blade, and Wendell wouldn't find peace until justice was served.

"Master Wendell," came a voice. Marcia, the most tedious of servant girls. She was as dull as pondwater at the best of times but insufferable since Prince Cyrus had departed the castle. She'd always had a certain mousy quality, but her lovesick puppy routine was becoming rather wearisome, and Wendell could hardly bring himself to address her despite knowing that she would remain at his door until he did. He caught her reflection in the mirror and supposed she was pretty in her own way. She was not his type. She was far too pale, her wavy auburn hair too unkempt, her body too slim. She was a girl, whereas Wendell favoured a woman. Besides, he had always preferred blondes.

"Yes, dear?" he called, his tone dripping with added pomposity. It was a weakness, but he did hold some sympathy for the girl. Her stock had risen immeasurably during her brief dalliance with the imposter king. It looked to be a real rags-to-riches story at one point, but therein lies the appeal of stories: they are so rarely a reflection of the real world. And so here they were, Marcia's gown stained by the day's labour while Prince Cyrus was likely rotting in Simeon's prisons. And that was the best-case scenario for the newfound prince.

"His Highness, King Augustus has summoned an emergency meeting of his most valued council."

"Has he now?" asked Wendell, a mischievous smile spreading across his face. "And why ever might that be, I wonder?" *Perhaps he needs help cutting his dinner or wiping his—*

"I'm not sure," Marcia interjected, "I was simply told to summon you immediately."

"Yes, yes, I hear you," spat Wendell, still facing the mirror. "Our king says jump, I say how high. I know the rules, child. I've served in this castle since before you were born, and I'll be here long after you go."

Marcia bowed, her face so low that Wendell couldn't gauge her reaction. "Sorry, my lord," she said absently, and then she was gone.

Emergency council meeting, he thought, straightening deep red silken robes. The day had finally come.

They had finally come.

⚜ ⚜ ⚜

"My lords, please stand for King Augustus, High Commander of the armies of Easthaven and hero of the eastern peoples."

Heavy doors crashed open, and Augustus was, for a moment, bathed in sunlight before he proceeded into the Grand Hall. The sound of cheering, clapping, and whooping followed him all the way to his gilded chair at the head of the table, where he seemed reluctant to sit and bring an end to the fanfare.

With the war with Auldhaven still fresh in the memory, Augustus was, among other things, revered as a man of the people. Here was a young king who was believed to have saved lives and defeated the most feared warmonger of an age with only a few fading scars around his temple and jaw to show for it. A surprising and inspiring story that Wendell knew to be total nonsense, and he wasn't alone in the knowledge. He forced a smile as the king looked in his direction, and when the king looked away, Wendell's eyes rolled as the decorative sword at Augustus's side became lodged in the intricate metalwork of his chair. It had been a rather rousing entrance, and Wendell had to credit his peers who never ceased in their applause, despite the fact that it took the intervention of two guards to finally free the sword and allow Augustus the comfort of his plush velvet seat.

Dressed in a bright white coat with gleaming gold buttons and decorative ribbons at the shoulder, King Augustus looked as ornamental as he did regal. He had a constant smirk that suggested confidence far exceeding his credentials, and in him, Wendell saw everything that he had hated about Anselm.

"My lords, please," Augustus finally said, raising a hand and inclining his head in his very best attempt at humility.

The room fell silent immediately, and Wendell took a moment to survey the assembly. It was little different from any other such gathering. Broderick and his captains sat beaming at the king; Cornelius, Master of Prayer, pored over religious texts in front of him; and Thaddeus's face was set in a characteristic frown. At Augustus's side sat Seth, who was something of a mystery to

Wendell but certainly preferred to the ever-meddlesome Garrett. If the recent conflict offered any cause for celebration, it was the absence of Anselm and his pet. It was a shame that Wendell hadn't been there to see it, a heroic death by all accounts, Garrett full of arrows like a novelty hedgehog. Enemies as they might be, Wendell felt a great deal of gratitude for Simeon. In their collective efforts, they had emptied Eldred's Keep of any resistance, clearing a path for better men to rule.

His lips started to curl into a smile, but at that moment, his eyes met with another's, and his face fell, expressionless.

Adaline.

A dazzling gem in a room full of shingle, she seemed more beautiful with every day. Her hair fell upon her shoulders like rivers of gold, and Wendell's heart doubled its efforts, beating twice as fast as she gave him a small smile. She was perfection, in spite of Anselm's interference. Surely now she would see what a fool the man had been and see Augustus a constant reminder of the former king's prideful ignorance. She would likely thank Wendell one day, when all this was over. He had worked so hard and for so many years. It was the very least that he deserved.

"Somewhere you'd rather be, Wendell?" It was Augustus's voice, and Wendell smiled at the king—though it pained him to think of a mere boy with such a title—to offer the full extent of his attention. After glaring at Wendell for another half-second, Augustus continued with whatever he'd been saying before, words that Wendell had missed in his revery to Adaline.

"It was not so long ago that we gathered here to discuss our conflict with Simeon," said the young king, "and yet here we are once more, with wolves at the door!" He narrowed his eyes as if to impress upon those gathered that he was, in fact, an authoritative leader.

Sounds of outrage echoed around the Grand Hall, and Wendell tried his best to portray some semblance of surprise. *Who could it possibly be this time?* he thought to himself with an internal snigger. *Who could have predicted this?*

"What did I tell you, boys?" asked Broderick, whose smile full of pride for his king was long gone. He rose to his feet in a predictably cumbersome manner, plate armour rattling as an unwelcome addition to the din. "The only end to war with Simeon will be when his head decorates our ramparts."

Wendell struggled not to roll his eyes again at the general's quick assumption.

There was further outcry around the room before Augustus raised his palm once more. "Yes, thank you, Broderick. Your passion and…" he pursed his lips while reaching for the right word, "…enthusiasm, are appreciated. However, this is not the work of our friend Simeon. Thaddeus, if you would?"

All eyes turned to Thaddeus, who rose slowly from his seat. A man of great experience, Thaddeus was one Wendell had been careful not to underestimate. He was too old to present any physical threat, but his cunning had remained unchanged by time. The older man wiped moisture from his dewy eyes, and Wendell listened on as the last bastion of Anselm's administration gave voice to the impending threat.

"Ten thousand men, according to our reports," said Thaddeus, his voice tinged with sadness, in stark contrast to that of the king. "Verderans, led by King Ferdinand's sons, Alonso and Rafael."

Though he had only just gotten the words out, his voice was lost in a sea of speculation before Augustus slammed his hands on the table. The rabble fell silent once more.

"Please continue," said Augustus, and Wendell could almost have sworn that the king was enjoying himself.

"Thank you, my king," said Thaddeus, continuing. "We understand that the Verderans have divided their forces, with the larger number currently bound for Highcastle."

"And the rest?" asked Broderick, red-faced with a vein bulging upon his forehead. "What is this trickery?"

"To that, I am unsure," answered Thaddeus. "It is early days; however, it seems that they have left a number of their generals to lead a secondary army from the coastal city of Kingsport. It would appear that they have taken the town and control the harbour, with their ships in the shadow of our eastern coast."

"And the people of Kingsport?"

"Of minor importance," answered Augustus, stifling Broderick and Thaddeus whose objections appeared to fall on deaf ears. "I understand your concerns," continued the king, ushering silence, "but Prince Rafael marches across our lands bound for the capital, and your king's life is in danger. Lucky for me, I am in the company of Easthaven's finest military minds, so I invite you all to share your opinions on this rather pressing concern."

It was all rather amusing to Wendell. There was little to dislike about Broderick. He had certainly shown a greater level of respect than Wendell had experienced from any of the others in attendance. If Wendell had a friend in the castle, he supposed it was probably the general. And yet, the man was so very limited, a limited man with such an instinctive desire for war that it reminded Wendell of a dog with a bone. Wendell could see the frustration on Broderick's face as he fought to force his instincts down.

It was Thaddeus who finally spoke, and despite the old man's obvious frustrations, Wendell had to admire his calm and tactful approach when dealing with the king. "If I may," he said. "There are but two options. We march to meet the Verderans in open combat, or we prepare ourselves and the people of Highcastle for siege."

This was the final straw for Broderick. "Just one choice then, my king," he said, clearly not considering the idea of a siege much of an idea at all. "I will prepare our forces at once and—"

"Yes, yes, just say the word and you'll kill them all, etcetera," Augustus sneered, dismissing his general as he waved quiet from the room once more. "Thaddeus, please continue."

Thaddeus turned his sad expression to Adaline. His eyes lowered, his mouth a straight line, as he proceeded. "In this, I must agree with the general. For his many achievements, King Anselm planned for a peaceable future. I don't believe that Highcastle is in any condition to defend a siege, nor are we so rich with food that we can afford to feed a city for any sustained period of time. Put simply, we'd be trapped."

Augustus nodded soundlessly, biting the inside of his lip in thought before gesturing to Broderick to speak once more.

"He's right, my king." The general's words were calm and measured following his earlier outburst. He seemed to be buoyed by Thaddeus's agreement. "The walls of the city are in a very...mixed state of repair. There are large sections near the north gate in particular that suffered heavy damage during previous conflicts and have never been fully restored. In some cases, the stonework is low, and in others, it is entirely crumbled away. There are some more serviceable stretches, and the inner walls could be used to secure the old town and the castle in case of a tactical retreat, but…" He paused to shake his head as if the battle was already lost. "I fear that there is little hope for defending Highcastle against such overwhelming numbers."

"The city would be exposed, my king," continued Thaddeus seamlessly, as though he and Broderick had rehearsed this. "Rafael's men would take the streets and descend upon Eldred's Keep."

"Eldred's Keep, you say?" Augustus fired back. "A stronghold which has survived all manner of threats for many hundreds of years?"

"Yes, but—"

"No, Thaddeus, I've heard enough."

The king rose to his feet and pressed a finger thoughtfully to his lips. It occurred to Wendell that he had not contributed a word to their discussions, yet Augustus was increasingly difficult to read since his return from battle, and any friction within the castle would only serve his purpose in the long run.

"I did not choose this crown," Augustus finally said, "any more than I have chosen for Rafael to invade our lands and threaten it." He placed a respectful hand on the Master of Prayer's shoulder, and Wendell saw an admiration in the young king, admiration that Wendell had often sought to no avail. Augustus had noticeably spent more time in the basilica following his return to the capital, and it seemed that the young king had come to place his trust in a higher power. His relationship with Cornelius was not one of respect but reverence. It grated on Wendell's nerves.

"I am your king at the will of our God, blessed from the heavens and guided on my divine path to lead Easthaven against all evil." And there it was, the boy no longer a simple fool, but a religious one at that. It seemed that Wendell mightn't have to say a word after all, and that Cornelius was the king's new puppeteer.

"No, I have great faith in our God and in all of you," Augustus continued, "that we might defend this great fortress against the Verderan advance. I was only recently entrusted with this great responsibility, and I will not see it so easily surrendered. I believe our God wishes to see me on this throne for many years to come."

"My king," came a respectful if ambitious attempt from Thaddeus, who, to Wendell's surprise, was allowed to continue, "our defences are weak, and our forces will be outnumbered. Please, see sense and send word for help, as your brother would have."

Thaddeus stopped abruptly at the thunderous look on Augustus's face, a deep scowl, and silence descended on the hall. It was as if everyone present knew a line had been crossed at the comparison being made between Augustus and his brother. Thaddeus was a man of experience and principle, but he was not without passion of his own, passion that would be his own undoing and perhaps that of a nation.

His voice dangerously low and icy, Augustus said, "Need I remind you that it is I who wears the crown, not Prince Cyrus, who abandoned his responsibilities in favour of his own personal crusade?" The king cracked his knuckles, as if to add threat to his statement. "Rafael's actions have shown us that we have no help, no alliance, and that there is no trust among neighbours."

"And Cornesse, my king?" asked Thaddeus desperately, his face pleading as he fought to reclaim Augustus's favour.

Wendell could have laughed out loud. That love story was even more amusing than Prince Cyrus and the servant girl, and he knew it would only enrage Augustus further that this stain of embarrassment had been brought up. It had been a week of smiles and subtle touches before Augustus had stated his intention to marry the young queen, Mathilde. It would have been an occasion for the ages, a perfect love story. It only needed Mathilde's agreement, but sadly for Augustus, Mathilde had other plans and snubbed the young king. Wendell hadn't laughed that hard for years. He'd never forget the look on the poor boy's face when Mathilde announced her intention to leave.

Augustus took a deep breath through his nose. "Cornesse is, and always has been our enemy, Thaddeus." There was steel in his voice that left no room for negotiation, and Wendell stifled a laugh. It seemed that Augustus had suffered that rarest form of heartbreak, the one that also affects one's memory. Without Mathilde, Wendell doubted the king would even be here to worry about who was or wasn't an enemy. "A union with their sort would only lead to our downfall," Augustus finished pointedly. The prospect of improved relations with Cornesse washed away by a tidal wave of Augustus's pride. It really was too easy sometimes.

With the air of the discussion being closed, Augustus snapped, "Broderick?"

The general perked his head up in attention as the king shifted his stare. "Yes, my king?"

"You swore to my father, King Anselm, that you would protect these lands, and I expect you to make good on this promise." His face was stone.

"It is God's will," the Master of Prayer said unexpectedly as Broderick nodded in agreement. "Our king is a man of great faith, and he has entrusted this faith in you all."

"You see, Thaddeus," Augustus said, confident grin back on his face, taking strength from the Master of Prayer's words as though they were a tonic. "We do not fight alone but with a higher power at our back. Mother, you're no stranger to religion. Tell them."

Wendell looked across at Adaline, whose mouth had opened slightly in surprise as the room shifted to look at her. Clearly, she had not expected her son to ask her to weigh in, and Wendell wondered if the king had only done so because he assumed his mother would side with him without a thought.

Adaline moved to speak but paused briefly, as though struggling to find the right words. She sat with such elegance and poise, her skin pale and pure, her lips…

"I think," Adaline began again, this time assertively, adding another pause for effect. "I think that this is a choice that only a king can make. However," Augustus's grin fell as he anticipated his mother's next words, "it would be foolish to ignore the advice of such loyal servants. We will be imprisoned within these walls, outnumbered, overpowered, and left to die of hunger if the Verderans don't tire of the siege and kill us first."

Her voice had such authority, and she tucked long strands of golden hair behind her ears as she delivered her verdict. The sight had always driven Wendell wild with desire, and today was no different. He just wanted to support her, to spend the rest of his days watching her, agreeing with her every word. Looking after her…

"Wendell, you seem to lack focus today. Can't you see the importance of the decision that we face?" Augustus snapped. The king had caught him daydreaming for the second time in this short meeting, but at least—Wendell thought—Augustus was unable to read his thoughts. "Please be the voice of reason and tell them that we can do this."

Wendell froze. It was some relief to find that the king still valued his opinion, but Adaline had fixed him with her eyes, her stare narrowing as she attempted to convey her thoughts wordlessly across the room. She was right, of course, but if Augustus mobilised his troops and secured support now, Rafael's army would be cut short in their advance. Spread thin on foreign lands and tired from their journey, their numbers would be vulnerable to the sort of ambush that they themselves had set out to accomplish.

Wendell couldn't let that happen.

He looked back to Augustus, whose eyebrows were raised expectantly. Like it or not, Augustus was king of Easthaven and was the man that Wendell needed to control, if he was to meet the demands of his Verderan employers. Making sure not to look at Adaline, Wendell finally said, "I have absolute trust in our king's plan and believe that that he can overcome this enemy just as he did with Simeon."

"Impossible!" yelled Broderick, standing up from his seat and slamming his fists onto the table. "My king, you must see that we will not survive this!"

Augustus ignored him and sat back in his chair with a half-smile that suggested vindication.

"This is not Eriwald," said Thaddeus gravely, supporting Broderick once more. "The castle we can defend for a time, but the city limits practically welcome invasion."

"Your father chose to develop the city within, Augustus," Adaline said, adding to Thaddeus's words. "He believed that his treaty would hold and thought that improved relations with our neighbours would provide our greatest defence." She reached across to take the king's hand in her own. "The city is a sprawl too jumbled to defend, and while the outer walls can be manned with guards, perhaps even repaired to some extent, the eastern and western gateways were designed not for troops but for trade."

The king shook his mother's hand away and sat silently as he seemed to consider her words, the fate of a nation resting in his hands. It occurred to Wendell that this decision would cost countless lives, but he hoped in that moment that he had done enough to convince Augustus to proceed with his ill-fated plan.

"I thank you all for your thoughts," the king said eventually. "I understand that Highcastle is not the fortress that we would hope for, and that Rafael's men march with purpose." He took a moment to recline in his chair and scratch at the light dusting of stubble upon his chin. His stare was fixed, dead ahead, on the doors from which they had all entered, and Wendell sensed that the king was keen to complete his monologue without any further scrutiny from his council. Obligingly, everyone remained silent as the king considered his next words, as if they too could sense his wishes.

"You tell me that our defences are weak," Augustus continued. "I say, strengthen them. You tell me that we will starve.

I suggest that we fill our storerooms at once. You tell me victory cannot be achieved..."

He stood once more to survey the room as if from the back of a glorious mount, embracing his moment, chest practically swelling. "Well, follow your king, and together we will achieve the impossible!"

Wendell grinned. Just as he had planned it.

Adagio paused as she crested yet another steep stretch of mountain trail. Her hooves shuffled to a halt on a patch of loose gravel, and Cyrus's heart pounded in his chest as he looked over the ledge at their left flank, where stones tumbled down the mountainside and into the valley below. Despite the obvious peril of their journey, he realised that he'd been riding in a daze for some time now, still shocked by his meeting with Simeon in Ravensward. In the end, it had all been so simple. In exchange for the return of his long-lost son, Simeon had offered Cyrus peace and the freedom to return to Highcastle.

The air was noticeably thinner at this altitude, but Cyrus closed his eyes as he breathed deeply and reflected on how lucky he was to be alive. He was more than a little lightheaded, but a brusque wind caught him with painful clarity, and he pulled a woollen scarf tight around his neck to shut out the cold.

"Keep moving," came Colton's voice, his every word echoing against the rockface. "There's a storm coming, and we need to get ourselves off of this track before dark."

Cyrus turned and nodded to his companion before leading on in single file. He had intended to travel alone, but Simeon insisted that Colton join him as an escort. He could just as easily have sent Lambert, but Cyrus sensed that the general had instead used his influence to elevate his old friend. The border guard was certainly grateful for the opportunity to impress his king, and Cyrus had to admit that the company was welcome. He had become used to Colton during their journey to Ravensward.

It was already the third day of their journey away from Simeon's castle, and Cyrus found the atmosphere between he and Colton to be comfortable, if somewhat changed. Though the threat of impending danger had passed for Cyrus, their new task had made Colton more earnest and less sociable. As the conversation between them diminished, Cyrus came to accept that he, and indeed Brandon, were little more than a means to an end for Colton. He thought of the freedom that Simeon had promised him and accepted that the relationship between Colton and himself was a one of convenience, after all.

Colton was by no means a bad man, but he had little of Garrett's charm or humour, Cyrus thought. They had visited a number of small towns and villages to seek out word of Simeon's son, but Colton had brooded quietly with every disappointment, and Cyrus found that it was increasingly hard work to maintain his own morale. It seemed that their mission would not offer Colton easy passage into the King's Guard, seemingly much to Colton's dismay, and Cyrus started to wonder if they would ever find Simeon's elusive bastard.

"There, up ahead!" said Colton, drawing his horse close behind Adagio on the narrow path.

Cyrus should have seen it, but his head was lowered to brace against the wind, his skin stinging as the gale whistled and cracked like a whip. Colton was right, though: a fork in the road offered passage up into the snow-capped mountains, while a second, signposted path led through a gap in the rock, where the sounds of a town already rushed out to meet them. The town was called Crowmarsh, and the signpost that told them so signalled a timely arrival to their intended destination as giant hailstones began to fall from the sky.

"We need to get to cover," called Colton, stating the obvious.

The two of them raced into Crowmarsh's warm embrace, wary faces greeting them as they slowed to a halt in the market square. Hailstones continued to bounce from the ground as both riders dismounted and rushed their horses under the overhanging roof of what appeared to be a tavern. It had been quite the day for Adagio, but she followed Colton's steed, Morven, without hesitation, and both horses were soon fastened to the sturdy wooden supports of the tavern's porch.

A small boy approached expectantly, his hair shorn close to his scalp, his clothes a medley of materials sewn together in a style that reminded Cyrus of Farley's mother's patchwork blanket. Colton flipped a bronze coin in the boy's direction, tapping the pommel of his sword to complete their silent negotiation, and Cyrus followed Colton as he trudged away, leaving the horses in the boy's care.

"I don't know about you, but I need a drink," said Colton, gesturing toward a set of saloon doors. It seemed that they had done nothing but drink in recent days, yet Cyrus couldn't deny the appeal of another. Taverns seemed to offer their best chance at information as to Brandon's whereabouts at any rate, Cyrus reasoned. In fact, it had been a barmaid in the village of Blackwheat who had suggested, rather hesitantly, that they continue on into the mountains.

In the scheme of things, Blackwheat had been one of a number of pleasant stops along the way. Cyrus, who hadn't expected the journey to be enjoyable and was glad to be proven wrong, found himself increasingly frustrated that his travels were once more stricken by the pressures of time. He would have loved to be able to spend a few days at each stop. Instead, he noted small details in a journal and promised himself that he would compile them for Fran and Marcia one day, perhaps Adaline too. Though seemingly small and insignificant on the page, Cyrus was keen to savour the memories: the herd of bulls that broke free from their paddock to block the road outside of Milburn, or the knife juggler and the caravan of entertainers that they had passed on the road away from Ravensward. In the village of Casterthorn, Cyrus had silenced an entire tavern with stories of myth and legend, and the barkeep had offered them food and lodging in return.

So many miles and so many memories—but no sign of Brandon. That was, at least, until they met Cora, a redheaded barmaid at the Black Horse Tavern in Blackwheat. Her voice was as loud and confident as any that Cyrus had heard throughout the evening, and yet it dropped to little more than a whisper, her eyes twitching around the room, as she had uttered the name of this place: Crowmarsh.

Less than a day later, Cyrus watched the all-too-familiar sight of Colton stepping purposefully into yet another drinking hole, and Cyrus was looking forward to finding out what information Crowmarsh had to offer. The smell of ale and pipe smoke hung in the air as it did in all the taverns they'd visited along the way, but this tavern was not as dark and squalid as some they had seen. Here, wall-mounted candelabras brought a sense of warmth and light in contrast to conditions outside. Jovial conversation muffled the sound of hailstones crashing against the porch and paving stones, while friends played cards or sat before a crackling fire drinking to the sound of a jaunty musical quartet.

"Nice place," said Cyrus, reaching to brush his fingertips against a dark wooden beam hanging overhead which only added to the tavern's cosy atmosphere. "Let's see what they have to eat and start asking around. We must be getting close."

"Yes, my lord," said Colton with obvious sarcasm. Their meeting on the bridge seemed like a lifetime ago, as did the formalities between them, and Cyrus smiled as he turned in search of a table. The tavern was busy, but he soon found a small, round table in the corner, and the warmth of the fire prompted Cyrus to remove his coat and rest it upon a spare stool to dry. He retrieved his journal from a leather satchel and had only just arrived at the correct page when Colton slammed two large tankards onto the table, ale spilling from the top to create streaks in the ink of his most recent entry.

"I hope you like chicken," said Colton, wiping a foamy moustache from his face. "Also, I asked at the bar, but no sign of Brandon. I guess we are stuck with each other for a while yet."

"Lucky me," said Cyrus, rolling his eyes.

"Yes, I thought so."

"We'll keep asking around, maybe someone else will know something."

Colton shrugged. "Ever the optimist."

Cyrus recoiled at the thought that he could possibly be the more hopeful of the two, especially given everything that he had been through. He closed his journal and took a swig of his own drink. The bitterness of the ale made him grimace, but the drink was strong and seemed to smooth the edges of his concern with immediate effect. Colton appeared to be in one of his more talkative moods, but as Cyrus made to ask the border guard more about his history with Lambert, a group of men approached, and Cyrus placed his tankard down as the new arrivals stood ominously beside their table.

"Evening gentlemen," said the foremost, a lanky young man perhaps a few years older than Cyrus. He had dark, piercing eyes, slicked-back hair, and a gold chain hanging at his neck. "Sorry to bother you," he continued, his face expressionless and his tone not sounding very sorry at all, "but I noticed that you were asking for someone at the bar. What brings you boys this far into the mountains?"

Colton took a swig of his drink, and Cyrus wasn't sure if he was stalling for his own benefit or simply to make the man wait. "It's no bother," he said eventually, turning in his chair. "Just a couple of travellers from the city hoping we might see an old friend. We've no need of trouble."

At this the man only laughed. "Of course," he said, running a hand through his hair as he made to turn away. "Only, these are uncertain times. All this talk of rebellion and rumours of an uprising. It's hard to know who to trust."

"You're not wrong there," said Colton, standing to face the group. "A drink to peace, then, and may the right side prevail!" He extended his tankard toward the man, waiting for him to return the toast. "The name's Colton, and this is Cyrus. Pleasure to make your acquaintance."

"They call me The Shepherd," came the man's hesitant reply, eyes narrowed as he took a tankard from one of his men, a brutish character with a bald head and a nose ring. "Or just Shep. And this here is my crew."

"Well, cheers to you all, and to King Simeon. May his reign be long and prosperous."

"To King Simeon," Shep said flatly.

Without warning, Shep crashed his tankard into Colton's temple. Cyrus was caught off-guard, his mind not processing what had happened until the ale from Shep's tankard splashed onto Cyrus's own face. He made to stand, but the bald man lunged in his direction, wrapping thick hands around Cyrus's neck, rows of gold rings cutting into his skin.

"We don't want any trouble!" called the owner of the tavern, ducking behind the bar.

But as Cyrus snatched a glimpse about the room, he noticed that the damage was already done. The room was emptying, the saloon doors were swinging with the patrons' hasty exits, and the musicians stowed their instruments to make an escape of their own. Cyrus attempted to prise his attackers' fingers from his throat, but the man's grip was mercilessly strong, and his only reward for his attempt was a headlock that forced his chair onto its back legs.

"Oh, I'll see that the right side prevails," said Shep, crouching to place a burlap sack over Colton's barely-conscious face as Cyrus grew faint from the pressure on his neck. Shep continued, "The time of King Simeon is over, and you will both bear witness to the strength of the revolution."

Cyrus was released from his headlock momentarily as his head, too, was covered by a sack, his vision going dark. The woven material smelled like damp earth, and Cyrus was so focused on trying to tamp down his nausea that he was unable to object as his hands were tied behind him.

"You can't do this," he muttered desperately, but he knew it was a waste of breath.

A sharp blow struck unexpectedly on the back of his head, and his body went limp.

⚜ ⚜ ⚜

Cyrus opened his eyes and squinted into the darkness. He could see no more than a few feet at first, but shapes and forms slowly began to appear in his vision, and damp, stagnant air told him he'd awoken in a cave of some description.

Colton, he thought, casting his mind back to the attack in the tavern. Cyrus was propped against a cold, harsh wall, but chains pulled him back as he attempted to stand. His head throbbed from the beating it had taken, and he couldn't believe that after avoiding Simeon's dungeons, he'd ended up imprisoned after all. And by a bunch of rebels at that.

"He's awake," came a voice from the darkness, and as Cyrus leaned forward, he could just make out the silhouette of another person propped against the opposite wall. The voice was not familiar, but Cyrus recognised the man's accent to be Verderan, and his words echoed from the walls and low ceiling in a way that made Cyrus feel immediately claustrophobic.

"I wouldn't worry about escaping." The second voice was Colton's, and he appeared to Cyrus's left with similar shackles. "These chains are fixed into the mountain, and even if you were to escape, you'd do well to get through that!" It seemed that he'd been awake for some time.

Cyrus followed Colton's gesture to his right to what looked like a very heavy door appearing through the gloom.

"Wood that would bend an axe," continued Colton, his voice grim. "Steel bars on the window too. There's no escaping this one."

A small light appeared beyond the door, and an orange glow climbed the walls as footsteps grew closer, muffled voices becoming clearer all the while. Colton shuffled back at the sound of keys finding the lock, and the candle cast enough light through the window to illuminate their surroundings for the first time.

"Well, open it," came Shep's impatient voice from the other side of the door.

Cyrus snatched a candlelit moment to survey their cell and saw that the Verderan had a long, grey beard resting on his lap, and a calm expression that suggested that none of this was new to him. Colton, meanwhile, sat with his knees pulled to his chest, and, Cyrus saw the same fear upon his companion's face that he had worn as he had watched Flynn's body swaying in the wind back at Farley's.

The lock clicked open, and Shep entered the room. He was accompanied by the small boy who had offered to care for their horses outside of the tavern. "Well, look who it is," said Shep, oozing confidence. "Twice in one day, and to think that we were strangers only a few hours ago!"

"What is it that you want?" asked Cyrus, unwilling to play games. It was only then that he realised how sore his throat had become. His voice sounded scratchy and strained, and the rest of his body still ached from whatever beating he had taken whilst unconscious.

"Well now, isn't that the million-mark question?" Shep pursed his lips as he rested his head on one side. "I guess the short answer is to see King Simeon buried firmly in the ground." He wandered over to Cyrus and crouched before him. "We will see that fool from the throne, and in doing so, I will see our people prosper once more!"

"We meant no offence," said Cyrus as their captor stood to walk away. "It was only a toast. Perhaps we can come to some arrangement, for our freedom that is?" He noticed the desperation in his voice but saw few other options. "We have money—"

"*Had* money," Shep interjected, turning back to face him. "Yes, we have your little coin purse. A very welcome contribution to our cause, thank you."

Cyrus slumped back as it dawned on him: if they had his money, they had his bag, and if they had his bag, then they had his journal. It would only be a matter of time before they discovered his true identity, and that would surely be the end of them.

"We have this as well," Shep continued, dangling a small object that Cyrus could barely see through the light. "Might be important, maybe not, but I thought we should take it from you to ensure your…*cooperation.*" He stepped a little closer, and the boy raised the candle without instruction to bring Cyrus's worst fears into the light.

"My bracelet!" Cyrus called, straining at the chains. It was the last thing Fran had given him before he left her in Highcastle, and tears formed in his eyes with thoughts of home, thoughts of Fran. "What is it that you want?" he repeated in a shout, this time with far less composure.

"You cannot win against Simeon!" added Colton, with more vigour than Cyrus could have mustered. He couldn't question Colton's faith in his king, but Cyrus cursed inwardly at the rather churlish outburst.

He needn't have worried. Their attempts seemed not to affect Shep at all, his malicious smirk ever-present in the candlelight. He turned to Colton, "Now that's where you're wrong. The man is old and weak. My sources tell me he had the king of Easthaven in his grasp and let the boy go." He shook his head and tutted loudly, and Cyrus was keenly aware of his own sweaty palms. "He took superior numbers across the border and still lost. He made this country a laughingstock, lost countless lives, and worst of all," he paused for impact, "the people are still hungry."

"I know people within the castle," said Colton, sensing an opportunity. "I can get you an audience with the king. I can help!"

Shep burst into a bout of dramatic laughter, and Cyrus noticed that the boy with the candle had remained silent all the while. The

Verderan man watched on intently but offered no words as their captor made to speak once more.

"The time for talk is over," Shep began, returning to the centre of the room. "We have our friends, and I am in no need of your introduction. As to the question of whether we can beat Simeon," he paused again as he gestured the young boy back toward the door, "I tell you that we will, and that you are going to help me. Now get some rest," he said, as the door creaked open. "Work begins at dawn."

Morning arrived with the sound of keys plunging into the cell door.

"Rise and shine," came a voice, but as Cyrus sat up, wide awake and quite sore from sitting on the hard floor all night, he wondered how anyone could ever sleep in this awful place. Then again, Cyrus thought as he manoeuvred slightly to massage the cramp in his back, it didn't seem to have bothered his cellmates.

As if the damp and the rats weren't bad enough, Colton had spent the entire night tossing and turning and making awful sounds in his sleep, presumably from nightmares, while the Verderan stranger snored like a bear among fits of conversation in his mother tongue.

As the jailer entered, Cyrus yawned deeply, surprising himself. It was the same bald man who had attacked him the previous day, and the smug look on his face suggested that he had enjoyed it.

"Does sir require a little longer in bed?" he asked sarcastically, gesturing to leave before his face turned serious once more. "Time for work, traitors," he continued, shuffling a large set of keys in his hand. "No funny business, all right? Or else, we will have a repeat of yesterday."

Cyrus sat silently as the other two roused. He had no idea what to expect but felt a familiar sense of despair at his predicament. *Same old Cyrus*, he thought. *Always chasing adventure with little appreciation for the dangers.* He should have known, and his sister had said as much before he left Highcastle.

Fran's cautionary words echoed in his mind, and Cyrus felt sick with the realisation that her bracelet was gone. He found himself in a truly hopeless situation, and he was struck with a surprising pang of sadness for Simeon. His son was still out there somewhere, oblivious to his heritage and his father's failing health. While Cyrus spent time chained up in this mountain, he knew that Simeon might be running out of time to meet his only son. This, in turn prompted thoughts of Anselm, the father he had never known. While a younger Cyrus might have felt anger at the situation, this new, older Cyrus stood silently and without question as the bald man unlocked his shackles from their fixture on the wall, leaving his hands bound as they went.

"Where are you taking us?" asked Colton, his eyebrows narrowed in a look of concern.

"Oh, you'll see soon enough." The bald man yanked Colton as he gestured for Cyrus to move toward the door. "Shep will be more than happy to answer your questions, I'm sure."

The bald man pushed Cyrus forward and out of the cell. He had Colton by the arm and was dragging him in a similar fashion, while the Verderan was left to sit silently in the half-light.

"Why not him?" asked Cyrus, breaking his silence to nod back toward the Verderan.

The bald man ignored his question, and the three of them shuffled onward into the passage beyond. "Take a left!" the bald man said roughly, and Cyrus followed his order, turning to face a long, cavernous corridor. Candles lined the walls to add light, yet Cyrus could not see an end to their path, and he felt, more than ever, that he was walking towards his doom. Above them, sharp spikes of rock projected from the ceiling like spear points, while bat wings fluttered in the darkness and anguished cries echoed around them. With every step, Cyrus noticed more cells like his own, young faces staring back at him from each window, their hands gripped tightly at the steel bars as Cyrus passed.

What is this place? he wondered without ever breaking stride. They were certainly inside the mountain, but the intricate warren of pathways and doors was like nothing he had ever seen. To his right, a larger wooden door appeared. It didn't have windows like the others, and two armed men stood guarding the entrance. Probably a storeroom, Cyrus thought, and he felt certain his belongings were stowed inside.

Cyrus stopped for a moment, wondering about the room's contents, but a sharp push in the back knocked him forward, and he lost his footing to land awkwardly on the chalky ground. Both guards sniggered as he struggled to his feet, and he decided to continue without prompting further encouragement from any of the brutish men. The bald man continued to grunt instructions as they navigated the labyrinth before them.

It seemed that they had walked for an age, and when their escort finally instructed them to stop, Cyrus wondered how he would ever find his way back, or indeed out of the mountain. They had arrived at an enormous set of doors equal to the entrance of Eldred's Keep, and the bald man took this moment to take the lead, pushing through the doors and dragging both Cyrus and Colton into the cavern beyond.

"Apologies, Shep," he called as the lanky man appeared before them, bathed in candlelight. "This one has slow feet and wandering eyes." He pointed at Cyrus, who swallowed the instinct to answer back at him.

"It's no problem, Nelson," said Shep, nodding at his underling in reassurance. "In fact, you are just in time. Put them with the others."

Cyrus stumbled forward as Nelson nudged him toward the middle of the enormous room. It was like a dome in the heart of the mountain, with three sets of large doors distributed at even distances around the circular walls, including those from which Cyrus and Colton had just entered. The ceiling in the middle of the room was higher than the section that they had just walked through, and every sound seemed to reverberate in a way that reminded Cyrus of the small chapel he had always hated to attend in Corhollow.

In the middle of the room stood lines of other men, women, and children, numbering perhaps fifty in total. Their clothes were stained black, and their faces were smudged with the same grime. As they joined the end of a line, Cyrus noticed that the black dirt stained the hands and nails of all those around him, but, he realised, only the adults were chained.

"Good morning, all," began Shep, and Cyrus snapped to attention, along with all the others in his line. "I wanted to take this opportunity to visit you all in person. You'll notice that we have some new arrivals, and I want to ensure that we are all clear to our purpose."

All eyes fell upon Cyrus, and it was all that he could do to maintain a blank expression under the weight of their stares.

"This," Shep continued, raising a clump of white rock in the air, "this, is why we are all here." He turned the rock in his hand, and Cyrus noticed, even at a distance, that it sparkled in the candlelight, like large salt crystals clinging to stone. "We have powerful friends that will use this to destroy the foundations of the old world and build it anew, friends who pay us good money for nature's bounty…money that allows me to feed you all and spare you the suffering of the thirst and hunger that epitomise Simeon's reign." He smiled as he tossed the rock in the air before catching it and holding it aloft once more. "Even as we speak, the Verderan army is marching on Highcastle, where they will harness the power of this very rock and with clever alchemy create a powder that will blast through the walls of Eldred's Keep, razing Highcastle to the ground!"

Cyrus stood, careful to keep his face expressionless and his stare ever-forward even as he felt Colton's eyes upon him. It felt as though he had turned to ice inside. So, this was the princes' plan and the reason behind their timewasting in Casarossa with all their riddles and games. The war with Simeon had only ever been a distraction, and Cyrus cursed himself for deserting the castle in their time of need. Once more, he thought of home, and his concern spiralled for the wellbeing of all those living in the capital, oblivious to the danger that was heading in their direction. He knew now, if he hadn't before, that he had to escape from this prison. He had to save them all.

"So, your efforts here are most valuable," Shep began once more, his voice reminding Cyrus of Augustus's victory address after their army's recent encounter with Simeon. That speech already felt like a lifetime ago, though in truth it had only been weeks. Shep's enthusiasm seemed to grow as he continued, "Together we shall see Highcastle fall and in doing so begin a chain of events that will see Simeon follow!"

His words prompted applause from Nelson, and Cyrus noticed even through his panic that the bald man was joined in celebration by the unshackled children. Though the sound of applause echoed around the chamber, the atmosphere was eerily muted. As Cyrus tried to pinpoint the reason for this, he realised that the children were clapping but otherwise made no noise. They certainly weren't vocalising anything. They were, to all intents and purposes, silent, while the faces of the men and women around him seemed to mirror his concern.

"To work then!" Shep called in a final attempt to rouse the assembly. With that, a set of doors creaked open on the far side of the room, signalling Nelson to step forward and motion the workers row-by-row toward two other guards who stood waiting for them.

"Keep moving!" he called, his hand hovering over his sword as a means of encouragement. It was all remarkably orderly, and as Cyrus joined the line with Colton behind him, he noticed the small boy in patchwork clothing distributing pickaxes from a large wooden crate as the workers passed through the doors.

"We're going to die here," whispered Colton, but with guards nearby, Cyrus decided it was better not to answer. In the end, he simply took his axe and descended into the darkness with everyone else. Though he didn't say so, he privately agreed that Colton was probably right.

⚜ ⚜ ⚜

"My hands," cried Colton, dropping his axe onto the ground in frustration. Cyrus stopped chipping at the fissure for a moment and turned to Colton to inspect the weeping callouses on his companion's hands.

"Three days, Cyrus. We've been here three days already! Nobody even knows where we are, and every success puts the lives of innocent people at risk!" He kicked his bucket of rocks over, scattering the crystalline contents across the ground. It felt like a moment of small victory until one of Shep's guards wandered over, looked down at the spillage, and landed a heavy fist in Colton's kidneys. This wasn't the first time.

"We'll find a way," said Cyrus, kneeling to help Colton up from where he'd fallen on the ground. Together, they gathered the fruits of his labour back into his bucket. "We just need to ask around. Someone must know the way out of here."

Colton dusted himself off as he rose to his feet, adding another streaky black handprint to his trousers. He glanced around wearily and kept his voice low. "It's not that easy, though, is it? We were just *asking around* in the tavern, and look where that got us. As for our Verderan cellmate, I don't trust him one bit. Face it: we're trapped."

"We'll find someone," said Cyrus, solemnly, turning back to the wall to avoid further suspicion from the guards. He put on his best, most confident voice and said, "I can get us out of here. I'm sure of it."

⚜ ⚜ ⚜

"Hey," Cyrus said, sidling over to a boy who was using the point of his axe to dig the white crystals out of the mountain. "I see you've had a good haul today. Shep will be pleased." Cyrus pointed towards the boy's full bucket, glinting in the candlelight. The mineshaft was barely taller than head height at the best of times, but this was an especially low section, and the air was humid and full of dust.

When the boy only grunted in response, Cyrus tried again. "How long have you been here? I'm new, you see, and—"

"He won't answer."

Cyrus turned to see a man approaching, and he was relieved to find that it was not a guard. The man wore a scarf about his head despite the humidity, and he had a small patch of beard beneath his lower lip.

"He won't answer, or rather he can't," the man continued. "The poor boy has lost his words. He's—"

"A *Shadow*," finished Cyrus, eyes narrowed as everything fell into place. The disappearances in Ravensward, the young faces at the cell windows, and the children at Shep's speech days before. Shep was building a revolution on the back of these poor children, using them for cheap or possibly even free labour while he seized power for himself with the help of the Verderans.

"A Shadow, exactly," answered the man, ducking into the alcove as the boy took his bucket and moved further into the mine. "Best you keep your volume down, though. If the guards hear you talking, they'll have your tongue, and you'll be facing a similar problem." He stepped shoulder-to-shoulder with Cyrus, facing the rock, and raised his axe to the section that the boy had been working on. "You're playing a risky game, new guy. Most of us have been here for months, and let me tell you, the sooner you accept your fate, the better."

"My fate?"

"Yes, your fate, and whatever you're thinking, I assure you it's no different to the one that faces rest of us."

"But there must be a way out," he said weakly. It was meant as a question, but it sounded little more than a hopeful statement in the moment. "There's another door in the main chamber," Cyrus continued, "There has to be a way in…a way *out*."

The man considered his words for a moment and parted a section of rock from the mountain with admirable technique. Cyrus glanced down and noticed that his own hands were shaking after three long days behind the axe, and his stomach sank as he was momentarily and painfully reminded of Garrett.

"Oh, there's a way out of course," said the man eventually, dropping another slab of sparkling stone into a bucket. "But you won't be leaving this place, not alive anyway. Now, out of my way. I'm taking this haul to Nelson. I suggest you do the same and try to eat something. You're looking a little shaky."

“Disgusting, isn’t it?” a woman said.

Cyrus had never spoken to the woman before, but he’d noticed her at the morning assembly on a couple of occasions, and it was the first time he had heard her speak. Her blonde hair was stained with the same dirt that seemed to cover every conceivable surface here, and her hands, though small and delicate, carried the scarred story of a history in the mine.

“Three months I’ve been here now,” she persisted, through a mouthful of stale bread. “Three months working all hours with nothing but bread and rancid water as a reward. It’s okay for them,” she gestured to where a group of Shadow children huddled silently, devouring their bread as though it were a delicacy. “They don’t know anything else. But I can’t do this anymore.”

Cyrus looked around warily. They were permitted a short break for lunch each day, but they had their meal in the main chamber above the mine, and the room was well-guarded by Shep’s men. The cavernous nature of their surroundings meant that voices carried easily to unwanted ears, so Cyrus lowered his voice as he leaned in to respond. “I’m told there is no way out of here, at least not alive.” He took a bite of his own bread and frowned at the flavour, though he was grateful for the sustenance as his stomach rumbled loudly. “I’ve only been here four days, but so far, I’ve learned nothing.”

“Hmm,” began the woman, with a swig of brown water to wash the taste of the bread away. “Well, perhaps you aren’t asking the right people. There are too many in here that have given up.

That fool calls himself 'The Shepherd.' Well, I'm no lamb to slaughter. Here, look at this." She rustled in her pockets to pull out a filthy-looking piece of parchment.

Cyrus took a cautious look before huddling closer. "What is it?" he asked. At first, it looked like little more than a jumble of lines sullied with dirt, but as his eyes focussed on the details, he found that he had already answered his own question.

"A map," he said excitedly, before clearing his throat to lower his voice. "A map of the mountain. But where did you get it?"

"I may be ragged now, but I didn't always look like this." She turned and cut her eyes toward Nelson, who was laughing with one of the other guards. "Our friend Nelson used to bring me all sorts of treats. It was mainly food and drink from the outside, but I helped myself to one or two other items." She folded the map and pressed it into Cyrus's hand. "Shep punished him when he lost the map, and he hasn't been the same since, but he never asked me about it. Maybe he doesn't want to know the answer."

"So, we can escape then?" asked Cyrus, his brain still catching up. "With the map that is, we can find a way out?"

"Well, I'll need your help for that. Your friend," she pointed at Colton who was collecting his own scrap of bread from the guards. "I hear he used to train with the King's Guard. Is that true?"

Cyrus nodded.

"Well in that case, the name is Maida, but there is someone else you need to meet."

⚜ ⚜ ⚜

Cyrus approached the man from behind, Maida's password bouncing around his head like a bright idea, and in truth it was. His name was Abel, Maida had told Cyrus, and he had been one of the earliest to arrive in the mountain. As he approached Abel, Cyrus noticed lengths of greasy hair upon Abel's shoulder, streaks of grey nearly hidden by the pervasive filth of the mine. He was, to Cyrus's thinking, similar in age to Garrett, and he hoped that the man had at least half of his old friend's spirit. He was going to need it.

Cyrus continued forward slowly, and it seemed that Abel was oblivious to his presence as he continued to chip away at the mountain. With five days of experience, Cyrus could already appreciate the precise nature of the man's strikes, and as a large section of white crystals fell from the wall, Cyrus knew he had found his man. A momentary pause allowed Cyrus to cover the last few yards, but as he reached to touch the older man's shoulder, Abel turned suddenly to place his axe at Cyrus's throat.

"What is it that you want, boy?" he growled, his eyes narrowed, and jaw clenched.

Cyrus knew he would need to answer promptly, but he was taken by shock. He'd been forced back against the wall, and he wondered if he was going to die alone in the darkness. "Freedom," he spluttered in desperation. "Only freedom…don't you?"

Abel's eyes twitched, glancing around them, before the axe lowered and a brief smile calmed Cyrus's thudding heart as the older man backed away. His face was a mass of dark beard with wiry grey protrusions, and though he had the appearance of a wild animal, there was a kindness in the man's eyes that put Cyrus at ease.

"That's a big idea you have there, boy," said Abel, letting the axe fall at his side. "Is it worth your life?"

"What life?" asked Cyrus, straightening his soot-stained shirt before realising the futility of his efforts and turning his attention back to Abel. "It means nothing compared to those of the innocent people in Highcastle or Ravensward. The Verderans won't stop because Shep tells them to. I know the princes, and they will see us all in chains. Out of the cooking pot and into the fire!"

"And how is it you know all of this?" Abel asked, a brow raised.

Cyrus froze at the question. "History," he said eventually, his heart racing once more at the thought of his identity being discovered. He remembered a time when he was just Cyrus from Corhollow and wished for a simple life without secrecy and lies, a time when he wouldn't have to obscure his identity for his own safety. "Obviously, I don't *actually* know the princes," he said, stumbling over his words in an attempt to move the conversation along. "I've read about people like them. This is how it starts, and soon enough we will all be beneath a Verderan heel!"

"Hmm," Abel muttered, biting at his lower lip in thought. "Your accent is Low Country, but there's something about you…" He circled Cyrus like a man surveying an ox at market. "You've got a certain poise, boy, that distinction that you only find in the city. There's a story here, but you aren't going to tell me, are you?"

Cyrus remained silent as the man paused to consider him.

"Okay, I'll help you. As it happens, I think you're right about the Verderans, and I have no intention of being burned by the flames of their mad ambition. I presume that Maida gave you the password, and if she trusts you, that's good enough for me. What do you need?"

Cyrus's shoulders slumped with relief, and he huddled closer to Abel, lowering his voice as he spoke. "We're getting out of here," he whispered urgently, conscious that they would only escape the guards' attention for so long. "I'm going to try and find a way to get us all out of here, but we'll need weapons. The guards take the axes back at the end of each day, and we won't manage it unarmed."

"So, she sent you to old Abel the stonemason?" Abel chuckled quietly, stroking the knots out of his hefty beard. "I might have something," he said, rolling his right sleeve as he spoke. "It's no less than Shep deserves, arming a skilled man with an axe. It may not look like much, but it's sharp. It will do the job."

Cyrus watched as Abel rolled his sleeve to the shoulder. The man's upper arm was tied tightly with criss-crossed string that might once have been a boot lace, and Cyrus noticed that the string was being used to hold something in place. Without hesitation, Abel took the end of the string and pulled it lightly so that the binding began to unravel, leaving deep impressions on his skin once it had fallen away.

"A blade?" asked Cyrus as a piece of sharpened stone fell away from Abel's arm. It had been fashioned into the shape of a large arrowhead and bound to a small wooden base, which acted as a handle.

"Not quite," Abel answered, placing the makeshift weapon in Cyrus's hand, "but it was the best I could do with a pickaxe and some flint. It'll take some force, but only a fool would underestimate the damage it can do."

Cyrus ran his fingers along the point of the knife and, though modest, it was more than he could have hoped for in the circumstances.

"Make them pay," Abel added ominously. "I haven't the mind to plan this escape, but when the time comes, you can count on me to stand beside you."

⚜ ⚜ ⚜

"Long time, no see, gentlemen."

A solid nudge in Cyrus's back caused him to fall forward into his cell, where Shep was crouching in front of the Verderan with his head turned to face them.

"Thank you, Nelson," Shep said, nodding his head toward the cell door. "Outside will be fine." Nelson trudged away, almost as though he was being denied a real treat by not being allowed to stay and watch.

It was the first time that Cyrus had seen Shep since he had revealed his plot with the princes four days earlier. His appearance in the cell was unsettling, especially since their Verderan cellmate wore a carefully blank expression, which only made Cyrus more suspicious still. Behind Cyrus, Colton stepped into the cell, and Nelson closed the door from the outside.

Shep was accompanied by the boy that Cyrus had begun to think of as Patch, owing to the piecemeal nature of his clothes, and as usual, the boy held a candle that illuminated the cell with a dim glow.

"Please, sit," Shep continued, gesturing Colton and Cyrus to their respective shackles hanging loose from the wall. "You must be tired after a long day. Rest and eat."

Cyrus shuffled over to his position against the wall and noticed that his usual heft of stale bread was accompanied by a bowl of thick brown liquid. It didn't look like a broth, but Cyrus judged by the smell that that's what it was supposed to be.

"You see," said Shep, "work diligently, and you will be rewarded. A little taste of my vision for the future!"

Cyrus gathered that the broth was meant to be a reward, despite its revolting appearance. "The future?" he spat, sitting without contest. "What future is that, Shep? War promises nothing but destruction."

Shep tutted loudly as he rose from beside the Verderan. He shook his head, the picture of a disappointed father. "And there I was thinking that we might have…changed you these past few days. Has the enthusiasm and productivity of my workforce had no effect upon you?"

"Children," Cyrus corrected him, with fire in his voice. "Not a workforce but prisoners and children. Shadows, who you treat as slaves."

Shep snapped forward and pointed a bony finger in Cyrus's face. "Lambs!" he yelled. "We don't call them Shadows here. They are naught but lost lambs. I am The Shepherd and they are my flock."

"You're insane," answered Cyrus, in spite of Shep's threatening figure looming over him. He couldn't help himself. "You pretend to care about them, provide them with a little freedom and barely edible food, but this is no kind of life for these children."

He looked across at Patch, who lingered for a moment before averting his eyes. "It isn't real freedom or opportunity, but slavery," he said, directing his words at Patch to try to drive the point home, before turning back to Shep. "And I will play no further part in it!"

"You will do as I say!" Shep took another step forward and squeezed a tight grip around Cyrus's throat, his other hand on the hilt of his sword. He paused for a moment; eyes bloodshot as he fixed Cyrus with a stare. "It seems I may have been wrong, though." He reached to collect the bowl of broth before tipping the liquid onto the floor. Despite how unappetising the bowl of broth had looked, Cyrus's stomach grumbled in protest, and Cyrus was taken aback by the blatant waste of food when all Shep seemed to talk about was the lack of food in Simeon's kingdom.

"You do not deserve my generosity," Shep continued. "You will return to basic rations tomorrow, and I don't want to hear of any further outbursts, or I will make your life extremely uncomfortable."

Shep extended the empty bowl in Patch's direction, and the boy ran over to collect it before continuing to secure Cyrus and Colton to their irons. Shep watched on, all the while, hand still hovering ominously over his sword. Once they were both secure, Shep and Patch made to leave, and the cell became darker with every step as the candle went with them. Shep banged on the cell door with a heavy fist, and Nelson welcomed them back into the corridor.

"Rest well," came Shep's final word, his voice echoing in the passageway as the door slammed shut behind him. "Tomorrow is a new day."

“Oh, it certainly is,” Cyrus muttered, manoeuvring his arm to check that the makeshift blade was still tied in place. “I’ll make sure of it.”

"It's time," whispered Cyrus as soft light began to reach their cell. It was Patch's morning task to light the candles in the corridors before food rations were brought to each cell. Cyrus's heart was beating fast, and he was full of nervous energy as he sat up and gave Colton a nod of reassurance.

"You can't do this, you know?" the Verderan said unexpectedly in his thick accent. "One mistake and you'll kill us all. Can you live with that much blood on your hands?"

Cyrus shook his head dismissively, not willing to let the Verderan's words rattle him from his purpose. "Rather that than see innocent people die in Highcastle," he said. "I have a score to settle with your princes—"

"The princes?" asked the Verderan, straightening his back with interest. "What do you know of the princes?"

Keys sounded in the lock as Cyrus made to answer, and Patch swept into the room with a customary sack of dry bread. He was silent as always, but Cyrus could sense uncertainty in the boy that he had hoped to goad during their last meeting.

"Thank you," said Colton, and his exaggerated smile was wide and appreciative as he took the bread. "You've always been good to us, and I know you'll have been looking after the horses too, just like I asked when we first met in Crowmarsh. Honest money for honest work."

Patch paused momentarily, and Cyrus noticed a subtle narrowing in the boy's eyes as Colton's words seemed to register.

"He's right, you know?" added Cyrus, seizing the moment. "You like horses, I imagine? The speed...the freedom. I knew a man who started out as a stable boy and became shield to the king of Easthaven!"

To this, Patch showed no reaction, and Cyrus sensed it was now or never as the boy knelt, seemingly unaffected, to offer bread.

"I can get *you* a job in the stables in Highcastle," he said desperately, reaching to grab the boy's arm. Patch tried to pull away in shock, but Cyrus's grip was too tight, and to Cyrus's surprise, Patch remained silent despite the constraint. "I can give you money and all the freedom you want," Cyrus continued, pulling the boy closer. Patch's eyes widened either in shock or fear. "This isn't living. You're enslaved to Shep, and he doesn't care about you, only what you can help him to achieve. Release us..." he added gently, and Patch's head lowered as though, for the first time, he was starting to see sense. "Set us free and we can save lives. I will see you safe—"

Patch's head fell limp as Colton's food bowl bounced from his skull with a sickening crunch and cracked into pieces on the floor.

"What are you doing?" Cyrus asked, venting his annoyance.

"It was taking too long!" Colton whispered urgently. "Get the keys, and let's get out of here."

Cyrus was overwhelmed with guilt; the boy was little older than Fran, and Cyrus was convinced that he had been getting through to him. He adjusted himself and rolled the boy's body onto the floor gently, reaching to empty the sack of bread before folding it to create a makeshift pillow in order to raise Patch's head from the cold floor. As he moved the boy's head, Cyrus felt small rushes of breath coming from the boy's mouth, though he was still unconscious.

"He's still alive," Cyrus said with relief.

"Well, good for him," answered Colton. "Now if it's all the same to you, I'd like to stay that way myself."

Cyrus nodded before reaching to take the set of keys from Patch's pocket. He'd been watching the boy for days and knew exactly what he was looking for. In only a matter of seconds, he arrived at Colton's side to release him, and as the two men stood, brushing themselves down, Cyrus suddenly remembered that they were not alone.

"What about him?" asked Colton, gesturing at the Verderan. Colton seemed to have remembered their cellmate at the same time as Cyrus.

"He's a prisoner, isn't he?" answered Cyrus. "We set him free."

"I'm not going anywhere," argued the Verderan. "You want to risk your own lives, be my guest. I'm safer here."

Cyrus unhooked a key from the chain and threw it at the old man's feet. "Do as you like, but we are getting out of here." He reached to untie the knife from his arm, but at that moment, a booming voice echoed in the corridor. Nelson.

"Everything okay in there, boy?" he called, causing Cyrus to freeze in place. He should have known Shep wouldn't send Patch alone.

"Give me the knife," said Colton urgently, reaching to take the handle from Cyrus. "Get on the floor with the boy. I'll take care of the rest."

Cyrus felt a little sceptical, but he didn't have too much time to question it. He hurried over to where Patch still lay on the floor and crouched down next to the boy as Colton pressed himself against the wall nearest the door, lingering ominously in the shadows.

"Help!" Colton called, unexpectedly, and as Cyrus panicked, scrabbling backward with his feet, the sound of heavy footsteps thundered down the corridor, Nelson's heavy breathing growing louder with every step.

It was only a moment before the bald man arrived at the door, and his eyes grew wide as he noticed Patch laid out upon the floor, Cyrus still crouched a few paces behind his unconscious body.

"What the—" Nelson began, but he never finished. Colton stepped from the shadows to drive the makeshift knife into soft flesh where his neck and shoulders met. His next words were gurgled as he sank to his knees, and the pressure of Nelson's thick hand did little to stem the flow of blood as he fell face-first onto the ground.

"We need to go," Colton said, offering Cyrus a hand to pull him to his feet before kneeling to collect Nelson's sword. Cyrus closed in behind his companion, and together they edged into the corridor. The path before them was clear, and Cyrus took a moment to review the map. He knew the path back to the main chamber well enough, but dark smudges indicated rows of cells where the other prisoners were being kept, and Cyrus was keen to make good on his promise to see the others free.

"Let's go," he said, folding the map once more and stowing it into his pocket. They took only a few strides before they reached the first set of cells, and though they remained undiscovered by guards, the faces of Shadow children peered back at them through the bars expectantly, watching in silence as Cyrus shuffled through the keys to find one that would deliver their freedom. Colton stood guard with Nelson's sword extended, and while his presence was something of a comfort, Cyrus still felt a wave of relief as the first lock clicked loose and he kicked the door open.

"Come on!" he said, quietly but urgently waving his arms to motion the children out before he moved on to the next cell. Door after door, Cyrus hurried to invite escape, yet with every backward step and fearful expression, he began to realise that none of them were coming, presumably because none of them actually wanted to leave. Cyrus thought of Maida, Abel, and even their Verderan cellmate—all the others who had been imprisoned by Shep's wild ambition and made to believe they were on a path to something greater. Some of them, Cyrus thought, knew what was best for them and wanted to go. Some of them—like these little ones—had never known anything else.

Cyrus glanced back at the children lingering in their unlocked cells once more before Colton nudged him. They didn't have time to stand around. Reluctantly pulling himself away from the children, Cyrus followed Colton along the path, and then they took a right turn toward the remaining cells, away from any route that Cyrus had taken previously.

A guard appeared unexpectedly. "Hey, you—" he said, noticing Cyrus and Colton, but that was all he could get out before Colton dashed forward to silence the man forevermore.

Maida's cell was ahead on the right, and Cyrus rushed ahead of Colton to fidget at the lock. Maida's hands gripped the bars tightly as Colton snatched keys from the fallen guard to follow Cyrus's lead with the surrounding cell doors. Within minutes, the doors were all open, and Cyrus curbed the rising fervour of their growing crowd, which appeared to number around thirty at first glance. He knew there were two doors outside of the main chamber, one of which led to the mine and the other marked as the exit. He just had to get them there without detection. He pulled out the map again, just to glance over it one more time, his heart racing.

"The guards chambers are all here," he said, pointing at an area on the map as a number of the escapees gathered around him. He knew that Maida had warned the others to be ready, but Cyrus was suddenly struck with a weight of responsibility, as their expectant faces stared back at him, their path to freedom almost solely in his hands. "Stick together," he continued, composing himself. "Colton here will lead the way," he said, nodding to his friend. "Move quickly, and we head straight for the exit." He paused for a moment, watching as Colton dashed away in the direction from which they'd come with a number of the others in tow.

I can't leave without getting my things back, Cyrus thought, and he grabbed the dead guard's sword. It was no use to him now, after all. With a look back down at the corpse, Cyrus hurried along to catch up with the others.

It took them no time to reach the main pathway, retracing Colton and Cyrus's steps as they went, and the lack of guards highlighted Shep's inflated self-confidence. By the time Cyrus re-joined the group, they were huddled and crouched in the shadows a short distance from the storeroom door that Cyrus had noticed on his first day. Colton peered around the corner and looked back at Cyrus, raising two fingers to indicate the number of men guarding the door.

It wouldn't be easy, but they wouldn't be expecting it. The two guards were engaged in lively conversation that echoed all around them, and as Cyrus edged forward to take a look for himself, it was clear that they were entirely unaware of his presence and that of the other escapees. Cyrus glanced back at the others a final time and then at Colton, who gave a silent nod, sword already raised with purpose. It was all a matter of timing now, and Cyrus braced himself, waiting patiently, until the guard nearest them turned to expose his back before stepping toward his colleague, obscuring the other man's view of where he and Colton were hiding. This was the opportunity. They wouldn't see it coming.

Cyrus seized the moment and, with it, the element of surprise. He dashed forward to drive his sword into the first guard's back and breathed a sigh of relief as Colton dashed beyond him to silence the other man in similarly efficient fashion. "Go on ahead," he said in a raised whisper to Colton, with the bodies of both men slumped at their feet.

"But," Colton began, but Cyrus shook his head. Colton sighed, like he knew he wouldn't be able to change Cyrus's mind, and motioned the group forward with him, leaving Cyrus behind.

With the others gone, Cyrus pushed the storeroom door with all his bodyweight, and as the door screeched open, his jaw fell loose.

Daylight. The door was no storeroom, but an exit. He breathed in deeply and started to smile, but then it dawned on him: if this was the exit, where were the others heading?

He squinted toward the small, dusty square before him, snow-capped mountains looming ominously on all sides with a single path leading away and back down into the valley. This was it; this was freedom, his chance to warn those in Highcastle about the army that was heading in their direction. He noticed a corral for horses and registered Adagio and Morven immediately. He had to go—he knew it might be now or never—but as he moved a step further into the light, he knew that he couldn't leave. It was his plan that had led them this far, and the others would be relying on him to see them free.

Cyrus turned hastily, cursing the situation as he rushed back into the mountain. He no longer feared the presence of guards and ran without thought, sword outstretched before him. His breaths were short with panic as he ran, yet the sound of his panting was soon lost in what Cyrus realised with dread were the sounds of a desperate battle.

He could not let them die, and that knowledge was pulsing frantically through his head. His freedom, he knew, was no bargain for their lives. Adrenaline rushed through his body, and he could feel his anxiety spiralling with every stride as he moved toward the source of the sound. He ground to a halt as he reached the main chamber, and though he tried to prepare himself for the worst, his jaw still fell slack as he witnessed the slaughter unfolding before him.

All around him, the escapees were fighting for their lives. The box of pickaxes had been broken open, and some were armed, yet the majority ran with only hope as a weapon. Their numbers were dwindling with every passing moment, and Cyrus knew, without doubt, that they could never prevail.

"Get out of here!" Colton screamed at Cyrus, pulling his sword from the gut of one of Shep's men. Blood was splattered on his face, but it did not seem to be his own. Many of their fellow escapees hadn't been as lucky, Cyrus saw, his stomach dropping.

Meanwhile, Shep's men were everywhere. They were armed and prepared. Someone had tipped them off, but who? As Cyrus's eyes fell upon Maida's lifeless body, he knew she had played no part in this betrayal.

Had Shep overheard their plans? Or perhaps Cyrus's Verderan cellmate had given their captors prior warning? Was the map an act of contingency on Shep's part, the markings on the map altered to send any escape attempts awry? Or maybe it was just a case of poor timing, pure coincidence. Whatever the answer, Cyrus had offered freedom and delivered only death.

"I said get out of here!" Colton yelled as he continued to fight furiously.

Nearby, Abel spun in deadly circles with an axe in both hands. The old man's hair whipped through the air, and though Shep's men held back, they had fallen into a well-organised line that threatened to push forward and engulf the remaining prisoners in their wake.

"You!" came a thundering voice.

Cyrus's head turned to find Shep pointing a blade in his direction. His every instinct told him to rush across the chamber and face the man responsible for all of this, but Shep was surrounded by his followers, offering little hope of success. Cyrus's eyes locked Shep's stare for a moment before the line of guards began moving forward, and Shep's eyes narrowed before his attention switched to Colton.

A shriek of pain rose above the commotion, and Cyrus watched as Abel fell to his knees, three eager young guards circling and jabbing swords in the old man's direction until Abel let his axes fall and his arms hang loose. Cyrus felt a pang for the older man, but he couldn't linger on that for too long. From the corner of his eye, Cyrus noticed Colton still locked in combat, and as Cyrus's eyes scoured the room, he realised his companion was the last of them still standing.

Colton, a valiant fighter, was doing his best to fend off two guards. But just as Cyrus decided against his better judgement to try and help, Shep stepped forward to drive his blade into Colton's unguarded flank. Colton cried out and fell to the stone floor, his fight extinguished like a candle in the breeze.

Cyrus's jaw dropped as he stopped in his tracks. He'd only made it a couple of steps in his pursuit to help Colton when his companion fell, and Cyrus felt the breath go out of him as Shep grabbed a fistful of Colton's hair, pulling his head back and exposing his neck.

Colton, whose gaze was locked on Cyrus from across the room, smiled one last time, and then Shep sliced across his neck. He'd only ever wanted to earn his position in the King's Guard, but Colton died miles from the capital and with little to show for his sacrifice.

It was all Cyrus could do to fight back the anguish. He wanted to scream and weep like a baby simultaneously, and his throat felt immediately tight. He was so sick of seeing good men die, he despaired, and for a moment, he was transported back to that field of battle, back to holding Garrett's lifeless body. Despite the grief of the sight of Colton's fallen form, something told Cyrus he had to move, some ghost of self-preservation.

In an instant, Cyrus turned to run, making it only a few strides before a line of Shadows appeared to block his path. At the forefront stood Patch, and to his side, a large boy with dark skin and wide holes in his earlobes as was customary for the tribal peoples of the Kanthu Isles. Cyrus had learned about the people of the Kanthu Isles during his lessons with Thaddeus in what seemed like another lifetime. The recollection only seemed to make things worse.

"No more death!" the Kanthu boy called, his voice thick with accent but no less convincing. Cyrus realised with a shock that the boy was talking not to Cyrus but to Shep and his men. They were here to protect him.

Cyrus heard a thud behind him as Shep released Colton's body and it hit the floor, but as Shep urged his men forward in pursuit, the Shadows parted to allow Cyrus through, and Cyrus ran on instinct. When he passed the Shadows, Cyrus saw that they gathered up again, forming a line, blocking the way.

Cyrus counted his blessings with every step. He knew the way to the exit, and he knew the path was clear. He ran as fast as his tired legs would carry him, but as new sounds of struggle echoed behind him, he also came to realise that Shep's guards were no longer in close pursuit.

I'll come back to save them, he thought as he broke out into daylight. Even as he had this thought, he wondered how many of them would be left to save by the time he made it back, if indeed he ever did.

He didn't break stride, running to the spot in which he'd seen the horses tied. Adagio whinnied impatiently as he unclipped the lock on the corral gate and ran toward her. His saddle was gone, but his horse was no less ready. As Cyrus climbed onto Adagio's bare back, tangling his fingers in her mane to steady himself, a face appeared at the entrance.

Shep's glare was so hot that it threatened to burn a hole in Cyrus, and as the band of horses broke free to create mayhem about them, Cyrus suspected that this was not the last that they would see of each other.

Highcastle was a hive of activity, an entire city working tirelessly toward a common goal, the sound of their efforts carrying on a gentle late-summer breeze. It really was rather impressive, Wendell thought as he stood, lips pursed at the window of his chambers in Eldred's Keep.

Wendell surveyed the capital through a spyglass. The eastern and western gates no longer served as glorified archways, but were now heavily reinforced doors with thick wooden beams acting as barricades against prospective attacks. A trench had been built into the grassland beyond, with vicious wooden spikes to slow the Verderan advance, and repairs were underway on the most vulnerable stretches of the walls, adding new sections of stone or makeshift palisades of sharpened wood.

Back within the city, it seemed nobody was spared from the duty of work. Carts raced through the narrow streets distributing food and weapons, while windows were sealed shut and blockades were constructed of barrels, furniture, and other household items. These were simple people, blindly following the whim of their king, and though Wendell knew it to be futile, he felt a surprising wave of pride at their optimism and togetherness. He had spent the entirety of his adult life as an underdog, and these were his countryfolk, after all.

He shook his head and turned away from the window. A roaring fireplace was in the centre of one wall with a single chair before it, the perfect spot to read or enjoy wine as it was intended: without the encumbrance of company. His bed was a simple wooden frame with soft, down cushioning that helped ease the aches of his advancing years. A single rug added warmth to the flagstones underfoot. It was threadbare in sections and fraying at the edges, but it had belonged to his mother and brought with it memories of happier times. That only left his desk. His official offices were in the bowels of the castle, but some tasks were just a little too...*sensitive,* and the withered remnants of a burned-out candle attested to his unfaltering work ethic.

And that was all, after thirty years of loyal service to the crown. It would have been the dream of many, but to Wendell, it was still just the beginning. He smiled as he surveyed his surroundings, and it occurred to him that the Verderans would soon see the castle reimagined, anyway. High-spirits and hard work would not save the people of Easthaven from the princes, and all that was left, Wendell thought with glee, was to decide which chambers he would choose for his own next. *Maybe Adaline's...*

The unmistakable sound of swords cut Wendell's thoughts short. *Are they here already?* he thought, pressing an ear to his chamber door. It couldn't be possible, surely?

General Broderick had amassed the king's forces in the castle courtyard for drills, and there was no way into the castle without significant force and persuasion. But if not the Verderans, then who?

Life was a dangerous game that had earned Wendell many enemies. He hadn't raised a sword in anger for many years, not since the incident, and yet he reached to remove his ceremonial blade from a mount on the wall, just in case. This was not the time to take chances, and he wrapped his remaining fingers around the hilt of the sword as he pushed the door open slowly, stepping into the unknown.

"Good!" Seth's voice echoed in the hallway as Francine circled him with her own sword raised.

The king's shield was stooped in a defensive stance, while the girl was snarling playfully, her feet carrying her across the stone floor with admirable grace. Wendell rolled his eyes and let the sword fall at his side as Seth noticed him, raising an eyebrow at Wendell's weapon.

Wendell should have known that it would only be the imposter king's sister. It seemed that no matter where he went these days, the girl was there, swinging a sword, playing out some wild fantasy as shield to the queen of Cornesse. *A title not so glamorous as it might sound*, thought Wendell. Had the girl learned nothing from Garrett's passing?

"Wendell!" called Seth, in what was nearly a very costly lapse of concentration. It seemed that Francine's intent was as sharp as her imagination, and it took considerable swordsmanship to divert the girl's lunge as she attacked unexpectedly.

"Okay, okay," Seth said to her, surrendering and chuckling as he rested hands on his knees. "Keep on like this, and you'll be shield to King Augustus!" He traipsed over to ruffle Francine's hair. "That's enough for one day. Maybe Wendell here can give you some instruction?"

Wendell froze, wide-eyed as Francine turned her attention upon him. "Oh, I don't really—" he murmured.

"But you have your sword," Francine interrupted with a look of expectancy, Seth's laughter sounding as he walked away. "Adaline told me that you used to be a great swordsman. Show me!"

A great swordsman? he thought, as the corners of his lips curled uncontrollably. *Did Adaline really say that?* His skin prickled with an excited energy, and he wondered just how much had changed during the past few days. Perhaps she was moving on from Anselm even quicker than he had expected. Perhaps, he thought, he might be moving into Adaline's chambers even sooner than he had hoped…

"It has been quite some time," he began, raising his sword. He managed to lift the weapon no higher than his own waist before Francine leapt forward and smashed the elaborate blade from his hand and onto the floor.

"Too slow, old man!" she yelled, poking her tongue from her mouth in mockery. "Seth told me never to lower my guard around an enemy. I could have killed you!"

But how will I ever win Adaline if you do?

Wendell crouched to reach for his sword, but Francine attacked once more, her foot sweeping his legs from under him and dropping him awkwardly onto the floor. His cheeks flushed pink with embarrassment, and his frustration grew as he fought unsuccessfully to arrange his robes. He could only imagine how ridiculous he must have looked: a noble and esteemed member of the king's employ at the feet of a peasant girl. He had been easy on her until now, but she would soon know the very extent of his fury.

"I'm sorry," said Francine before Wendell could bring himself to unleash his rage upon her. She reached to offer a small hand. Her face was sincere, and she showed no notice of his missing fingers, a politeness that, Wendell conceded, most adults couldn't manage. Her attack had been an affront, of that there was no doubt, and yet as she smiled down at him with the naivety of youth, it occurred to him just how funny he would have found this as a child.

"It's no problem," he said, raising his palms to decline her offer of help. "I'm just a little rusty is all."

He returned to his feet and dusted himself down. The smile had returned to Francine's face, and in that moment, he felt an overwhelming familiarity in the girl that he had previously failed to notice. She reminded him in a way of a young Adaline, he realised, as he switched the blade to his left hand.

Francine had a mischievous smile that transported him back to the very first time he had met the dowager queen. They were only children themselves at the time; their parents had been guests at one of King Ailwin's feasts, and he remembered standing in the corner as the king invited his assembly to dance. Dancing was for girls of course, yet when the dashing Prince Anselm led the way, it seemed all of a sudden that Wendell was the only boy to have attended unprepared. It was every bit as embarrassing as it was impressive to watch. The girls' long skirts spiralled as the music played and laughter filled the room. He wanted more than anything to be part of it, and just when he thought that the moment would pass, Adaline had arrived to save him.

"Dance with me!" she had instructed, pulling him by the arm with no room for discussion. And before he knew it, they *were* dancing. He didn't know her name or any of the steps, but none of that mattered; he simply knew he would never let her go.

Fran's voice punctured his memories. "Are you ready?" She had a look of steely determination about her.

Wendell gave a smile of his own and raised his blade accordingly. "Ready."

The sword felt strange in his weaker hand, but a warrior's instinct is something that never goes away. Francine's first lunge was predictable, and Wendell deflected her sword with minimal effort. It was true that the girl had excellent footwork, yet her forms were limited and predictable, and as the next attack arrived, he knocked the blade cleanly from her hand, raising his own to point victoriously at the girl's unprotected neck.

"Wow," said Fran, head arched back and breathing heavily, "I didn't think you could do that!"

"And that there is your lesson," he answered promptly, lowering his sword. "There are times in life when it helps to have people underestimate you." He looked down and nudged Francine's sword back to her with his foot. "Learn to mask your strengths, and you will master the deadliest weapon of all: the element of surprise."

He smiled a final time before turning to return to his chambers, closing the door behind him without saying another word.

⚜ ⚜ ⚜

With the thought of Adaline's praise in his head, it was rapidly becoming one of Wendell's better days in the castle. He paced the hallways with a little extra spring in his step, and as he plunged the depths of his mind for something to feel aggrieved about, he found that the well had, at least temporarily, run dry. He felt a smile on his face for the first time in weeks and noticed that it was returned in kind by the people around him.

How unusual, he thought, that small gestures could make such a difference. There was the small matter of high treason, for which he was definitely guilty, and the encroaching Verderan army, but of his actions that day, Wendell found that he felt surprisingly good.

But where had it all started? he wondered. His breakfast had been the normal platter of smoked fish, while the fortification of Highcastle was, if anything, of a hindrance to his plan. *The girl then?* He replayed his time with Francine and felt his smile widen inexplicably. To him, she was bossy, tactless, relentless, and—though it pained him to admit it—fun. It occurred to him that the castle had been lifeless for too long. However much the people had adored Anselm, the late king had been so often occupied by official duties or the pursuit of vices with his bootlicker, Garrett. In his absence, Augustus had grown to become a joyless child, and despite all of life's luxuries, it seemed to Wendell that the boy had never truly laughed or experienced anything close to true happiness.

Wendell was mildly shocked by the sudden sadness that overwhelmed him at the thought of Augustus. Though foolish and misguided, King Augustus was hardly more than a boy, one that would ultimately suffer for his father's actions. It was a rare instant of doubt, but Wendell momentarily considered the alternative. Could he possibly reverse this sequence of events and become saviour to the people of Highcastle? Could he yet forge an honest path in the castle?

He laughed at the thought and shook his head as he continued down the hallway. *No*, he mused silently. *This is not a game for hearts but for heads, and I've already made my move.*

"Wendell, my lord!" a voice sounded from behind him, and as Wendell turned, he noticed a stranger of a man walking swiftly in pursuit. The man was dressed in the simple red tunic of castle staff, and on closer inspection, Wendell recalled him from dinner the previous evening. He had a young face with prominent cheekbones, and his eyes were ocean blue, despite his dark features.

"Wendell, I'm ever so glad I found you," the man continued.

A quick glance around confirmed to Wendell that they were alone, and there was something about the man that made him think this was no coincidence. He watched as the man's eyes twitched around them and took an instinctive step away, fumbling in his pocket purposefully.

"Oh, don't be afraid," the man said, just as he seemed to find what he was searching for. He unfolded his hand to present a Verderan coin to Wendell, along with a small smile. "We have the same employer," he said. "The same…vision."

The look on the man's face shifted into something hungry and somewhat menacing, and though Wendell knew this was the same man who had approached him only moments ago, his new expression rendered him almost unrecognisable to Wendell.

"I don't know what you mean," Wendell said, turning to walk away. But he made it only a few strides before the man pulled him back by the arm. Wendell's every instinct told him to strike out, but this was not the time for unwanted attention. He doubted that the man posed any threat to him, but it was no less unnerving to be blindsided after investing so much time and energy coordinating events within the castle. Had the princes sent this man? *Some show of faith*, he thought, and after all that he had done for them.

Wendell knew that a nearby door would lead to a storeroom, which would be a perfect sanctuary for delicate discussions, and he gestured the man forward before closing the door behind them.

"Why are you here?" he asked in an urgent whisper. It was one of a thousand questions in his mind, but since the room was not the storeroom he had thought but rather a latrine, he settled for brevity. His sense of panic was overwhelming and only heightened by the man's calm demeanour. He wanted to take him by the shoulders and shake the answer from him, but larger forces were clearly at play, and Wendell took a moment to compose himself as the man began to speak.

"I'm here to help," the man began quietly. "The princes are aware of the efforts to strengthen Highcastle and are concerned by the prospect of a lengthy siege. Though they travel with weapons capable of reducing the city to rubble, it is Prince Rafael's intention to sit upon Isidore's Chair and command unquestionable rule over the nation of Easthaven."

Wendell nodded, his brain working to anticipate his role in all of this.

"They ask, therefore," the man continued, "that you conspire to tease King Augustus from his shell. The Verderan armies are little more than a day from Highcastle, and the prince expects that your considerable cunning will see King Augustus ride out to meet him in combat."

"But—"

"Please save your excuses," the man said, his tone taking on an edge as steely as Wendell's sword, which was, he realised, now stowed safely back in his own chambers. The man continued, "I know all about you, Wendell. I know that you have lived your life in the castle and that you have known these people for many years. I don't doubt that I'd be having second thoughts if I were in your position, but this is no time for weakness. The princes will simply not allow it. You asked why I am here?"

The man opened his tunic to reveal a knife stowed away.

"The simple answer is: to ensure that you finish what you have started."

⚜ ⚜ ⚜

Wendell took a seat toward the front of the basilica. This was his first visit since Augustus's coronation, and though he had never considered himself a religious man, this seemed as good a time as any to start. The wooden bench was cold and uncomfortable, but the silence was welcome, and he reached forward to rest his elbows on the back of the bench in front of him before uttering a quiet prayer.

His eyes were drawn to Anselm's tomb, an ornate slab of glossy marble among the grey flagstones, and it seemed that no matter Wendell's actions, things always seemed to spiral, dragging him down. He had only ever wanted to do the right thing but had a bad habit of associating with the wrong people.

This will be the last of it, he promised himself. *One last simple act, and in the doing of it, closure.*

Footsteps sounded behind him, and Wendell turned to see the Master of Prayer in approach.

"Wendell, my dear boy," the old man said with his most pious smile. His face was gaunt as always, his hair and beard perfectly straight, his habit characteristically pristine. "What a pleasant surprise to find you in the company of our Lord. It seems that recent struggles have ushered many lost souls back into His holy embrace." He paused before taking a seat at Wendell's side. "You are a good man, Wendell, but one full of demons. The young king has shown us the path, and you are right to follow him into the refuge of this holy place."

Wendell smiled. "Thank you, Cornelius. It is great comfort." He turned to face the Master of Prayer. "I find the demands of office most challenging of late, and the right path is not always the easiest to take."

"An age-old problem, dear boy." Cornelius placed a bony hand atop Wendell's, each finger adorned with gold bands displaying a selection of precious gemstones. "I do not envy you but would encourage you to consider the example of young Augustus. It is only months since the boy was left fatherless. Even now, he stands little more than a child, yet one who has witnessed war and great suffering. Cut adrift from his people, it would have been easy to lose his way, but Augustus's strength and belief saw him returned to us victorious. Within the bosom of faith, true healing can begin."

Wendell nodded silently. It all sounded like riddles to him, and he knew better than to attribute Augustus's deliverance to divine intervention. "It is an inspiring story," he said finally, meeting the old man's stare, "and your support for the young king has been invaluable during this difficult time."

Cornelius inclined his head graciously as Wendell braced himself for the punchline.

"What a shame it would be then," Wendell said, "for the king to find that his most trusted aide has been…*misusing* church funds."

The Master of Prayer made to speak, his eyes were narrowed, and there was a look of panic in his face that Wendell knew all too well.

"The jewels and the robes…" Wendell continued, with perhaps just the slightest hint of enjoyment. "I've known you many years, Cornelius, and I for one would never deny you the benefit of such luxuries, but possessions like these..." He raised Cornelius's left hand to inspect his fine rings. "Well, they are not without considerable cost, and I would hate to see harmful accusations tarnish your name."

"Nonsense!" yelled the Master of Prayer, his voice echoing throughout the basilica as he snatched his hand away. The old man took a deep breath, which seemed to restore some of his decorum, though he scowled at Wendell before continuing at what passed as a conversational level of volume, "You can't do this. He will never believe you."

"Oh, but he will," said Wendell, turning to face ahead at the apse. "You may have wormed your way into the king's favour, but in matters of money, my word is divine. Augustus is no fool, you know that, but he is a young man driven by insecurities. Do you really trust your faith enough to take that chance?"

Cornelius sat wordlessly. If there was any proof of wrongdoing on the Master of Prayer's part, it had not passed Wendell's desk. This move was a speculative one by any standard, but Wendell had come to view doubt as a most dangerous weapon.

"What is it that you want?" the Master of Prayer asked, his voice quiet and defeated. It occurred to Wendell that he had, not too long ago, been asking the Verderan man the same thing in the same desperate tone, tucked away in a latrine. *Funny how quickly things can change…*

"Only the word of God," said Wendell, shaking the thought of the Verderan man away, his heart slowing with relief. "And with it, your help setting Augustus on the *right* path."

Cyrus raced into the courtyard of Simeon's castle, Adagio's hooves beating down as two unsuspecting guards parted to clear a path. To her credit, Adagio had shared his urgency every step of way during their two-day journey, and as a young stable hand rushed out to meet them, Cyrus leapt from his mount, knowing that she had more than earned her rest.

"I need to see the king!" he shouted urgently at a group of guards gathered idly nearby. His previous fear of Ravensward was little more than a distant memory, and he paused for a moment as he realised how much he was starting to sound like a character from one of his own stories. Eventually, one of the guards made to meet him. He was of a similar age to Cyrus and most notable for the gap between his two front teeth.

"Just this way," he answered hastily, and Cyrus followed as the guard led them into the castle, navigating a series of long corridors with beamed ceilings to match those in Simeon's throne room. It was every bit as labyrinthine as Eldred's Keep, and despite having visited once before, Cyrus found he still had no sense of his bearings when he arrived in the throne room to stand before King Simeon once more.

"Prince Cyrus," said Simeon hesitantly.

The king's voice was so quiet that it scarcely caused an echo, and Cyrus edged closer to Simeon's withered form. It had been less than two weeks since Cyrus had left Ravensward, and though decline in the king was to be expected from what he had told Cyrus about his health, it still shocked him to see how quickly Simeon had faded.

"My boy," the king continued. "Do you have news of my boy?"

All of a sudden, Cyrus's brain caught up with the conversation. In his haste to quell the uprising, he had given little thought to his original purpose: finding Simeon's long-lost son. A nauseating wave of despondency washed over him, and as General Lambert appeared at his king's side, the memory of Colton made things worse still.

"No sign of your son. I'm sorry." It seemed right to broach things head on, but this didn't make it any easier as he lowered his brow to deliver the news. "But I have urgent information of rebellion in the west. Their numbers are growing, and they are in league with the Verderans with plans to see my brother from his throne."

"And how does this concern us?" Lambert interrupted as though he spoke for the king.

"Because they won't stop there," Cyrus answered, his frustration growing with every passing moment. It seemed only yesterday that he had made a similar case in Casarossa, and the irony was not lost on him at all. "Their leader, Shep, is taking prisoners and brainwashing Shadow children. His numbers are small, but it only takes a spark to start a fire. He has access to materials that can blast holes in our cities. He will come for you next, Simeon."

"Impossible!" yelled Lambert, but Simeon remained silent and thoughtful before raising a palm to prevent any further outbursts.

"What would you have us do, Prince Cyrus?"

"Send a force," Cyrus answered without hesitation. "No more than fifty men, but those who are willing to march and ready to fight. Dowse the flames of insurrection before they catch light, and see justice for those already lost."

Cyrus's voice caught, and Lambert's head began to turn, scanning the room like an owl.

"Wait, where's Colton?" he asked, and it pained Cyrus to hear the panic.

Cyrus paused for a moment, but he knew there was no use running from the truth. "Colton's gone," he began, his every word like a knife in the heart. "I tried to save him, but he gave his life to see me from Shep's grasp—"

"It can't be true!" Lambert yelled as he drew his blade.

The light in the throne room was poor, but Cyrus noticed tears in the general's eyes, and he took a step back as Lambert approached him threateningly.

"It's all lies! Can't you see, Simeon? The prince is trying to trick us with his mind games. Tell me where he is, or I'll save the Verderans a job and kill you right here!"

"That's enough, Lambert!" Simeon said, slamming his hand down on the armrest of his throne. He tried to stand, but he fell back into his seat with exhaustion. "Prince Cyrus is many things, but I do not believe him to be a liar. These traitors," he said, palms extended, "can you lead my men to them?"

It was the question that Cyrus had expected but dreaded the most. The two days it had taken him to ride from Shep's prison back to Simeon's castle had left him with no desire to return to the mountain. Cyrus had hoped to free himself of his commitments and return home, perhaps with the support of Simeon's army. He now saw that things would not be so easy.

"I must return to Highcastle," he began desperately, "I know the destructive power that the princes possess, and though there is no love lost between the king and me, it is my duty to warn my brother."

Simeon sat back in his throne, his eyes narrowed, and Cyrus wondered if his heartfelt plea might garner the desired response, but these hopes were short-lived. "Be that as it may, you are still my…*guest* here, Prince Cyrus. You are yet to find my son, and it seems that this villainous uprising is as much a threat to me as it is your brother. I have every desire to grant your freedom, but I would be a fool to do so in these circumstances." He paused, and his tone turned serious. "I'm sorry, but I must ask again, can you lead my men to the traitors?"

Cyrus swallowed, accepting defeat. He realised that he had little choice in the matter but wondered if knowledge of Shep's whereabouts could still be used to his advantage. "Yes, I can," he started flatly. "I may not have found your son, but I will help your men to end the uprising and ensure that Colton is avenged. I will make sure that you can rest easy on your throne, but in return, I ask that you do the same for my brother."

Simeon shrugged. "Go on."

"If I make it back, you'll free me to return to Highcastle," Cyrus said, impassioned. "But whatever happens, I ask that you honour the terms you agreed with my father and send men to help defend Easthaven against the Verderans."

"And why would I do that?"

"Because if Easthaven falls, it will take a lot more than fifty men to secure your position. Power is a delicate balance. You know that as well as anyone, Simeon. Do you believe that Verderan ambitions will end at your borders? Do you believe they will let Auldhaven stay as it is?"

Simeon sat silent, scratching his chin in thought.

"You must do something," Cyrus pleaded.

"I cannot make any promises."

"At least consider it," he tried once more, and Simeon's face softened as though Cyrus was finally getting through to him.

"Do this thing, and I'll consider it," Simeon said, nodding slowly.

"And I'll go with him this time, my king," snapped Lambert. He sheathed his sword as he turned to the king. "I will escort Prince Cyrus and see the truth in his words. Allow me fifty of the King's Guard, and I will destroy any notion of sedition." He turned back to Cyrus menacingly. "That, or I'll ensure that the prince is handled suitably."

Simeon exhaled as he slumped more deeply into his seat. "I suppose I have little other choice," he said sadly. "A lifetime of death, and it seems that there is yet more to come. Take your men,

Lambert, but treat the prince as though he were my own. As for you Cyrus," he said, inclining his head slowly, "this is the second time you have entered my castle when most others in your place would have run. I thank you for your loyalty, and I will think on your request. See that you both return safely, and I'll have my thoughts ready when you do."

Cyrus nodded and bowed graciously before turning to leave. He wondered if he should have run after all.

⚜ ⚜ ⚜

"Colton was my best friend," said Lambert, drawing his horse alongside Adagio. He'd managed to maintain an uncomfortable silence for the first day of their travels, but with the western mountains coming into view, it seemed that there were a few things the general wanted to get off his chest. "We've seen less of each other in recent times, of course," he continued, "but we grew up together. The same village, the same upbringing, and the same dreams. Oh, we had some times back then." He broke off into a bout of laughter before clearing his throat to steady himself once more.

"He told me that he wanted to join the King's Guard," said Cyrus, seizing his opportunity, perhaps hoping for accord. "He hardly spoke of anything else, to tell you the truth."

Lambert smiled. "It's all he ever wanted, really. He changed a lot over the years, but he made some poor choices when he was younger, things that slowed him up. He used to act like good things were just going to happen for him, but he didn't want to work for them. I don't know if he perhaps had money problems or whether it was something else, but I remember the day he just gave up his dreams and left to become a border guard. I never gave up on him, though."

"Well, he spoke highly of you," said Cyrus, piecing together some of the few proper conversations he had shared with Colton. "I know he saw this as an opportunity to honour the king and perhaps earn himself another chance."

Lambert scoffed. "I thought the same when I told Simeon to send him as your escort. A futile search for a lost boy, I thought. What could possibly go wrong?"

"He died serving his king."

"He died for nothing!" Lambert snapped unexpectedly, his smile now a distant memory. "He died miles from anywhere, on a fool's errand and escorting an enemy prince." He breathed deeply, and Cyrus remained quiet with some sympathy for Lambert's loss and the pain it seemed to cause him. "It wasn't meant to be like this," he continued, tone laced with a desperate sadness. "He could have made it one day, one way or another. He was doing just fine manning the border until you arrived, until you…" He trailed off.

"I'm sorry," said Cyrus after a moment's pause. He thought back to all the people he had lost and the circumstances that had led him to this position, and found himself somewhere between anger and a sad appreciation for Lambert's pain. "I'm sorry that he died, but I didn't ask for any of this. We've all made sacrifices; Colton made his to fight against this resistance and set me free so that I could warn the rest of you."

"What happened?" Lambert demanded, with no improvement to his mood. "At the end, what happened?"

"It was Shep," Cyrus answered. "His men rounded on the prisoners, but Shep was the one dealt the final blow. I tried to save him, but there were too many."

Lambert considered this answer, and then slowed to draw his horse to a stop. "Shame," he said flatly, turning to face Cyrus. "Shame Shep got him instead of you."

⚜ ⚜ ⚜

The ground was dry and dusty as Cyrus crawled slowly forward, the mouth of the mountain becoming clearer with his every move. An early morning fog hung in the sky, but everything else was as he remembered it. Outside of the cave, a Shadow boy tended to the horses while a single guard paced the entrance, blowing smoke from a pipe.

"There, up ahead," Cyrus whispered, gesturing with a nod as Lambert moved alongside him.

They were obscured by the angle of the path, while the rest of their company remained further down the slope with the horses. Cyrus knew the layout of the mountain with some confidence, but he had every respect for Shep's cunning, so Cyrus was guarded. He wondered if any of the other prisoners had survived their attempted escape and felt a sudden tightness in his chest at the memory of Colton's passing.

"So, this is where he died?" Lambert asked, as if reading his mind. Maybe something had crossed Cyrus's face that had given him away.

Cyrus nodded wordlessly. He could sense the general's nervous energy but was keen to avoid underestimating Shep a second time, so he began to crawl from danger until Lambert followed in kind.

"The plan then?" spat Lambert. "You've been in there, so tell us your thoughts."

"There's a chamber," Cyrus began, pulling the map from his pocket to illustrate the layout. "If we're going to face them, that's where they'll be."

"And these pathways?" Lambert pointed at the web of corridors that seemed to cover the page.

"Cells." Cyrus was surprised by the sadness in his voice and the anxious feeling that came with it. "This is where they kept us. I've no idea if any of the others survived, and then there's the Shadow children. We have to set them free."

"I don't know," said Lambert, scratching at his chin. "Remember that we are here to suppress a rebellion and find some justice for Colton." Lambert said firmly. "This is not the time to relieve a guilty conscience or to make a name for yourself."

Cyrus's heart sank as Lambert unsheathed his sword with purpose before standing to address the troops. "Our enemies hide within these mountains," he called in a voice quiet enough not to be overheard by the guard above but still forceful enough to drive his point home. "They are cowards without courage or honour who would see your king removed from this world and our freedoms challenged."

Cyrus could see the men's jaws flexing as they clenched their teeth, their hands tightening around swords as they stood ready to storm the mountain.

"This leaves us but one choice," Lambert continued. "We will march into the jaws of the beast, and in doing so, we will see the sharpest teeth of rebellion removed forevermore!"

The men raised their swords and growled in support before Lambert gestured forward, and their company descended on the enemy, first approaching the single guard that Cyrus and Lambert had seen before.

"Who are—" the man said in alarm before Lambert's sword saw the guard to a swift end. The Shadow boy darted into the corral to hide behind a water trough.

"Too easy," the general scoffed, crushing the guard's pipe underfoot. "I want three groups," he called to his men, and he knelt to collect the guard's key as the others split their numbers accordingly. "The first of you will follow the main path. Secure passage, but do not—I repeat do not—engage the main chamber. Your task is to ensure that nobody leaves the mountain without my say so. To the second of you…"

The next group stood to attention, as if wanting to outdo the first.

Lambert nodded approvingly and continued, "Inspect the cells in the eastern section and see if there are any survivors. The rest of you," he looked to Cyrus and the soldiers that surrounded him, "follow me, and we will clear the west. We're lucky to have the prince with us. He's recently returned from a relaxing stretch in these dungeons, so I've no doubt he'll be keen to show us around."

Laughter broke out among them, heavy hands shaking Cyrus by the shoulders as he stood frozen in place. He had never wanted to return to this nightmare, let alone the cell that had detained him, yet here he was, watching as Lambert's men poured into the mountain.

"Get moving, boy!" said Lambert, nudging Cyrus back into the darkness. Once inside, Cyrus took a left turn and moved quickly toward the Shadow cells.

"We're here to save you," he whispered to the children once they'd made it to the cells. He pressed his face against the bars of the first. The light was dim, but he could see their small forms sprawled on the floor, their hands and legs now bound in chains, a likely consequence of his own actions.

"We need to find the keys," he called out to no one in particular. There was no response, and when he turned to search for them, he found that Lambert and the others had already pressed on further into the shadows. *So much for following me*, he thought, chasing them down the corridor. It seemed that Lambert truly had no intention of saving the Shadows, and Cyrus felt entirely helpless. Colton's dead face stared back at him from every cell that he passed, and the walls seemed to close in on him with every stride until he caught up with the others.

"I think this is the last one," said Lambert as he gestured to the cell that Cyrus had occupied only recently. The sight of it made him feel sick in an instant. His chest tightened, his breathing grew shallow, and then the sound of chains rattled like a memory from within.

"What was that?" Lambert spat, pointing his sword at Cyrus in anger. "If this is a trap, I'll see that you never leave this place."

"How would I know?" Cyrus raised his palms in innocence. "There was a man, our cellmate. A Verderan man. Perhaps he's still alive."

"A Verderan man?" Lambert grabbed Cyrus by the shirt before pushing him toward the cell. "Well, perhaps you would be kind enough to introduce us."

Cyrus wondered if this might be another of Shep's games. Perhaps it *was* a trap? Though, he thought, it wouldn't be Cyrus's trap on Lambert; it would be Shep's trap on them all.

Cyrus hesitantly reached for the door and pulled it slowly open, forcing himself not to wince. Inside, he found little more than the ragged Verderan staring back at him.

"See? I told you, this is the—"

Lambert smashed Cyrus out of the way and stepped into the cell beyond him. "Ferdinand, is that you?" he called, clearly astonished.

"General Lambert," the man said warmly, the sound of chains rattling as he rose to his feet. "You'll have to excuse our surroundings. It's no match for my palace in Casarossa, but it has a certain charm, don't you think?" The man was speaking more than he ever had to Cyrus or Colton.

Ferdinand? thought Cyrus, his heart beating a little faster. *Casarossa?* It couldn't be. "You're King Ferdinand?" he demanded, stepping forward to stand at Lambert's side. "All that time, and you failed to mention that you're King Ferdinand?"

"You never asked…oh, and welcome home, by the way!" the Verderan said, his response trickling with arrogance. "We are here because my sons are invading Easthaven. I didn't see any gain in revealing my identity to a son of Anselm."

"But—"

"I may be old, but please don't think me a fool," Ferdinand continued. "I knew your father for many years, and you share more than his appearance." He extended his shackled arms before him, eyebrows raised at Cyrus. "As much as I am enjoying our reunion, I presume you are here to set me free?"

"Yes, absolutely!" Lambert jumped at the king's instruction. He handed the heavy ring of keys to one of his men, who moved to crouch beside Ferdinand and try the various keys in the lock one by one.

"So, you knew who I was all along?" Cyrus asked, turning his attention back to Ferdinand.

"From the moment you arrived," the king said, his expression saddening, and then his voice turned sincere. "I heard about your father, and now this horrible business with my sons. It's hard to know whom to trust these days."

The lock of Ferdinand's shackles clicked open, and Lambert wasted no time helping the Verderan king to his feet.

"But why would they do this?" Cyrus asked feebly. He knew things had been amiss when he and Garrett were in Casarossa, and it dawned on him now that Ferdinand might have been here in this foul place all along.

"Ambition," the king answered. "The ambition and greed of two young princes. You try to encourage your children…" He grimaced as he stretched out the stiffness in his legs. "You try to tell them that anything is possible, but this…" He winced more as his joints made popping and clicking noises at the slightest stretch.

Cyrus knew that Ferdinand wasn't exaggerating his pain and discomfort, and he felt awful for interrogating the king so soon.

"At first, they blamed the heat and the dry conditions for my poor health," Ferdinand said. "They kept me locked up for months, my condition worsening with every day." He paused, stood up fully, and threw the last of his shackles onto the dusty floor. "I knew they were up to something, and when you arrived in Casarossa, that's when I realised they were keeping things from me. My captain, Lorenzo, made mention of your visit, and when I asked my sons why I wasn't informed of a royal visitor, they had me sent here!"

"But your sickness," Cyrus protested.

"Poison," he said sadly. The king's voice lost all its confidence. "That's the one mercy of being in this place. Here, I am at least safe from their attempts to steal life away from me." He breathed deeply as if to steady himself. "For all their brave words and sharp actions, they never had it in them to see me killed. In the end, it was easier to send me here—where Shep, their ally, was preparing to aid them in their fight—and let me rot while they ruled unopposed in my name."

"They were wrong to underestimate you," Lambert said. He placed a reassuring hand on Ferdinand's shoulder. It seemed to Cyrus that the general's sycophancy knew no bounds, though Cyrus had to admit that even he felt some sympathy for the king.

"We shall see you free from this place," Lambert persisted, "and when all is said and done, I've no doubt that you will sit upon the throne of Verdera once more."

Ferdinand smiled and made for the door, taking only a few strides before the sound of swords and screams began to echo throughout the mountain.

"Shep," Cyrus muttered grimly, but Lambert was already off in pursuit.

The main chamber was a battleground when they arrived, and Lambert showed no hesitation in rushing to join his troops. The similarity between this moment and Cyrus's last time in the main chamber were frightening, but he knew he could not allow the same outcome to happen again. He raised his sword instinctively to fend off an attack, and before he knew it, the blade ran red with the blood of one of Shep's guards.

"To victory!" Lambert screamed as he tore through the enemy, his voice acting as a rallying call to his men. There was no sign of Shep, but Cyrus had known it wouldn't be that easy. He looked at his wrist, where Francine's bracelet had once been, and cursed the man responsible as he plunged into the mayhem.

"Watch out!" Cyrus darted forward to intercept a blade bound for Lambert's back. The guard was young and thirsty for blood, but he was no match for Cyrus's superior technique, and Cyrus twisted his opponent's sword from his hand before burying his own in the man's unprotected stomach. It was all over in an instant.

A subtle nod was the extent of Lambert's gratitude, his panicked eyes glancing to Cyrus's left as another attack rained in, forcing Cyrus to duck and roll away. Where was his attacker? Cyrus looked up as Lambert ran the man through, the all-too-familiar smell of blood and death hanging in the air. Cyrus gave a short nod back at Lambert to match the general's own sentiments.

The opposition was thinning already, and Cyrus parried another strike as he gazed back to see Ferdinand still safe at the door.

Cyrus turned back toward Lambert. "We have to find Shep!" he cried to the general, dropping a shoulder as he twisted to force his sword into the small of a man's back. Once the man had fallen, Cyrus had a chance to breathe and take in the scene. Several of Shep's men knelt before Lambert. They were disarmed, their hands locked behind their heads, but Shep was still nowhere to be seen.

Coward, Cyrus thought to himself as he pressed ever-forward. Only a handful of guards remained, and they backed fearfully toward the door that Cyrus had once thought an exit.

"Where is your leader?" Cyrus barked, sword raised and patience wearing thin. It was clear that the guards' cause was lost, and it came as no surprise when the first of them dropped his blade to the floor, hands raised in surrender as others followed suit. Still, no one answered Cyrus's question.

"I said where is your—" Then it dawned on him.

"Keys!" he yelled, and a nervous guard obliged with shaking hands. The door before him had an unusual cross-shaped keyhole, and he had no trouble finding its counterpart before pushing it open with a shoulder. Though the heavy door groaned with every inch, Cyrus soon achieved a gap big enough to step through and continue into the room beyond. It was little more than a common storeroom in the end, but as Lambert secured the captives behind him, Cyrus's eyes fell upon a series of large carts full to the brim with crystalline white stone.

The power to destroy a city, he thought, observing a cluster in the candlelight. It was some relief to find that the materials were still in Auldhaven—a long way from Highcastle—and Cyrus felt renewed hope for those back home. But where was Shep?

He glanced around the room and noticed a small desk in the corner. He raised his sword in approach but lowered it at the sight of his own journal on the table. Rushing over, he found that the book was open at his account of Ravensward. His bag was also on the floor, and Cyrus slammed the journal shut before opening the bag to reach inside.

"Looking for something?"

Cyrus turned toward the voice and into a heavy fist that slammed him back onto the desk. The punch landed right between his eyes, and his head screamed with pain as Shep pressed it further into the woodwork.

"Did he send you?" Shep asked, and his breath was hot and stale as he drew closer to whisper. "Did our beloved king send you? Answer me!"

"Yes," Cyrus managed despite the unrelenting pressure of Shep's assault.

"And do you think he'll care about you if you make it back? Do you even think he'd care if I killed you right here?

"Shep—"

"No, he wouldn't! The man is a selfish fool that uses good people but cares only for himself. There are others like me, you know? Men who will stand up and make a difference. Simeon's time is coming to an end."

Cyrus began to feel faint as his breaths grew short and desperate under Shep's interrogation.

Shep continued, apparently unaware that Cyrus was on the brink of unconsciousness, "I started all of this to ensure that nobody would ever be hungry or alone, and I will yet see Simeon to the grave!"

"Cyrus!" someone called, but Cyrus couldn't quite make out who it was. Shep's grip relented as footsteps rushed into the room, and he turned to meet Lambert's attack.

The sound of swords crashed behind Cyrus as he rolled over on the desk, his head resting against the soft leather binding of his journal. He breathed deeply, and as his vision drifted slowly back into focus, he found himself considering what he would write about all of this, if he survived, and his mind replayed his journey since Highcastle. He wondered what had happened to Farley and whether Colton would have been happy with his noble ending. His thoughts moved to Simeon and the search for his son. What kind of man might Brandon be? Had he grown up resenting an absent father until illness tore his mother away from him?

The faces of Shep's men suddenly appeared in his mind: young, misguided men. Lost souls comforted by the companionship of their cause. Likely, Cyrus thought as Lambert and Shep fought on, Brandon would find common ground with these men. But he was Simeon's son. Cyrus was sure Brandon would have the same streak of ambition as his father.

Brandon wouldn't fight alongside men like these, Cyrus thought. He would lead them. He wouldn't have simply suffered life's injustices; he would have avenged them. Simeon's son was no soldier. He was a general.

A man like his father.

A man just like Shep.

Cyrus's vision returned in full, and he leapt to his feet, only to see Shep crumbling to the floor, Lambert's face twisted with bloodlust as he circled his defeated enemy.

"What have you done?" asked Cyrus, hands tearing at the very roots of his hair, but Lambert's expression showed no remorse, and it was clear that the general was oblivious to the consequence of his actions.

"Hang in there!" Cyrus yelled to Shep as he pushed Lambert aside to raise Shep's head from the ground. His brown tunic was dark with blood, and his skin was already turning pale.

"What did you expect?" Lambert's eyes narrowed as he wiped his blade clean on the leg of his trousers. "We came here seeking vengeance, for Colton, for the king!"

Cyrus peered into Shep's bloodshot eyes. In the end, Cyrus and Shep weren't so different, Cyrus thought: two boys set adrift, deprived of their birth right, and left to forge a path of their own. Cyrus could sense Shep's life slipping away, and his own breathing slowed as the dying man reached out to hold his arm.

"It's all right," Cyrus said with a smile, even though he knew it wasn't. He'd seen the same look on Garrett's face once, and he cursed the world for the suffering that seemed to follow him around, landing on so many who came into his life.

A crowd of Shadows rushed past the soldiers at the door to join Cyrus at Shep's side. Foremost of them was Patch, and tears streamed from the boy's eyes as he sobbed before letting his head fall upon Shep's chest. "Shep!" he wailed, the words muffled by Shep's tunic as the boy finally broke his silence.

But as Cyrus adjusted the man's tunic, he knew for sure that this was not his name, and it never had been. Cyrus's fingers prised a gold chain free from the bloody mess of Shep's wound, and on this chain hung a gold ring inlaid with an emerald stone.

⚜ ⚜ ⚜

Lambert sat in shock as Cyrus covered Brandon's body with thick woollen blankets and closed the man's eyes for a final time. The remaining insurgents were bound, but their fight had died with their leader, and the Shadows were left to console each other after the loss of their adoptive father.

"I didn't know," Lambert said, his voice aghast. The general's expression was one of sadness, but Cyrus knew that it was only a mask to his fear. "I thought he was a murderer, a monster…he killed Colton..."

Cyrus sighed. He and Lambert were far from friends, but he regretted that the man was suffering as a result of saving Cyrus's life. "I didn't know either," Cyrus said. "Not until it was too late."

"They loved him," said Ferdinand, standing in the doorway. "To us, this was a prison, but to those children, it was home. The only one they'd ever had." The old man moved to place a hand on Lambert's shoulder. "Don't blame yourself. You weren't to know." He had obviously overheard the revelation about Shep's true identity.

Cyrus walked back over to the desk and packed his journal into the bag. Fran's bracelet was buried at the bottom, and he felt a surge of optimism that contrasted greatly with the mood of the room as he tied it around his wrist once more. He had never planned for things to end this way, but Brandon's passing had ended their search, and with the rebellion silenced, he was ready to go home. He weighed the gold ring in his hand, observing the intricate green stone before placing it into his pocket. "Make ready to leave," he called, but he made it no more than a few strides before one of Lambert's men rushed breathlessly into the room.

"Men…approaching from the mountain path!"

The man's eyes were wide with panic, and Lambert rushed past him as the man crouched to catch his breath.

"To the entrance!" barked Lambert, his worries about Brandon set to one side as he made to deal with the immediate threat. A crowd of Lambert's men had already gathered by the time they reached the entrance, and though their weapons were raised with deadly intent, the men parted to allow Lambert and Cyrus through.

"What is the meaning of this?" began Lambert, but Cyrus only laughed.

"They aren't men," he interjected. "They're pirates!"

⚜ ⚜ ⚜

"Well, if it isn't the king…or prince…or whatever you are!"

Roscoe covered the final few yards to wrap Cyrus in tight embrace. Cyrus didn't need to look at Lambert's men to guess their reactions, and he pulled away from his old friend to ensure a peaceful exchange.

"Good to see you, Roscoe," Cyrus said with a genuine smile. He looked around to see that Roscoe was joined by a far larger complement of around thirty men, and his hands were decorated with precious stones. His very appearance spoke to his successes since their last meeting, and Cyrus was pleased to find that his friend had fallen on better times. He thought with a pang that it would make Garrett happy to see his old friend doing well. Still, it was a welcome relief to see a familiar face after all that had happened, but before Cyrus could even bask in the feeling of relief, his eyes narrowed as he considered the unexpected nature of their reunion.

"You'll be wondering why I'm here," Roscoe said as if on cue. He straightened his tricorn hat as his crew watched on, sun glinting from the ring in his eyebrow. "I learned a lot during our time together, and with the news of Garrett's passing," his smile dropped as he paused to push tobacco into this pipe, "I've realised that life is too short to spend it on the run. I'm not a young man anymore, and it seemed like the right time to pursue more, shall we say, *honourable* endeavours."

Cyrus smiled. It seemed that some things never changed. "I'm pleased for you," he said, the question of Roscoe's appearance still a mystery to him. "These *honourable* dealings, though, how did they come to include Shep?"

"Well, that's simple," Roscoe's face regained the same mischief it had carried when they had first met. "There I was, sitting at the docks in Casarossa, waiting for you and Garrett while you met with the princes, just minding my own business," he paused before a trademark smoke ring floated into the air, "when a man approached me enquiring about the Dagger. At first, I thought he was trying to pin something on me, but it turned out he needed someone to shift some old stone between Auldhaven and Verdera. Apparently, the king's fleet was busy with something or other."

Cyrus closed his eyes before lowering his head into his hands.

"I thought you'd be happy for me," Roscoe said. The disappointment was clear in his voice, and Cyrus was beginning to wish he hadn't asked. "It seemed like good honest work," Roscoe insisted, "and the money was too good to refuse. This is our third trip, but Shep normally meets us at the base of the mountain. How do you know Shep, anyway? Is he around?"

Cyrus glanced back at Lambert, dread growing with the realisation that the stones he'd seen in Shep's storeroom were by no means the only ones, not if this was Roscoe's third trip to the mountain. By the time his gaze returned to Roscoe, he felt that the answer to Roscoe's question was probably painted on his own face.

"I don't know how to tell you this," he began hesitantly, "but Shep was providing the Verderans with weapons to destroy Highcastle and take over Easthaven. The princes tricked us in Casarossa, and they are already on their way to destroy the capital. The rocks that you've been transporting," he stopped to gesture back at the mountain, "Rafael and Alonso are using them to create a blast powder capable of destroying Eldred's Keep."

Roscoe's jaw dropped; all traces of humour gone.

"Shep has been giving them the raw materials," Lambert added, moving to stand at Cyrus's side. "He has been using you to transport them, and in return, the princes were going to support Shep's attempt on King Simeon's throne."

"Simeon?" asked Roscoe, sending a questioning glance to Cyrus.

"Yes, Simeon," answered Cyrus with a sigh, knowing how confusing it must have been to Roscoe. After all, they had departed each other's company with Simeon as the enemy, and yet here Cyrus was at the man's behest. "He sent us to intercept the rebels, and here we are. We were about to return to Ravensward when you arrived."

"Well, don't let me hold you up." Roscoe grinned as he swept his hat from his head, mocking Cyrus with an extravagant curtsy. "I presume this means we aren't getting paid. Only, I've a few more mouths to feed these days." He glanced around at his men.

Cyrus rolled his eyes at the gesture before surveying Roscoe's retinue. "Take whatever you can find in the mountain," he answered. "See Shep returned to the earth and that stone disposed of. Anything else is yours. Visit me in Highcastle when all of this is over, and I'll see that your men are rewarded."

"You're too kind," said Roscoe, "and look, I'm sorry, I had no idea..."

"It's fine," Cyrus responded flatly. "Can't change what we've done, only what we choose to do next." It struck Cyrus that this was something Garrett might say, and he wondered if the pirate was thinking of his old friend too.

Roscoe said nothing, but he nodded and then gave a sincere bow. The hair at the top of his head was thinning, and as he rose to full height to replace his hat, his eyes glanced beyond Cyrus to where a group of Shadows had gathered at the entrance. "And what about them?" he asked, pointing to Patch, who stood at the front of the group. The boy's eyes were still pink from Shep's passing, but he showed no fear under Roscoe's gaze. "What do you think, boy?" the pirate called. "Do you want to see the world? There's always space for a few more in my crew!"

Cyrus stood almost protectively in front of Patch, but the boy stepped around him, pausing in front of the pirates. He looked so small in their shadow, but in the past few weeks, Cyrus had begun to suspect that the boy was, in fact, spirited and brave.

"What's your name?" Roscoe asked, crouching to meet him at eye level.

"He won't answer," said Cyrus. "I don't know his real name, but I've taken to calling him Patch."

"Patch!" Roscoe's laughter was so loud that it startled them all. "A name for a pirate if ever there was one! Join us if you want, boy, but don't ever let anything happen to your eye. The rest of the crew would never let you live it down!"

Patch grinned and reached his hand out to shake Roscoe's, accepting the deal.

Cyrus smiled. "You're free," he said turning to the remaining Shadows. "I know you never wanted any of this, but you are free to leave this place and live your lives. Roscoe is a good man, but Highcastle will always welcome you, I've no doubt that Ravensward is the same." Cyrus wasn't sure what sort of life would await the children in Auldhaven's capital; after all, that's where they had come from in the first place. But he couldn't worry on that too long in that moment. There just wasn't time. He turned back to Roscoe, who gave him a nod of approval. "It's good to see you, old friend," Cyrus said, "but for now, I've got a city to save."

"Always so dramatic," said Roscoe, rolling his eyes. And with that, the men embraced a final time before going their separate ways.

As Cyrus glanced back a final time, he found the Shadow children already crowding around Roscoe and his men. In the wily old pirate captain, it seemed that the Shadows had found a new home.

CHAPTER X

"The wolves are at the door!" King Augustus said before covering his mouth as an audible belch echoed around the room. The Grand Hall was a melting pot of silent concern as the king sat awkwardly in his chair at the head of the table. It was a warm day, and the king's face was pale with sweat beading on his forehead as he gulped down a full glass of wine, swallow after swallow, presumably in an attempt to rid himself of his ailment. Everyone gathered exchanged worried looks.

"Are you okay, my king?" Broderick asked, the first to break the silence. They had been summoned to discuss the arrival of the Verderan army, and it was by no means an ideal time for Augustus to fall ill.

Concerned for the king, Broderick, or for yourself? thought Wendell through a sip of his own wine. Augustus's condition had been worsening for days, and the king's own physicians were at a loss as to the reason behind his decline. It had started with a temperature, and then the sickness and cramping had followed. He had scarcely risen from his bed in recent days, and it was becoming quite the mystery, at least to those who didn't know where to look.

Poison was an art, of course. Too little, and the results were ineffectual; too much, and you have another Anselm on your conscience. It had taken years of practice, but with the benefit of experience, it seemed that Wendell was becoming a veritable expert.

"Rest, my king," Wendell said, and Augustus forced a grateful smile. Wendell rose to address the assembly. "As our king said, the wolves are indeed at the door. The Verderans have taken residence beyond our city walls, and though we knew this day would come, the question remains as to what they will do next."

"Their numbers stand at around eight thousand from our estimates," added Thaddeus, remaining seated. "They have established camps in view of the city, and it seems that they mean to lay siege."

"But why?" Broderick was not so boisterous in the face of long odds, it seemed. "They hold the greater number. Why not attack now?"

"Perhaps they are waiting for something?" Adaline guessed, offering a rare contribution as her hand rested on her son's arm, her brow creased with worry for the boy. "We have prepared the city for battle, but perhaps we should take the fight to them?"

Unexpectedly, her words fell on deaf ears, and Wendell had to swallow his anger as Augustus gestured for him to continue once more.

Wendell said, "We have enough food and water to last a couple of weeks, but the city is yet vulnerable. Perhaps there is some merit in the queen's suggestion." He was rewarded with a small smile from Adaline. Bolstered, he continued, "With our new fortifications and our knowledge of the field, there is every chance of victory despite their greater number. Only you can make the decision, my king," he said, bowing at Augustus, who looked like he might fall asleep at any moment, "but I think that we should remain open to all options at this time."

The room fell silent, and attention turned upon the king. His bloodshot eyes were drooping, and Wendell wondered if he'd overdone the dosage after all. "It's a shame Cornelius cannot be with us today," Augustus began, speech akin to a drunken stutter, "for he would remind you that our fate is not decided in this room but by the hands of God." The king spoke with conviction, and yet it was all Wendell could do to keep from rolling his eyes as the young man continued with his religious tirade. "We chose our path at the last meeting, and I see no good reason to change. Great work has been done to strengthen the capital, and the Verderans may yet be surprised by our resilience."

Broderick and his generals applauded as expected, and though Wendell clapped along, his expression was blank.

Not if they surprise you first… he thought silently, and as the assembly parted, he knew it would take divine intervention to see Augustus moved from his decision.

⚜ ⚜ ⚜

Wendell was running out of time. Despite his highly commendable efforts, he knew Prince Rafael to be an impatient man with a disposition ill-suited to siege conditions. He had hoped to manoeuvre Augustus with gentle persuasion, but desperate times called for desperate measures. It was time to pursue a rather different approach to force Augustus out into battle.

In the end, the result would be the same. The hand of God himself would not deliver victory to Augustus, and it was a matter of self-preservation as much as anything for Wendell. Then there was Adaline. Wendell couldn't save Augustus in all of this, but if the king were to leave the castle and meet the Verderans, at least Adaline would be spared. Prince Rafael was a ruthless killer, but he had always been true to his word.

Wendell picked up his pace to begin the next stage of his plan, but as he turned a corner into the long corridor that led toward Augustus's chambers, he found Francine perched on a window ledge, sword in hand, displaying a rather impressive pout.

"Nobody to terrorise today?" he asked, slowing with no intention to stop. The girl's face had none of her normal vibrance, and as he moved closer, he realised that it would not be as simple as a flippant remark while passing by. He stopped.

"Just bored is all," came Francine's monotone reply. She had transitioned into a moody teenager overnight, and the act was complete as she blew out her cheeks dramatically. "I miss Cyrus, and Seth is busy with Broderick. All of the men are preparing for war. Nobody in the castle knows what to do with me. I'm not staff, and I'm not a princess. I'm—"

"A nobody," Wendell finished with a sad smile.

"Thanks." Francine rolled her eyes at his frank words, letting her sword drop so that it dangled by her legs.

"No," he said, shaking his head. "I'm not saying that you are. I just know how it feels. I've been in this castle many years now, and do you want to know why people pay attention to me?"

Fran glanced over at him and then nodded with a silent reluctance.

"Because I worked hard to make myself a somebody." He raised his right hand to draw attention to the two missing fingers. "You see this?" he asked, "I was going to be in the King's Guard once, perhaps even a general." He laughed, and then his thoughts turned to Anselm, and his smile soured. *A story for another day, perhaps...* "I never wanted to be Master of Coin, but I took my setbacks. I made a life for myself here in Highcastle, and now I have the ear of the king!"

A strange feeling washed over Wendell as Francine smiled back at him. He *had* worked hard over the years, and no doubt his story would be an inspiration to any child. He recoiled at the unexpected warmth of yet another exchange, recalling a memory of his own: a young man with an injured hand, his promising future snatched away. Old friends newly absent as he suffered through his recovery alone. A young man with an injured hand, a nobody. Invisible.

"Success is not about making excuses but rather seizing chances. So, Seth can't train with you? Fine, train by yourself. Could there be a more fearsome opponent than your own imagination? Your own shadow?"

Francine laughed, and her nose scrunched at Wendell's unexpected monologue.

"Take it from me," he continued, "if you want to be the very best at whatever it may be, you'll need to work morning, noon, and night. 'Trust, commitment, and honour,' that's what Thaddeus always used to say." He chuckled, forgetting himself for a moment. "Pick yourself up and earn their attention. I don't want to see you without that sword in your hand from now on, understood?"

"Understood," Francine said as she jumped down from the ledge. She flashed a toothy smile before running in the direction from which he had arrived. Once she was gone, Wendell was left with nothing but another inexplicable grin on his face.

The siege! he thought, smile fading as he scolded himself. The lives of thousands were on the line, and there he was wasting time on a child. No good could possibly come from his efforts to help the girl, he knew. But if helping Francine in some way was truly a waste of time, why did it feel like the right thing to do?

"Inspiring words," came a voice.

Wendell startled as the Verderan assassin appeared from behind a stone column. He looked every bit as sinister as he had during their previous meeting, and he proceeded to goad Wendell with a round of mock applause.

"Forgive me," he said stepping into the light, "but perhaps I am dealing with the wrong person. Maybe the girl would have been a better choice. She at least seems to demonstrate the required sense of urgency." He moved closer to Wendell and whispered in his ear. "Time's up."

Wendell's eyes squeezed tightly shut as he flinched, expecting the man's blade. He remained this way for a few long moments before opening them once more to find that the man had gone. He had expected swift action from the princes, but they had sent their assassin back far more quickly than even Wendell had anticipated. His plan was well-considered and close to bearing fruit, but the art of subtle manipulation cannot be rushed, and at the man's hard words, Wendell feared the alternative.

I can still do this, he thought, continuing toward King Augustus's chambers. *I've come too far to fail.*

⚜ ⚜ ⚜

Despite great confidence in his own abilities, Wendell really was starting to worry about the king's health. Even as a warm summer carried on outside, a roaring fire raged in Augustus's chambers, and Wendell was forced to loosen the collar of his robes as he sat patiently at the king's bedside.

"More water, my king?" he asked, deciding that water alone was best suited to his current predicament. The boy was still sweating profusely, all the while complaining of cold from beneath a pile of thick bedsheets. He had none of his usual prickly nature, and he seemed a million miles from being able to walk the length of the castle, much less into a field of war.

When Augustus finally answered, he did so wordlessly. His hand flung out limply as he reached to take the glass from Wendell's grip. Augustus wasn't going to die, of course, but Wendell winced as he watched the young king choke down the water, coughing much of it back up and onto his bedsheets. It was one thing to poison someone, but it was something else entirely to watch them suffer. Wendell turned his face away, mentally urging the next stage of his plan to commence.

A sudden knock at the door startled the king, even in his half-conscious state.

"Can I come in?" asked Cornelius, Master of Prayer, his head poked through a gap of his own making. Whatever Wendell thought of the old man, he couldn't question his timekeeping.

"Cornelius," he responded with his very best impression of surprise. "The king is not well at present, but I'm sure he would take great comfort from your company."

At this, Cornelius sidled over to the bed. Wendell made no offer to relinquish his chair, and the old man was forced to his knees, resting elbows on the bedframe to utter a prayer.

"What word from above?" Wendell probed, nudging Cornelius with his foot. The king sat up in his bed silently, his reverence for the old man undeniable.

Cornelius shot Wendell a sharp look before standing to approach the fireplace. "It seems the king is being punished," he ventured, turning dramatically to catch an expression of relief on Wendell's face. "This illness is a message from God that we should not allow the Verderan heathens to attack our freedoms. No!" He stamped sharply, and Wendell was surprisingly taken by the old man's performance. "We shall not sit idly by as they see us to starvation within these walls." He returned to the bedside and took Augustus by the hand, the king shaking like a leaf in the harsh wind of revelation. "Take the fight to our enemies, Augustus, and see your health restored. If you choose to remain in the comfort of your bed, know that you will never leave."

The silence after Cornelius's words was louder than the sounds of battle, which were ringing sharply in Wendell's mind as he thought of what must come next.

Cornelius's speech had been more than Wendell could have hoped for, and after a moment, Augustus's face spasmed with fear, his eyes going wide.

"Fetch Broderick," the king muttered after some consideration. "Tell him it's time to do the Lord's work."

⚜ ⚜ ⚜

Twenty odd years of service. Almost half of Wendell's life, and if nothing else, he concluded that his luxurious down-cushioned mattress had been worth it all. He nestled contentedly into his pillow and breathed a deep sigh of relief. People had often asked him how he slept at night, and he lamented that he had not yet found the words to capture the sheer luxury of his sleeping arrangement. It was like sleeping on a cloud—not just any cloud but the best, most perfect cloud in the sky—and with the successful outcome of his meeting with Augustus, that's exactly how Wendell was feeling.

Broderick was no fool. He knew Augustus's new plan to be insanity, but when a man prides himself on a willingness to do battle, it is very difficult to deny the ardent wishes of a king. So it was, then, that the armies of Easthaven would ride out to meet their Verderan rivals, abandoning the security of the city walls and with only the word of God for protection. It would be a massacre, of course, but armed men fight willingly. This reckless approach would at least ensure the safety of the castle and those who resided within its walls. It would take some doing, but Wendell knew Adaline would thank him for all of this one day. The destination had always been unavoidable. It was simply Wendell's duty to ensure the safest route.

He rolled over onto his back and looked up at the ornate arches of the ceiling, his eyes growing heavy in the darkness. Tomorrow would bring about the culmination of all of his efforts and with it, his just rewards. He tried to imagine a life in which Anselm's face didn't seem to stare back at him from every wall, every corner, eyes pitying him and judging his every action. He imagined life with Adaline. A dream, just he and…

Adaline! Wendell sat bolt upright at the sound of a scream erupting down the hallway.

He swung his legs from the bed and rushed to his sword on its mount. He'd know her voice anywhere, and it had always been his job to save her, especially when men had started to notice her as a younger woman. A stream of bad sorts with worse intentions, but he'd always kept her safe, hadn't he? At least until Anselm, anyway. It couldn't be anything too serious, though, he assured himself, even as he ran toward the sound of the scream. She was safe here in the castle, surely. Her doors were always attended by two guards. It was probably just a bad dream or perhaps an unwelcome rodent. He had to check, though; it was the very least a gentleman would do.

"Is everything all right?" he called, bare feet slapping against the flagstones. He imagined he looked rather comical in his bedclothes, but there was no humour in coming around the corner to find Adaline's guards dead at her doorway. A pair of gaping throats, oozing quietly as dark blood pooled around them. He froze, blade shimmering in the moonlight. The doors were partly open, and he could hear the sound of gentle sobbing from within.

She's alive, he thought with a wave of relief. He made to enter and embrace his moment of gallantry, but the sound of urgent footsteps caused him to pause before Thaddeus and Seth rushed by with a handful of the King's Guard.

"She's alive," he said aloud this time, albeit weakly, as the last of the guards passed him. The doors were wide open, and he inhaled the sweet scent of Adaline's perfume as he followed suit. The men were all at the dowager queen's bedside as he entered, but Wendell's eyes were drawn to a third pool of blood forming on the floor before him, coming from a man who was all-too-familiar, one who had only recently filled Wendell with dread.

Time's up, the man had said, but he hadn't known how right he was.

The assassin's face was twisted in a look of surprise while a small, vicious blade stood upright, buried in his chest. Wendell worked to mask any recognition of the man's face, but the sword itself carried a vague familiarity of its own. Whose was it? He glanced back to where Thaddeus held Adaline, and his eyes narrowed with confusion. If the guards were both dead and Adaline remained bedbound, then who had killed the assassin?

He wanted to run to Adaline to comfort her, but a gentle sob sounded once more, and Wendell turned slowly to find a small form shaking in the corner.

"I didn't mean to kill him," Fran wept, tears in her eyes, her lips trembling with every word. "He killed the guards, and he was going to—"

"Shh," Wendell smiled as he crouched down to comfort Fran instead, patting her dark hair as she continued to sob. "He was a bad man. You did the right thing." Fran reached out toward him, and Wendell found that he didn't have the strength to deny her. He hugged her against his torso.

"You saved the queen," he said, holding her tightly, his words ringing with truth. And for this, he knew that he would always be in Francine's debt.

Rain lashed down on the city of Ravensward, King Simeon's castle creaking and groaning under the onslaught. Cyrus felt as though he could hear every raindrop as it slammed against the stonework, and an unexpected crash of thunder startled him, his breath short and pitchy as he stood, full of sympathy, before the king.

Simeon's condition seemed not to have worsened since the last time Cyrus had seen him, but Cyrus feared this would only be a small mercy in the face of the news Cyrus had come to deliver. The king's appearance remained pale, and his skin was beginning to fall slack upon his shrivelled frame as he slowly and tenderly inspected the gold ring between his fingers, its green stone glinting in the light. The silence was excruciating, but Cyrus dreaded the questions to come even more. He had come so close to freedom, but here he was, stood once again before his adversary and this time with word of the man's dead son.

"Tell me how it happened," Simeon croaked, breaking the silence. He shed no tears, but it seemed to Cyrus that the king's spirit had died along with the son he had never met.

"It was an accident," began Lambert, with more than a little fear in his voice. "We had no idea that Brandon was acting under a different name. Shep. We engaged the rebels, naturally, and his identity wasn't clear until it was too late." Cyrus could tell Lambert was on the edge of apologising, but he sensed that the man wasn't yet ready to admit whose blade had done the job.

Simeon threw the ring across the throne room, his chest heaving as he fought to keep his breathing regular. "I asked how it happened!" he barked, and it seemed to use up all of his remaining energy. His voice was quieter when he continued, "I never gave that boy a damn thing. It's no wonder he hated me. He was doing just fine without me. Then I come along, sending you two after him, and now look where he is. He's dead." Simeon's voice nearly broke on the last word, but he kept his gaze ahead, staring at Lambert for further explanation.

"I'm sorry," said Lambert finally, and Cyrus noticed the general shaking as he tried to steady himself. "He attacked Prince Cyrus," he continued, pleading with arms outstretched, his tone giving away the bits of the story he had left out. "We didn't know who he was, and he was about to kill the prince. It was—"

"An accident," Cyrus finished solemnly. "It was an accident." He paused to let it sink in. "Brandon attacked me while Lambert was securing the prisoners. I never saw who killed him, but we would never have let it happen if we had known who he truly was." Silence fell upon the room, and though Cyrus could feel Lambert's eyes hot upon him, it was Simeon's reaction he feared the most.

"Your son was a fine man," Cyrus added with more veneration than Brandon perhaps deserved, at least from what Cyrus had seen of him. "A leader of men, a general in his own right, and loved by those who knew him best." He walked across the throne room to collect the ring from the flagstones before offering it back to the king in kindness. "He was every bit his father's son, but he's gone now. I know it is of little consolation, but I have reason to believe he read my journal before…" He paused to consider his words before continuing, "He knew you were searching for him. He died knowing his father cared. You did all that you could…"

That was it. Another man had died, and that was all he had to say on the matter. Cyrus thought back to his parents in Coldwynne and Osbert afterwards, wishing that someone had been there to provide similar comfort. It wouldn't bring any of them back to life, but surely there was some solace to be found in reliving a person's finer points. It was likely, Cyrus thought, that Simeon would see him to the dungeons because of Brandon's death, but Cyrus had to do what he knew to be right, whether it damned him or not.

"Thank you," said Simeon unexpectedly, reaching to take the ring with a sad smile. "Not just for this but for everything. It seems I will leave this world with nothing, but in the two of you at least," he gestured at Cyrus and Lambert, respectively, "I know I have a most loyal servant, and the rarest of all gifts: an enemy turned friend. I have asked much of you in recent weeks, Prince Cyrus, but I think the time has come to deliver my side of the bargain."

Simeon rose to his feet slowly, and Cyrus, stomach lurching, braced himself for another of Simeon's treacherous plots.

"You are free to leave Ravensward at your will," Simeon said, "and in doing so, I hereby renounce the claim of Auldhaven on any future second-born prince. These terms were decided at a time rife with mistrust, but your actions have shown that this is no longer the path forward for a brighter future between our two nations."

It was all Cyrus could do to keep his jaw from dropping as the king extended a hand in Cyrus's direction. His nails were unkempt, and blue veins bulged through unexpectedly liver-spotted skin. It seemed only yesterday that Cyrus had planned Simeon's demise, but in that moment, he felt nothing but warmth toward the king he had come to know.

"We are perhaps the very best of enemies," Simeon said. He laughed as his hand met Cyrus's. The man's grip remained firm, and it was a surprise to Cyrus when the king pulled him closer for a heartfelt—if slightly awkward—embrace.

"Thank you, Simeon," said Cyrus, stepping away from the king. "A great deal has changed, and you have been most generous, but I must know your thoughts on my other request." He was reluctant to push his luck but knew that if he was going to secure help for Easthaven, it was now or never. "Will you uphold the promise you made during the treaty and send troops to help Augustus defend Highcastle against the Verderans?"

Simeon opened his mouth to speak, but Cyrus would not be slowed.

"You are a good man, Simeon. I see that now. Make your final act one that will leave history with the same impression, one that will secure your legacy and save my people." It was optimistic at best, Cyrus knew, and it took all of his energy to ignore his quivering nerves and force a look of confidence onto his face.

The king's reaction was delayed at first, his eyes narrowed as he looked beyond Cyrus, and his face settled into a thoughtful expression, his chin in his hand. For a fleeting moment, Cyrus's chest felt fit to burst as he imagined that he might actually achieve the impossible, but then Simeon's expression turned from contemplative to serious, and Cyrus felt his hope falling away strand by strand.

"Your actions are admirable, young prince," Simeon began, hobbling back to his throne. "Your brother is a deceitful fool who sold you out at the first sign of threat, yet you still petition for support to save him." It was Simeon's turn to silence Cyrus as he tried to interject, raising a palm as he shifted in his throne, and then lowering his hand as he found the comfort to continue. "There is no finer end to this story than for our two nations to join in union. Perhaps together, we could defeat the Verderans and rewrite history. Who knows, I might even live long enough to celebrate!" He laughed briefly before the corners of his mouth fell once more. "I would like to help you, Prince Cyrus, truly I would. Yet I fear that I must use this time for the betterment of the people, rather than my own legacy. Our soldiers are only recently returned from the campaign in Easthaven, and with the prospect of my passing, the priority must be to prevent any further battles within our own borders. I hope you understand?"

Cyrus's head lowered. Simeon's answer was a crushing disappointment, but it was also what Cyrus would have done in Simeon's position.

"It is not the answer that I had hoped for, but I wish you all the best," he said, eventually. "There was one other thing…" He paused, choosing his words carefully. "During our assault on the mountain, we found that Brandon had been holding King Ferdinand captive at the request of the Verderan princes, Rafael and Alonso. We were able to liberate the king, and he has consented to help bring an end to this war, one way or another. Perhaps his presence will shift the balance."

"And I thought *I* had family problems…" Simeon shook his head slowly. "Well, if anyone can do this, it's you, Cyrus. Truly, I wish I could do more, but my role now is to heal the wounds of my people so that we may lend support to our brothers and sisters in Easthaven for generations to come…Now!" he called abruptly, clapping his hands. "Where is that bearded oaf, Ferdinand? I would share words with him before your departure."

Simeon, temporarily restored of his good humour or perhaps too stubborn to give into grief, made to leave, but then he turned to face Cyrus once more. "Oh, and Cyrus, I almost forgot." He reached into his jacket and retrieved a roll of parchment, leaning forward to hand it over. "This came for you. Hopefully it will provide the good news that I could not."

Cyrus took the parchment from Simeon and gave a silent nod as he turned away, a smile playing at the edge of his mouth despite the bad news from Simeon. He didn't need to look at the letter to see who'd sent it. He'd know that sweet scent of flowers anywhere. She hadn't forgotten him. Marcia.

⚜ ⚜ ⚜

Cyrus was free to leave Ravensward with Simeon's blessing. He had disrupted the Verderans' supply of blast powder and would return to Highcastle with the most powerful weapon of all: King Ferdinand. For all of their bluster, Cyrus knew that the princes had been unable to stomach killing their father and that the return of the king would undermine their ruthless plans. The princes had inherited their pomposity from their father, but Ferdinand seemed nevertheless to be a decent man, and as Cyrus left the bearded king to his goodbyes with Simeon, he felt a sense of hope descend upon him for the first time in—well, he couldn't remember how long. He was ready to get back to Highcastle, and he believed, perhaps optimistically, that the battle could still be won.

He wondered when he would return to Simeon's castle and who would sit upon the throne when he did. As always seemed to be the case during his travels, it occurred to him that he had spent little time actually exploring the capital, and with Marcia's parchment protruding from his saddlebag, he decided to leave Adagio with a fresh-faced stable hand as he wandered to discover Simeon's gardens while the two kings had their meeting. Perhaps, he thought, he should eventually do some travelling without the pressing needs of war following him around.

The first thing that caught him was the smell. He ducked through a stone archway wrapped with vines and into the vivid oasis of the walled garden beyond. The lawn was trimmed short, the edges precise, and recent wet weather was responsible for vibrant colours the likes of which Cyrus had not seen since Casarossa. He took a delicate orange flower in his palm and closed his eyes, allowing its sweet scent to fill his nose and thinking of the instantly familiar scent that had come with Marcia's parchment. Standing in the garden, Cyrus knew this was the calm before the storm, but he had seen enough death to know that life can be snatched away in an instant. He wanted to make this one moment of peace count.

He walked on through another narrow archway and into a tunnel of sorts, where flowers hanging from a wooden frame cascaded all around him. The space was small, but Cyrus felt none of his usual nervousness at the sense of confinement. This place was ethereal and heavenly, a stark contrast to the hopeless passageways of the mountain and the mines. He wondered why Simeon would ever leave this hideaway, and as he emerged into the sunlight, he felt refreshed by the experience. His hand fell upon the parchment in his pocket, and an ornate bench provided him with the opportunity to sit. Though it was damp with morning dew, Cyrus marvelled at the intricate carvings of rearing warhorses that served as the bench's legs as he wiped the seat dry and took a moment to rest.

The most beautiful things, Cyrus reflected, always seemed to remind him of Marcia, and a stupid grin unfolded at the same time as the parchment. Her neat, curling script was elegantly written, and he ran his hands over the twists and turns of her letters as he made his way eagerly down the page.

Dearest Cyrus,

I suppose it is my turn to apologise. I should have written back sooner, but I wasn't really sure what to say. I am writing this more in hope than expectation, but if you're reading it, then I guess that means that everything turned out all right?

It was wonderful to hear about your appointment of Merrill as Magistrate in Eriwald. He is kind and caring and seems to be perfect for the position that you've given him. Meanwhile, here in Highcastle, King Augustus is the same as always. It seems that Simeon was not behind Anselm's murder after all, and the armies of Verdera are marching toward the capital. In truth, I am sending this now because I'm not sure when, or if, I'll be able to write again once they arrive.

Anyway, the king—your brother, I should say—is placing his faith in religion. It's his answer to everything these days. Thaddeus is trying to make him see sense, and even Broderick seems scared at the prospect of war. Your mother is well and trying to see the best in Augustus, but we appear to be condemned to siege conditions. If only we had a steady hand in the castle, someone who could think or at least talk their way out of this. Know anyone?

I know you asked about your sister, and she is doing splendidly. She's a natural around the castle. I even noticed Wendell of all people practicing swordplay with her the other day. Perhaps she will be our protector now that you're gone.

I've been spending a lot of time with Adaline lately, and she misses you greatly. We all do. I should have realised that you weren't Augustus from the beginning—I can't imagine now how anyone could get the two of you confused—and I regret that I didn't share my feelings with you in the end. I think about you all the time and hope you'll come back to us someday.

I can't wait to hear of your adventures, and who knows? Maybe I'll be part of them one day. It all sounds very exciting, but after these last few months, I'll be happy with a simple life when all this is done. Death, deceit, and war. I'm starting to wonder if excitement is really that exciting after all.

Wishing for your safe return,

Marcia

Cyrus rolled the page and held the scroll to his forehead with a smile and an ache somewhere deep inside himself. Marcia's words surged through him like early morning energy, and he felt, for a moment, that things really would be all right. He had known about the Verderans already, but in light of Marcia revealing her feelings for him, he knew it would take more than a few thousand soldiers to keep him from her. It was madness, of course, but maybe there was some truth in all the love stories he'd heard growing up. Perhaps the two of them were simply meant to be. It made his chest swell just to allow himself to hope for it.

Setting aside his racing heart, Cyrus thought through the rest of the letter's contents. News of his family had come as a great relief as well, and Cyrus looked down at Francine's leather bracelet, proud if unsurprised to hear of her progress. He had been too preoccupied to consider how much he truly missed his sister and his mother, but his heart skipped again, and a wave of excitement washed over him as he contemplated home.

Home, he thought as he had done so many times before. *Where is home?*

When he really thought about it, he found Eldred's Keep at the forefront of his mind. He would never forget those he had lost or the other places he had called home along the way, but in Highcastle, he had found a fresh start, and it was not one that he would give up so easily. Not without a fight.

He stood and stowed the parchment safely back into his pocket. It was tough to leave the tranquillity of Simeon's manicured gardens behind, but he tore himself away to face the road ahead. By the time he returned to the courtyard, he found Ferdinand already waiting in his saddle purposefully. It seemed that he, too, was focused on the road ahead instead of what lay behind.

Though the king's face was shrouded in facial hair, Cyrus noticed that Ferdinand had tidied his appearance immeasurably in the short time since they'd arrived. His beard had been shortened to his collar, and his hair had been cut and tied so that grey strands now fell uniformly down the back of his neck. The fresh set of clothes that Ferdinand wore were clearly the work of Simeon's tailors, and the man looked every bit a king, his silk shirt iridescent as he sat astride Morven, the same horse that had carried him away from the mountain.

"Ready to go?" Ferdinand asked as he ushered Morven forward.

Cyrus took a moment to turn and nod back toward Simeon, who stood by the grand castle doors. The king leaned on his wooden walking cane for balance with General Lambert at his side. Lambert gave a nod of his own in Cyrus's direction. The respect between all of them was an unspoken yet welcome change from their first meeting, and with the loose ends tied, it was finally time to go.

Adagio, impatient as ever, snorted as if to express her own readiness, pulling Cyrus back into the moment. He smiled, recalling that this stubborn mare had been his one constant on this long journey. He stroked her mane as he once again returned to his mount.

"Ready," said Cyrus, and they raced through the gates, leaving the City of Spires behind them.

⚜ ⚜ ⚜

They took the most direct route back to Highcastle. The horses rode hard, and though Ferdinand called for regular breaks, they made good progress retracing Cyrus's path across Auldhaven until the border was in sight once more. Though purposeful and efficient, Cyrus found Ferdinand to be far more talkative than he had at first imagined. The two of them discussed the wonders of Verdera at great length, both on the road and in taverns along the way, where Ferdinand spoke with a twinkle of nostalgia in his eyes.

"The great cascading waterfalls of Analdas!"

"The lava flow of the Arasca volcano in the eastern mountain ranges of Valentera!"

"You've not lived until you've seen the great rock formations of the Estaga Desert!"

The prospect of seeing any one of them excited Cyrus, and his imaginings provided a welcome distraction until they arrived to take rest in the small town of Bransdale, where Ferdinand moved to speak of his sons' irrepressible ambitions and how the loss of their mother had hardened them to the world.

By the third day, their conversation had progressed to Augustus. Keen to learn of his counterpart in Easthaven, Ferdinand asked questions of Cyrus that called upon the very limits of his creativity.

"What kind of man is the king?"

"Where do his thoughts lie on Anselm's treaty?"

"Will he ride out to meet the princes or endure a siege?"

Cyrus thought he would run out of variations on ways to say, "Sorry, I don't really know." He would have loved to answer Ferdinand's questions in more detail or do more than speculate, but it occurred to Cyrus that he knew extraordinarily little about his brother. What he did know, he didn't trust, and that fact didn't make contemplating Ferdinand's litany of questions any easier.

Cyrus always kept Marcia's parchment close, tucked into the pocket just over his heart, and though the letter may have offered some insight into developments in Highcastle, he never discussed the contents with Ferdinand, feeling that her words were intended for Cyrus and Cyrus alone.

When they approached the border crossing, Cyrus felt a pang at seeing the two figures standing guard in the same place Flynn and Colton had stood on the bridge. This sadness was immediately replaced by nervousness as he wondered if the guards might question him on the whereabouts of the two previous guardsmen, but thankfully, they passed without question. It was a relief, if somewhat disconcerting, Cyrus thought as he turned to look back at the fading silhouettes of the new guards once more, to see how easily men can be replaced.

As they travelled through the Whitewood, they avoided Farley's house at all costs, and Cyrus fought to clear the image of Flynn's swaying, lifeless body from its place in his mind. It was no more than half a day before they broke through the shimmering maze. Ferdinand demonstrated great skill for navigation, and though the Whitewood was labyrinthine in its design, the old king remained ever watchful, using only the sun in the sky to guide their way.

From there on out, the journey was relatively simple: a straight race across the western prairie lands, bypassing Eriwald in their haste for home. Cyrus's mind replayed Marcia's letter over and over, her voice growing clearer with every stride. He had thought about their reunion a thousand times, and his excitement grew as his mind turned to Fran, Adaline, Thaddeus, and all the others in the castle. Mile after mile, he urged Adagio forward. He proudly realised that his mare seemed to grow faster and stronger with each passing day, and Cyrus marvelled at her lean physique as they paused to let an exhausted Morven rest.

The morning of their fourth day brought with it a glimpse of Highcastle, the low sun gleaming from the tall towers of Eldred's Keep. The grey stonework of the castle appeared on the horizon, and though Cyrus wanted to leap from Adagio and sprint the final distance, he found an army in his path that was deterrent enough.

"Oh my," said Ferdinand with a quiet gasp, drawing up beside Cyrus. The king was using a hand to shield his eyes, but no glare of the sun could hide the scale of the force before them. The north of the city was surrounded, and the morning air was thick with the smell of campfire smoke and cooking meat from the Verderan forces, which were split between three separate encampments. The largest of these encampments sat beyond the main northern entrance to the city, while the two smaller divisions had been positioned to prevent movement from the eastern and western gates. Invading soldiers swarmed around the city like ants, and it was the first time Cyrus had looked upon Highcastle and found it seeming small and fragile. There was no way they would be able to ride into the capital like this, and it occurred to Cyrus that he was foolish for thinking it would be possible in the first place.

"We have to get you to safety," Cyrus said, scouring the landscape once more as though searching for an answer. He could see that great work had been done to fortify the outer limits of the city before the Verderans arrived, and though he was glad to see Highcastle better protected, this would not help him as he tried to find a way inside. He considered trying to negotiate with the princes, but it wasn't worth the risk they posed to their father. After all that he had been through, Cyrus thought, he was going to be thwarted within sight of the city gates. But as Cyrus let his head fall in disappointment—all but pulling his own hair out in frustration—it was Ferdinand whose own frustrated remark provided the answer Cyrus sought.

"It would be easier to walk through stone," the king said flatly.

Cyrus's eyes widened as he sat upright in his saddle once more, all traces of despair immediately erased. That was it. That was the answer. Walking through stone. Garrett's voice suddenly echoed in Cyrus's memory. *"It's prudent for a king to have a means of entering or exiting the castle in times of need."*

Cyrus turned Adagio to face the Dalhart Forest, gesturing for Ferdinand to follow him. "A secret door," he said with a wide smile, hoping that it was still there. "I think there might be a way."

⚜ ⚜ ⚜

Adagio slowed as she broke through the trees and into the clearing. "This is the place," called Cyrus, jumping from her back. When Ferdinand drew level, his face was bemused, and Cyrus hoped more than ever before that Garrett had not been joking. He had shown Cyrus the hidden door during their previous visit, but whether it truly offered passage into the castle was yet to be determined.

Everything was as he remembered it, from the moss-covered boulder to the impressive rockface and its trickling water. Cyrus's eyes found the section of glistening stone, and it seemed only moments ago that he had been here. With Marcia. With Garrett. Sun shone through the branches overhead as if highlighting their path to freedom, and Cyrus tied Adagio to a tree before rushing over to place his hand against the rock. *Moment of truth*, he thought. And, with Ferdinand watching on expectantly, he closed his eyes and pushed on the door.

"What the—"

Cyrus gave a sigh of relief as a gap appeared in one side of the rock as the door opened inward just like any other door would. Cobwebs broke away as he used a shoulder to push it open more widely. The rock scraped with every inch, suggesting that the entrance had not been used in some time.

"It's real!" he said, turning to Ferdinand, who remained open-mouthed where Cyrus had left him. "I mean, of course it's real. This is our answer." He pointed back at the opening. "It leads all the way to the castle, and—"

Cyrus froze as Verderan voices sounded nearby. A flock of birds fluttered into the air noisily, and sounds of movement in the trees indicated that the newcomers were close. Cyrus's heart pounded. He turned back to Ferdinand, who stood stock still as if expecting instruction.

"Into the tunnel," Cyrus whispered urgently through gritted teeth.

Ferdinand wasted no time in darting into the dark space, bracing himself against the wall, plainly ready to see the door closed behind them. The footsteps were growing louder now, but Cyrus remembered the journal and his other belongings, which were back in his saddlebag. He rushed over to Adagio, and it dawned on him that this might be the last that they would see of each other.

"Go, old girl," he said affectionately, his throat unexpectedly tight. "Be free." He untied her tether, and though he wished her to run, she only nuzzled him before trotting over to Morven. Ferdinand's face was barely visible in the shadow of the tunnel, but his eyes were wide with concern. Cyrus knew he only needed to free Morven and both horses would run, helping to conceal Cyrus and Ferdinand's presence in the forest, but Ferdinand had tied the knot tight. Cyrus wrestled with the thick rope, but it showed little sign of loosening. His hands were sweaty with nerves.

"Is anyone there?" came a Verderan voice, closer this time, and as Cyrus reached for his sword in desperation, two guards appeared through the trees with halberds fixed in his direction.

"I suggest you drop that!" said a grizzly old guard with a scar upon his cheek.

It was a hopeless situation, and Cyrus could not risk the tunnel being discovered. He dropped his sword to the mossy forest floor and raised his hands in peace. As Adagio moved to stand resolutely at his side, Cyrus noticed Ferdinand's shadowed face fade fully into the darkness of the tunnel as the door edged slowly and silently closed.

The atmosphere in Eldred's Keep was uncharacteristically sullen. Though mindful of Cornelius's words, Augustus, to Wendell's surprise, had decided to delay his offensive actions against the Verderans. Whether this was down to the shock from the attack on Adaline or the miraculous improvement in Augustus's own health, it seemed that logic might finally prevail with the young king. None of this was helping with Wendell's nerves, of course.

The whole affair was a disaster, and the attack on Adaline had been a most treacherous betrayal to Wendell. The Verderan princes, Rafael and Alonso, had promised Adaline's safety as a reward for Wendell's hard work and personal risk. Had the princes reneged on their word and ordered the assassin to murder Adaline, or was it the mindless act of a man desperate to please his employers? The assassin's passing brought little comfort in light of the likely repercussions. The Verderans now had little option other than storming the city. Losses on both sides would be innumerable, and in the event of a Verderan victory, it seemed highly unlikely that the princes would be willing to share their hard-earned success with Wendell.

Adaline was alive, though. And as Wendell stood surreptitiously peering around the corner of the doorway to Adaline's room, watching as Marcia laughed with the dowager queen while she brushed Adaline's golden hair, he knew that he still had at least one reason to be thankful.

"Wendell, is that you?" Adaline said, seemingly having caught a glimpse of him in her mirror.

He stepped back into the shadows just as Adaline turned to summon him. She was never meant to see him there, and he decided that this was as good a time as any to leave. He needed some time to think, to get things under control again. He had allowed himself to become distracted of late, and the consequences had been dire, nearly catastrophic in the case of Adaline. As he scurried away from the dowager queen's quarters, instinct took him through the castle. He made his way down a set of winding stairs toward his offices, a dark section of the castle illuminated only by dim candlelight to which the old and unsightly were condemned. He shared this space with Thaddeus, but they each had their own rooms, and it was rare that he would see the old man here, leafing through his dusty tomes. Wendell moved quickly, and though he walked with his head bowed in thought, a sudden sound alerted him. The commotion seemed to be coming from one of Thaddeus's libraries, and Wendell blew out his cheeks in frustration. It seemed there was no place for peace in this castle.

Now was not the time for Thaddeus's unnecessary interruptions, and Wendell banged on the closed door of the library before turning the handle to force his way in. "Do you mind?" he called in frustration, but as his eyes adjusted to the dimly lit room, he found that it was not Thaddeus that stood before him.

"King Ferdinand?" Wendell said with a light gasp. Wendell's eyes narrowed as he spoke, yet the man only smiled back while brushing himself down. Wendell remembered the king being remarkably well-maintained during their previous meetings, and though he now looked somewhat dishevelled, his identity was in no doubt.

"Is that you?" Wendell asked, though he knew the answer, puzzling over the possible reasons for the man's appearance. Prince Rafael said that his father had been "dealt with," but perhaps the Verderans were working together once more. They were decidedly fractious people after all. Maybe Ferdinand had been sent as an assassin to punish Wendell for his failings or perhaps even to kill King Augustus. This turn in the game was so unexpected that Wendell couldn't seem to stop the questions falling from his mouth despite the fact that he had given Ferdinand no time to answer.

"But how did you…" Wendell began weakly, his voice trailing off as his eyes fell upon a large wooden trapdoor embedded in the stone floor. The pitted wood and rusted metal told Wendell that it was not a new construction, and a misplaced section of carpet indicated that it had been covered in secrecy.

A way in and out of the castle? thought Wendell, his mind boggling with the possibilities. Could this be the answer for the Verderan forces, or better still, for his own escape? Perhaps he had been wrong to place his trust in the princes. What he needed, he thought, was a way to see Adaline and himself to safety, and here it was, staring back at him. His eyes returned to Ferdinand, who smiled at Wendell's barrage of questions.

"Where to start?" he began, lips pursed, eyes rolled upward in thought. "Yes, I am King Ferdinand—well, at least the last time I checked, anyway! As for the question of how I find myself in the castle…" He raised his eyebrow and turned to point down at the trapdoor. "I think you have figured that one out for yourself."

Ferdinand bent down to adjust the carpet back over the trapdoor, a cloud of dust rising as the carpet thumped back into place. He dusted off his hands for a few moments and then turned back to Wendell. "I escaped the Verderan army with Prince Cyrus," Ferdinand said, and Wendell's breath hitched at the mention of Augustus's brother, "but the prince was caught in the process."

Wendell swallowed dryly at Ferdinand's words, wondering wordlessly if Prince Cyrus was still alive and what this would mean in their efforts against the Verderans.

Ferdinand continued, "Now, if you don't mind me asking, who exactly are you?"

It was an insult, of course; they had met on multiple occasions. But Wendell was still too distracted by the mention of Cyrus to be affronted.

"Wendell," he answered, trying to hide the note of uncertainty in his voice. "We've met before, though the last time would have been some years ago. I'm sorry, did you say Prince Cyrus?"

The king nodded, and his face turned serious. "The prince lives. Well, at least for now. He helped me escape a rebel group in Auldhaven where I was being held prisoner, and we were returning to the castle to warn you of the Verderan advance when he was captured by some of my sons' men." He paused thoughtfully and then corrected himself, "My men, I suppose."

Wendell could never have predicted this most unexpected turn of events, not for all his planning and calculations. How had Prince Cyrus possibly survived Simeon's wrath, and how much did Ferdinand really know? He glanced back at the trapdoor before his eyes fell upon a candlestick holder on Thaddeus's desk. It occurred to him that the weighty metal would make it an effective weapon…

It would be the easiest thing in the world to do, he thought. The princes had clearly spared their father, for whatever reason, but it had been a mistake and one that could prove costly. Perhaps killing Ferdinand would save them a job. It might earn him a way back into their good graces, while the trapdoor would see him safely from the castle before anyone noticed. He edged wordlessly toward the desk, his mind whirring at what seemed an impossible speed. It felt foolish to rely upon anything other than his own instincts, and Wendell realised it was self-preservation alone that had seen him this far. He leaned upon the desk in a way he hoped seemed casual, his expression thoughtful. His eyes fixed on Ferdinand's as his hand searched for a grip on the intended weapon. He couldn't take any chances.

"It is a blessing that you have returned to us," Wendell began, killing time if nothing else.

Ferdinand nodded as he turned to survey the selection of books, leaving the back of his head momentarily exposed. The base of the candelabra weighed heavy in Wendell's left hand, and he knew it was now or never. He rose to his feet and stepped toward the king. Ferdinand would never see it coming. Just one quick action. A simple strike to the temple. He raised the candlestick high into the air, but movement caught the corner of his eye, and he quickly stepped back as Thaddeus appeared in the doorway.

"Wendell, is that you?" the old man asked, squinting and stepping into the room holding a flame of his own. His face was puzzled, but Wendell sensed and hoped that this was due to Ferdinand's appearance and not because Thaddeus had seen what Wendell was about to do.

"Ah, Thaddeus," Wendell said, his voice straining slightly over his dry throat. "Yes, it's me."

"I never took you for a scholar," Thaddeus continued, moving forward hesitantly. "I see you have a friend with you. Perhaps there is something that I can help with?"

Wendell still wasn't sure how much Thaddeus had seen, and he turned to place the candlestick holder inconspicuously back on the desk. He found himself uncharacteristically short of words and more than a little relieved when Ferdinand took the initiative.

"As a matter of fact, there is," the king's words came unexpectedly. "Thaddeus, my old friend, it has been far too long!"

Thaddeus's smile broadened with sudden recognition. It seemed Ferdinand was able to remember *some* of the people he had met previously, Wendell reflected with an internal pout.

"Ferdinand?" Thaddeus said, stepping forward as the king moved to meet him with an outstretched hand. "I thought you were dead!" he continued with greater confidence. "I'm sorry, the light is so poor down here! What a wonderful surprise to see you, and what impeccable timing. You always were a man of high drama!"

The two men laughed as they shook hands, and Wendell stood considering the situation silently, feeling like a spare wheel. He privately thought it was Thaddeus who had impeccable timing.

Wendell used this moment to gather his thoughts. He doubted that the princes would be working with their father. Not after what they did to him, sending him off to rot in Auldhaven, Wendell decided. Besides, their prideful ambition would never allow it. Wendell had missed his chance to kill Ferdinand and correct the princes' mistake, but perhaps the Verderan king was unaware of Wendell's efforts to bring about Augustus's downfall. Likely, Ferdinand would encourage Augustus to take offensive action in an effort to defend the capital and reclaim the Verderan crown. What would happen in such a case? Augustus remained heavily outnumbered, but King Ferdinand's reappearance could very well derail the Verderans, whose soldiers had sworn fealty not to the princes but to their king. Wendell thought they would be most likely to surrender the princes if the soldiers learned of their wicked plot to usurp the throne. Rafael and Alonso had demanded battle, but the outcome was no longer certain. Wendell hadn't come this far to see Augustus remain on the throne, and there was still the question of how much Ferdinand might know about Wendell's involvement with the princes.

It was all agonizingly unpredictable, and as Wendell looked to the gap where his fingers should be, he thought back to that moment of injustice, many years before. He had knelt, defeated, beneath Anselm's blade, vulnerable, and entirely out of control. It was the moment for which he could never forgive Anselm. The moment where Anselm took Wendell's fingers and his future along with them, and everything had changed. Wendell had sworn that day that he would never lose control of his own destiny, and he sighed deeply at his more immediate predicament. How had it come to this?

"We must take you to the king at once," said Thaddeus, gesturing Ferdinand back toward the door. It was as though Wendell wasn't even there, as though Wendell hadn't been the one to find Ferdinand in the first place, and as he scurried along behind them, he scolded himself for not getting to Ferdinand sooner.

He had made another mistake, he knew, and he feared it might be his last.

⚜ ⚜ ⚜

Wendell's chair scraped on the flagstones as he moved to take his place at the table. The smell of roasted meat hung in the air, and servants dashed around diligently, leaving a banquet in their wake. It was a feast for the ages, another of Augustus's nightly extravaganzas, and to Wendell's mind it was an altogether inappropriate event for a king to hold when he was ruling over a city under siege.

"A truly magnificent offering," he said nevertheless, pulling himself closer to the table.

"Hard to believe that it is even possible!" Adaline added with a subtle roll of her eyes. Augustus only smiled, and Wendell gave a smirk of his own at the king's ignorance to his mother's clever double-meaning.

"The king should be here at any moment," Wendell continued. "King Ferdinand, that is," he added, and with his last word still echoing out, the doors swung open to reveal Ferdinand's distinctive bearded smile.

"King Ferdinand," said Augustus, rising to his feet. "We are privileged to have you join us." The young king paused to raise a glass in Ferdinand's direction. "I see that you have been well tended to. All traces of the forest are gone from you, and a king has been unearthed once more. Please, join us." He gestured to an empty chair at the high table.

Ferdinand bowed, and if he was insulted by Augustus's words, it didn't show. The Verderan king sauntered into the room wearing a white shirt of the finest Easthaven cotton beneath a black jacket emblazoned with gold. It was an ensemble from Augustus's own collection, but Ferdinand had a confident swagger that carried the look effortlessly, one that even the sometimes-pompous Augustus couldn't quite pull off.

"Most kind," Ferdinand said, arriving at the table with Seth in tow.

Augustus inclined his head graciously, flicking his hand lazily to dismiss Seth, who closed the doors quietly behind him. "Useful chap to have around, that one," Augustus said, "but hardly ideal dinner company." He gave a half-smile and gestured for Ferdinand to be seated. "It is just the four of us this evening, I'm afraid. Thaddeus is discussing strategy with Broderick, so I have invited Wendell to join us instead. I must say that my Master of Coin took little convincing, though I suspect that there may be an altogether less *innocent* reason for his attendance!" He glanced knowingly toward Adaline.

Both kings laughed, and Wendell's skin turned pink under the queen's puzzled expression. Forget Ferdinand alone; he could have killed both kings in that moment. A dreamy smile formed as he thought of what a great pleasure it would be to see the Verderan king consigned to history and Augustus dethroned to face a similar fate. His short-lived smile began to wane. It was already starting to look an unlikely outcome, and what if the Verderan princes *were* responsible for the attack on Adaline? They were, at the very least, unpredictable. Was Wendell truly sure that life would be any better under Rafael and Alonso's charge?

He shook the doubt away and chose to laugh as though Augustus's remark didn't bother him, raising a glass at the young king's slight.

"Ferdinand, I hear you have news of Cyrus?" Adaline said, leaning forward expectantly as she asked.

The Verderan king smiled as he made to respond, but Augustus interjected, slamming a hand on the table to silence him.

"Enough of that, Mother," he responded abruptly. "Can't you see that the man has just escaped an ordeal? There will be time to catch up on the comings and goings of my dear brother later. A toast!" He rose to his feet emphatically. "To victory in the coming days and peace between our two great nations."

"To victory," said Ferdinand, standing to echo his host.

"To victory," muttered Wendell, and as he looked back at Augustus, he wondered why he had ever stopped poisoning him.

It wasn't until a few moments later that Wendell realised that while the room had echoed Augustus's call for victory, no one had remembered to echo his call for peace.

"Delicious!" Ferdinand exclaimed, relinquishing his cutlery as he sat back and rested his hands on his inflated stomach. His jacket was only hours old, but its buttons were already fit to burst.

Ferdinand wasn't wrong. The selection of meats, cheeses, and pastries was a credit to the kitchens of Eldred's Keep, and while most of the city was struggling on rations, there was no sign of a siege at the king's table. It was, of course, a rather painful affair to have to survive the king's company, especially when he was peacocking in front of another king, and Wendell wondered how he might have survived the evening without the large quantity of wine on offer. The boy's lack of humility was so great that Wendell almost admired him for his obliviousness, and despite his better judgement, Wendell laughed at all the right moments as Augustus regaled Ferdinand with exaggerated stories of his victory in the war with King Simeon.

"A truly wonderful evening," Ferdinand surmised as Augustus paused for a long-overdue breath. "I hope you don't mind, but rich food like this..." he swigged his wine as he gestured about the table, "well, it makes a man tired. Especially one so newly restored to such luxuries!"

Augustus rose to his feet. "Be my guest. You are not a young man anymore, nor are you expected to compete with one." He smirked smugly, tilting his glass toward Ferdinand. "I suggest you take water before bed. It would be a shame to miss you at breakfast!"

It was Ferdinand's turn to smile, and Wendell had to admire the Verderan king's tact. Wendell himself had suffered no end of Augustus's heedless slights, and it was no easy task to swallow your pride and smile with such grace. Wendell had no doubt that Ferdinand saw Augustus for the fool that he was, but the king hid it with aplomb.

"Good night, Dowager Queen," Ferdinand said gently, moving to kiss Adaline's hand with a little too much affection for Wendell's liking. "And to you King Augustus." Ferdinand offered a hand in courtesy. "I wish you peaceful rest."

Augustus took Ferdinand's hand before the old king pulled him close in embrace. The look on Augustus's face was priceless, but Wendell's amusement soon turned to confusion when Augustus gasped and blood began to pour from the young king's lips.

"Mother," gurgled Augustus through his own blood, his expression one of shock as he fell suddenly at Ferdinand's feet.

"Silence the queen!" Ferdinand shouted unexpectedly at Wendell. Though he was struck by shock, Wendell immediately rushed from his seat to place a hand over Adaline's screams before she could alert the guards outside as to what had happened. He was unsure as to why he was taking orders from Ferdinand, the king he had considered killing, but after all, Ferdinand was the only king left in the room, and Wendell's credence had always been to position himself with the most powerful ally in any given situation.

Perhaps Ferdinand really is working with his sons after all, Wendell thought. Augustus was no longer moving, but blood bubbled around the knife in his chest, and Wendell struggled to control Adaline as she fought to break free, her screams muffled by Wendell's hand pressed tightly to her face and her pristine nails digging into the skin on his arms.

"You think that I don't know you, Wendell?" asked Ferdinand, dragging Augustus's lifeless body along the floor. "I know all about your schemes with my sons. I had no love for Anselm, but I was prepared to honour the treaty. I told them to stop, but what's done is done, and I see that my biggest mistake was underestimating them. Augustus will die like his father, and with Simeon at death's door, it seems that the game has changed. My sons may think me a fool, an old man turned weak, but I will show them the error of their ways. I will take my crown back, and with it, the throne of Easthaven. As for you, Wendell," he paused to look Wendell up and down with a sneer. "You will help me just as you helped them to kill Anselm."

Adaline kicked out at Wendell, the heel of her shoe digging into his knee as she snarled in an attempt to escape his grip. When he looked down at her, he was met with an expression of pure horror. Her eyes screamed, *How could you?*

"You see to the queen," Ferdinand ordered, dropping a bloody knife on the table beside him. "I'll deal with the brute outside." Wendell assumed that Ferdinand meant Seth, the king's shield.

The door swung open behind him, and Wendell felt like his head was about to explode. He had no choice other than to silence Adaline—not if he wanted to live, at least—yet in that moment, he intensely felt her every wail, her every spasm of grief. He wanted nothing more than to make things right.

"Get off of me!" yelled Adaline, stamping down on Wendell's toes to break free. He expected her to lash out or to scream at the top of her voice, but the queen only sobbed as she rushed across the room to hold Augustus's lifeless body in her arms.

"How could you?" she wept, speaking the sentence her eyes had already said to him aloud, blood pooling all around them.

How could I? thought Wendell, shaking his head in disbelief. Was she so naïve to his feelings? "I never meant for things to end like this, Adaline. I loved you, and—"

"You loved me and what, Wendell? I was your friend. Was that not enough?" The question hurt more than Wendell had expected, and for the second time that day, he was lost for words. The dowager queen gave a slightly maniacal laugh before saying, "No, of course that wasn't enough. You were my best friend, Wendell, once upon a time. People warned me. They told me that you wanted more, but I thought you respected me." She laughed again, a cold, spiteful laugh, tears still falling from her cheeks onto Augustus's unmoving chest.

"I did," said Wendell desperately, "I do."

"You don't, though, do you?" continued Adaline ruthlessly, saltwater tracks down the powder on her cheeks. "How could you have done this if you did? You are a nasty, jealous fool! You threatened every man I ever spoke to. You warned all the others away. You marked me as your own and decided that if you couldn't have me, nobody could. But then Anselm came along and ruined your little plan, didn't he?"

"That man was a damn fool!"

"He was your friend, Wendell. Or at least he thought he was."

"He was nothing more than a smile and a crown. He was never good enough for you. Or maybe he was. I never expected you to be so shallow."

Adaline looked as though she had been slapped. "Anselm was a great man," she said, shaking as she pulled Augustus's body closer to her own chest.

"He was worse than a fool. He was a fool born with all the advantages, all the privileges, and he took everything from me!"

"I was never yours to take!" she said, her voice venomous.

"He cut my future away from me, all of my hopes and my dreams. Anselm made me this way!"

Adaline, clutching her dead son to her, broke once more into laughter as Wendell stared longingly at the gap where his fingers had once been. "Do you even believe that, Wendell? No one forced you to challenge Anselm back then. It was your own vanity, your own jealousy. And still, he was able to look past all of that to give you a place in our household."

"Lies!" Wendell yelled, slamming a fist down onto the table just as Augustus had done only a short while before. "He wanted to humiliate me. It was never enough to have you. He wanted to grind me under his heel and keep me in line, to show me who was king."

"You actually do believe that, don't you?" asked Adaline, lowering Augustus's body to gently lie him on the flagstones, the boy's face fixed in a permanent look of surprise as the last of his colour drained away. Adaline rounded on Wendell, and it occurred to him that the only thing fuelling her, the only thing keeping her from collapsing, was the rage she felt towards him.

"You actually think the whole world is out to get you," she said, walking towards him, eyes narrowed, jaw clenched. "The sad thing is, Wendell, that the enemy isn't out there." She gestured around the room, pointing towards a window. "It's inside of you. The real rot is in your insecurities, your jealousy, your self-loathing. And it isn't you who has paid the price." He could see that she was doing everything in her power not to look back at Augustus's body.

"He crippled me, Adaline," said Wendell pleadingly, his voice lowered in sadness. "He made me half a man, a laughingstock."

"Anselm did nothing of the sort!" She was right in front of him, specks of spit showering Wendell's face, her eyes wild. "You made yourself a laughingstock. You challenged him, and for what? It was a fool's errand."

Her voice seemed suddenly distant as Wendell stood blank-faced, his memory winding back through the years to find that fateful day. Was she right? Could it have been him? He remembered envying the new king, Anselm, who, in Wendell's memory, resembled Augustus. Anselm was a young man who had it all: the crown, the girl Wendell loved, and the power to shape Wendell's own future. Wendell had no ambition for Anselm's throne, but in the training circle, they would be equals. The circle was Wendell's kingdom and his opportunity to teach Anselm a little humility. The man was nothing more than a preening dandy, and Wendell was going to prove it to everyone, to Adaline. Sure, Anselm was strong, but was he brave?

"Brave enough to fight with real swords?" Wendell had challenged him.

Anselm's face had creased with fear as he looked across at a young Adaline, tears upon her cheeks as she pleaded them to stop.

"You don't have to do this!" she had called as Anselm took the blade. As Wendell had taken his own.

"You remember now, don't you?" asked Adaline, calling Wendell back into the present. "You brought this upon yourself. You challenged Anselm, and you lost. Fair and square." She grabbed Wendell by the shoulders to shake him hard. Wendell was so aghast that he didn't even fight back. "He never meant to hurt you," she cried. "He never even wanted to fight you!"

"I lost, did I?" Wendell asked with a sneer, his pride stinging from Adaline's words, true as they might have been. His voice was ice. "He may have taken my fingers, but here I stand before you. Where is your brave husband now?"

The sting of Adaline's slap was sobering for Wendell, and he had to duck to avoid another.

"You killed him. You betrayed me by killing him. I hope you know, for every day for the rest of your pitiful life, that his death doesn't change anything, not for me. I will always love him, and I will always think of you as nothing more than a coward."

"You will be mine!" Wendell called out suddenly in a fit of rage, grabbing her by the arm. "Just as things should have been!" He looked down at his grip around her forearm and winced as he noted his absent fingers, remembering the moment when he met Anselm's sword with a block, blades grinding together, before his feet went from beneath him, the edge of Anselm's steel cutting through his hand, through his bare flesh and bone.

"I will never be yours," said Adaline, snatching her arm away from him, her head held high as though she meant to look down upon him. "You must know that. You can manipulate, cheat, and trick people all you like, but you can never make me love you. Is this what you want? To live like this for the rest of your life?"

He paused for a moment and realised he had no idea what he actually wanted. Was this how he had expected things to work out? Had he expected her to understand his pain, to sympathise with him, to forgive him? He had done it all: killed Anselm and his foolish son, conveniently blocking out the fact that it was *her* son too. He had invited an army to the very gates of the city, but the pain was still there. She was right, and she always had been. A nostalgic smile crossed his face as he gazed at Adaline and saw the little girl, as strong-willed as Francine, who had dragged him to dance with her all those years before. She had always been able to see right through him. She was extraordinary then, and she was extraordinary now.

"I.... I don't know," he muttered absently.

"You destroyed my family, and you still don't know?" She grabbed him by the throat and forced him back until his foot caught a loose flagstone, and then it was Adaline who stood over him. "Why stop there? You heard Ferdinand. It's me next, surely. Why not prove how brave you really are and kill me next, Wendell?"

She grabbed the knife from the table and dropped it beside him, the metal of the blade ringing on contact with the stones. He nearly winced, but he stopped himself. Despite all that had happened, he couldn't bear for her to think him weak.

"Get up and finish this," she said, nodding at the knife beside him.

She stood over him as he climbed to his feet, their eyes meeting as he drew level. He had imagined this moment for most of his life, but never had he dreamt to face such scorn. Such hatred.

"I love you," he said feebly. "I could never hurt you. You must know that."

At this she only sneered. "How can you say that you love me after all you have done to me? How can you say you would never hurt me after all the hurt you have brought to my door? You couldn't love anyone, Wendell. You don't even love yourself."

His chest tightened with the truth of it, and a tear of his own fell slowly and heavily onto the floor. Even after all this time, she still knew him better than he knew himself, and she must have known deep inside that he wouldn't kill her, couldn't kill her.

He reached for the knife, maybe for effect, but mostly to buy himself time. He couldn't change what had come before, but he alone would decide what happened next.

"I love you," he repeated, much more convincingly this time around. And Adaline flinched as he stabbed the knife into a joint of mutton, blood gathering around the blade as it had in Augustus's chest.

"I'm going to make this right," he finished, reaching to remove the knife slowly. "I'll show you."

⚜ ⚜ ⚜

"It's done then?" asked Ferdinand as Wendell rushed out into the hallway to find the Verderan King manoeuvring what Wendell recognised as Seth's body to rest against the stone wall. The king's shield had a knife wound in his stomach, and Ferdinand was reaching to take the man's sword.

"We need to get out of here," came Wendell's response as he dodged the question while drawing as much attention as possible to the streaks of red upon his knife, hoping Ferdinand would assume it was Adaline's. The pretence alone made him feel sick, but as always, he had to play his part. "I hope you have an idea to avoid the guards, or this will all have been for nothing."

"Do you think me a fool?" asked Ferdinand with arched brows. "We will use the door in Thaddeus's library. It will lead us to the woods, and we will be back with my people before anyone realises what's happened." He placed a hand on Wendell's shoulder as the Master of Coin nodded in recollection of the evening's events. "It's time to take my crown back," Ferdinand said, his voice steely, "I will bring my sons to heel, and Easthaven will become another jewel on the Verderan crown."

With this, the old king turned and sprinted down the corridor with surprising agility. He kept low to avoid detection, yet the sound of military manoeuvres echoed from outside the castle, and Wendell knew that there was little within to prevent their escape. They slowed and nodded as they passed two guards who had no reason to suspect any wrongdoing, and in a matter of moments, they were back in the Thaddeus's offices, where Ferdinand threw the carpet back to further their escape.

"I won't forget what you've done here today," said the king, reaching to open the heavy wooden door. The hinges creaked with every inch, and the sound tormented the developing pain in Wendell's head. He looked from the open trapdoor, back toward the door through which they'd entered, and then back again. Was this really what he wanted? He'd promised Adaline that he would make things right, but how? And was it even possible? To leave the castle was to accept responsibility for Anselm's murder and Augustus's since. His knowledge of Highcastle would be a priceless weapon for the Verderans, but it would mean death and suffering for those still in the city. Augustus was gone, and Cyrus was already in the hands of Prince Rafael. Anselm's lineage had been destroyed. Must Adaline, Broderick, Francine, and all the others in the capital suffer for their king's mistakes? For the sake of Wendell's petty, ill-conceived revenge?

Ferdinand climbed down a small ladder into the tunnel, leaving little time for Wendell to stand around thinking. There was no changing the past now, and Wendell suspected that the Verderans still offered him his best chance at survival. He could never have killed Adaline, but his decision to leave her alive signalled the end of his time in the castle. He only hoped that his actions wouldn't lead to a far more gruesome death at the hands of another.

No, surely I can still save her. There must be a way. Think, think...

Wendell stepped down into the tunnel, pulling the door closed just as the first voices of panic began to ring out around Eldred's Keep.

"You did the right thing," said Ferdinand, raising the very same candlestick that Wendell had contemplated using to kill him only hours before. It felt like a lifetime ago. The hidden passage itself was like a mineshaft—a tunnel carved into the rock and supported by thick wooden beams on all sides. Wendell couldn't help but wonder when the tunnel had been built and by whom. The earth was chalky underfoot, but the tunnel was tall enough for them to remain upright, and they moved quickly, the Verderan king leading the way.

"Here, just up ahead," Ferdinand said after several minutes spent trawling through the darkness. The air was hot and humid, and Wendell felt sticky with sweat as Ferdinand stopped to pass him the candle in order to free up his own hands so he could begin climbing another small ladder before them. "And just like magic…" he said from a ledge above Wendell, "Light!"

Wendell used a hand to cover his eyes as he ascended the ladder, unused to the light as he had become during their time underground. When he reached the top, he found Ferdinand already basking in the mild early evening air.

"Where are we?" Wendell asked, but his eyes widened as the sound of trickling water provided an answer. He had been here many times before, the most recent of which had been for his meeting with the Verderan princes after Cyrus and Augustus had returned, victorious, to Highcastle. Looking back at the stone door, which was still ajar, Wendell shook his head, thinking of the legacy of Anselm's arrogance. The tunnel had been here all along, right under everyone's noses.

"What now?" he asked before Ferdinand had opportunity to answer his first question. The king made to speak, but his words were interrupted by the impatient sound of a horse's nickering. "Is that Prince Cyrus's horse?"

"I believe her name is Adagio," the Verderan king said as he strolled over toward the mare and a second horse, a stallion, who stood by her side, the pair of them tied to a tree. "Seems these two are inseparable," Ferdinand continued, taking Adagio by the reins, and stroking her muzzle briefly. "Fine horses, the both of them. My son's men must have tied them up out here when they took Prince Cyrus." He shook his head. "Their folly is our favour. It's not far, but why walk, eh?"

Wendell nodded, but despite all his previous actions, the idea of riding Cyrus's horse troubled his conscience inexplicably. It seemed, somehow, a step too far.

"You take Adagio," he said, reaching to untie the unfamiliar stallion from the tree. The knot was tight, and he resorted to burning the rope with the candle before extinguishing the now unnecessary flame. It was early evening, and the sky was orange with a dash of red, as if hinting at the blood that had been spilled. Wendell swallowed hard as he climbed into the saddle and followed Ferdinand toward the Verderan camp.

⚜ ⚜ ⚜

Wendell had never doubted the princes' convictions, but as he and Ferdinand sprinted into the heart of their encampment on the backs of stolen horses, he realised for the first time that he had certainly underestimated the depth of those convictions. The camp itself was a sprawling mass that surrounded the north of city. He had seen it swell from within the castle, but to be among them—well, that was something else entirely.

The pair rode fast, and though tents flew past in a blur, there was no mistaking the grizzled faces of the warriors that inhabited them. These were hard, angry men, Wendell thought. Impatient men keen to end their foray into foreign lands, to claim victory and return home to inevitable glory. Weapons glinted in the corner of

Wendell's eye as he pushed on after Ferdinand. Men bearing swords, halberds, pikes, and bows practised with deadly precision. Enormous battering rams were mounted on wheels for easy mobility, while imposing catapults sat in waiting, their accompanying carts full of deadly boulders at least three times the size of a human head. It seemed the princes had prepared for every eventuality, and Wendell's eyes narrowed as he considered the reason behind the delay in the Verderan attack. When he'd last met with the princes in Dalhart Forest, unknowingly near the hidden door, Rafael had spoken of weapons *the likes of which this world has never known.* It had seemed a blusterous brag at the time, but Wendell's heart sank as he wondered what could be more destructive than those laid before him now.

He slowed his horse as doubt clawed at him once more. He hadn't saved Adaline or any of the others; he'd only delayed the inevitable. And with Ferdinand soon to be reunited with his sons, there was no longer any doubt as what to the outcome of a battle would be. He had thought himself worthy of lecturing and instructing Francine, yet she had shown more bravery in saving Adaline than he ever had. Wendell regretted that he had never said goodbye to the girl he had somehow come to think of as a friend, perhaps the only person left who saw any good in him. He thought of turning his horse to run back, but Ferdinand suddenly slowed ahead of him as a group of guards rushed out to meet them. Wendell recognised the man at the front as Captain Lorenzo, a loathsome toad whose waxed moustache and shining black boots demonstrated the captain's limited experience as to the true horrors of war. It had been some years since their last meeting, and the

Verderan had made some gains around the waist, but he had a face that was not easily forgotten.

"My king!" said the captain, his tone one of unquestionable surprise. He dropped automatically into a bow.

Ferdinand stepped from his horse without hesitation, gesturing back at Wendell to do the same. Two guards accompanied Captain Lorenzo, one at either flank, and Ferdinand was ushered hurriedly toward a large tent nearby. Wendell realised he had no idea what to expect from his journey into this tent, and as he ducked his head through the flaps, a few steps behind Ferdinand, he regretted the loss of his knife.

The tent folded open to reveal the princes staring back at them.

"Father, Wendell, what a lovely surprise," Rafael said, standing up from behind an ornate desk as he spoke. His face was the picture of happiness—as though he was genuinely glad to see his father—but something behind his eyes belied his inner dismay. Prince Alonso sat in a chair of his own in the corner, and Wendell noticed the young prince edge forward in his seat, eyes wide as Wendell and Ferdinand arrived. He was seemingly less schooled than his brother at masking his true emotions. Prince Rafael motioned for Captain Lorenzo and his underlings to leave, so that only the Verderan princes, their father, and Wendell remained.

"A truly momentous reunion," Rafael continued, scratching at the dark stubble on his chin as he stepped around his desk to approach them. "The ghost of the old king riding through camp on the eve of battle. A great omen, wouldn't you say, Wendell?"

Wendell's eyes twitched anxiously as he froze in place, unsure as to how he should respond. His gaze fell upon maps of Highcastle on the prince's desk, and his stomach fell as he realised the maps were there as a direct result of his own actions.

"A good omen indeed," Wendell said almost absently. "Your family is reunited, and King Augustus is dead. Perhaps now is the time to let old wounds heal and build toward a more peaceable future?"

Rafael's eyes widened at Wendell's revelation. "Augustus is dead?" he asked before breaking into laughter, while his brother's face remained expressionless. "King Augustus is dead, and you speak of peace?" Rafael continued in his most condescending tone. "That's the thing about your generation, Wendell. You place too much emphasis on fanciful hopes and pretty ideas."

"Enough!" said King Ferdinand suddenly, striding across the tent to stand toe-to-toe with his eldest son. "I can understand and perhaps even forgive you for sending me to that Auldhaven prison—and don't pretend you weren't behind that—but this all ends here. I have killed Easthaven's king and discovered a way into the castle. We will see this debacle to its inevitable end together, but you *will* fall in line behind your father. Behind your king."

A momentary silence followed, and then Prince Rafael licked his teeth before turning away from his father. It was all Wendell could do to stop himself from running headlong in the opposite direction. Perhaps, he thought wildly, he could still warn them in the castle. Maybe there was time. Maybe Adaline could forgive him after all, and with what he knew of the Verderan camp, there was every possibility that Easthaven could yet prevail. Would the Verderan royals even notice if he left? This was family business, after all.

Wendell winced as the pain in his head flared up with a vengeance behind his eyes, the ache further aggravated as Rafael began to clap his hands slowly but loudly in an unmistakably petulant effort to mock his father.

"That was quite some speech," the prince said, turning back to sneer at the king. "I must admit that it was a mistake to send you away." He circled his father slowly, eyes narrowed, his jaw a hard line. "To let sentimentality stand in the way of progress," he paused, tutting as he shook his head, "well, that is unforgivable."

"Brother—" Prince Alonso cut in.

"No!" Rafael shrieked, raising a hand to silence his younger sibling. "You know, Alonso, I start to wonder if you have the stomach for this. I told you that it was a fool's move to send Father away and leave him in the hands of that dolt Shep."

Alonso rose from his seat. "He's still our father!"

"Pah!" Rafael scoffed. "The man is a relic, devoid of any ambition."

"Watch your words, son. There are limits to my mercy," said Ferdinand, if only to remind Rafael that he was still in the room. Wendell's heart was thumping in his chest. He hadn't known what to expect from the reunion, and the outcome remained balanced on a knife's edge.

Alonso's eyes lowered as he shook his head. "You've gone too far, brother. Father is back whether you like it or not. Maybe we can still make this right?"

"You really think so?" said Rafael, and he gave a quick laugh before his face turned serious once more. "I think the real problem is that you haven't come far enough. I, for one, will not sit in an old man's shadow any longer. Anselm is dead, Augustus is dead, and that charlatan Cyrus is bound in Verderan chains." He paused for a moment to let his words hang in the air. "Contest me if you wish, brother, but our dear father is right: this ends here."

Wendell's mouth fell open as he watched Rafael lunge forward to drive a spiteful knife deep into his father's stomach, Ferdinand's eyes bulging in surprise as he fell forward onto Rafael's shoulder before collapsing lifelessly to the floor of the tent.

Alonso stepped forward instinctively, but his advance was halted as Rafael extended the bloodied knife in warning. "I will see this city fall," said Rafael with a maddened air, veins protruding in his neck as his chest heaved. "I'll show Father that we have no need for his secret 'way into the city,' and I will sit upon both thrones, ruling over Verdera and Easthaven as one. Now, will you contest me?" he asked as he turned toward his brother, who had been stunned into silence. When no answer was forthcoming, Rafael shouted, "I said, will you contest me?"

Prince Alonso swallowed hard before he spoke. His answer was short and quiet, but the look of defeat—etched into the faint frown lines around the corners of the younger prince's mouth—told its own story. Wendell wondered if he would have given a different answer if he had found himself in the prince's position, but no matter how many times he asked himself, the answer was always same.

"No," said Alonso, casting his eyes downward, away from his brother. Rafael nodded contentedly as Ferdinand's body turned cold and pale on the floor between them, but Rafael wasn't looking at his father. His eyes were focused ever forward.

It seemed that Wendell had been right back in the castle: there was no place for peace after all.

Cyrus sat up as the tent swung open. His latest accommodation was a large triangular structure supported by a wooden column at the centre. The tent itself was nothing remarkable, but the support was as wide as a tree, driven deep into the ground for sturdiness. It was an immovable object, fixed in place. Cyrus would know; he was chained to it.

"Good evening," said Rafael, stepping forward like an entertainer basking in the praise of his adoring crowd. The prince had the remarkable ability to seem more despicable with every meeting, Cyrus thought as he pulled at his shackles, hopeful that he might break free and wipe the smile from his captor's face.

"It really is beautiful out there," the prince continued. "Easthaven is little more than a slum compared to Verdera, but those sunsets…" He lingered, if only to enjoy his moment. "Well, they are truly beautiful. Unmissable, even." A bout of awkward, forced laughter followed, and Rafael only ceased when Prince

Alonso stepped into the tent, bringing with him much less presence than his brother.

"Well, if it isn't the ugly one!" said Rafael, shoving his brother playfully. It was clearly meant as a joke, but Rafael's push was not without force, and Alonso managed little more than a half-smile as he steadied himself for a wordless nod in Cyrus's direction. "We'd have brought our father along, of course, but he is suffering from a most…*debilitating* condition. You may have heard of it. It's called…death. I hope you understand?" He smiled coldly at Cyrus.

Cyrus's eyes twitched to Alonso, who only turned away. "Lies!" Cyrus yelled without thought, unable to restrain himself any longer. "Ferdinand is alive and safe in Highcastle. I sent him there. He'll be telling our generals all your secrets and weaknesses, and we will see King Ferdinand restored to the throne!" He sat back with a smile, eager for the prince's reaction, but to his surprise and dismay, Rafael only laughed.

"You know, I almost believed you," said the prince, his confident tone setting Cyrus on edge. "You speak with such poise, such conviction. I could very well believe that Ferdinand is in the castle right now conspiring against me. It wouldn't be without reason, after all." Rafael wandered over to Cyrus, where he drew a small knife and crouched before him. "But if Father is in Eldred's Keep, then who did I just kill with this very knife?" He pursed his lips and paused for a moment before standing to turn away. "I don't expect you to believe me, but perhaps there is an old friend who might be able to convince you. Guards, send him in!"

Cyrus could hear muffled conversation outside the tent, and then the tent flaps parted slowly as a third man entered to rapturous applause from the would-be king.

"Wendell?" spat Cyrus, heart pounding as he pulled at his restraints once more.

"I see no introduction is needed, but perhaps this will go some way to earning your confidence, Prince Cyrus." Rafael pulled Wendell close, his arm tight around the bald man's shoulders as though the pair were old friends. "The time for games and riddles is over. My father is dead. Your father and brother are dead. Do you know what that means?"

"Augustus?" asked Cyrus, his glare hot upon Wendell, who looked away, seemingly unable to meet Cyrus's gaze. "My brother is dead?" he asked, his voice hoarse. His head was spinning, and a wave of guilt washed over him with the thought that he was somehow responsible for all of this. He pictured Augustus—Cyrus's mirror image, a half of him even if he was unlikeable, perhaps even detestable. Even if they hardly knew each other. His twin.

"The king is dead, but don't worry, everyone else in the castle is safe. For now." Rafael smiled with the confidence of a man in total control. "Congratulations, Cyrus. We finally speak as equals, one king to another. I had hoped for a more, shall we say, extravagant setting, but these are the times we live in!"

One king to another. It was as though the fight had been beaten out of him, and Cyrus slumped down as he fought to hold back tears. He had perhaps never felt less like a king than in that moment, the moment he learned he might actually be one.

"So why not kill me then?" Cyrus said, his voice sounding small and frail in comparison to Rafael's boisterous bluster. "You have what you wanted. Why not end it here? You've won."

"Oh, that's very kind of you to say," said Rafael as he prowled around the tent, the others watching on in silence, "but we know very well that things must be seen in order to be believed. It would be all too easy to kill you now and seize your city, but you have a habit of appearing unexpectedly, and I will not allow you to become a symbol of hope." He walked over to rest an elbow on one of several carts that filled the tent. "No, you will watch me raze Highcastle to the ground, and when your people finally relent and place the crown upon my head, they will see you executed in the streets of the capital, ending any question over the legitimacy of my rule."

"The people of Highcastle will never allow this!"

"Oh, but they will." Rafael turned with a handful of fine black powder sifting through his fingers. It was, Cyrus presumed, a product of the alchemy that Shep had spoken of in the mines. The white salt-like substance, transformed into something dark and deadly. "We will dowse the city walls with this remarkable powder, and when fire is added to the mix? Boom!" Rafael threw the powder into the air dramatically. "There is no army that can resist our destructive power. The time for peace is over, King Cyrus. Rest well, for tomorrow is the beginning of the end for your family."

Before Cyrus could gather his thoughts to put another sentence together, to protest, Rafael turned away and walked out of the tent, leaving the others to follow. Wendell was the last figure to retreat.

"You are a coward, Wendell!" Cyrus shouted as the bald man skulked out of the tent. "A coward, you hear me?" he repeated with only himself now for company. "You were always a coward," he said gently for a third and final time, too quietly for anyone but himself to hear. But as tears fell helplessly down his cheeks, Cyrus wondered at whom his words were truly aimed.

❧ ❧ ❧

It was hard to imagine how things could get any worse, and Cyrus fidgeted as night encroached on the tent around him. Was Rafael actually telling the truth? Augustus was a self-serving fool, but he was the rightful king and the only man capable of uniting Easthaven against the Verderan threat. Twins as they might be, the two boys had only spent a couple of days in each other's presence, and they hadn't gotten along well…but Gus had at least committed to protecting Adaline and Francine. Wendell had betrayed them all, but what if there were others in the castle of a similar mind? Were there others that Cyrus should be wary of, even now?

Cyrus realised that by opening the door in the woods, he had exposed everyone he cared about, and at least one man had already died for another of his mistakes. Had Ferdinand told his sons of the secret door before he died? He wondered what part Ferdinand had played in all of this and recalled the old king's amiable relationship with King Simeon. Perhaps Simeon was somehow involved, Cyrus thought wildly. Perhaps this was the last deceitful act of a dying man. It dawned on Cyrus how reckless he had become. *King Cyrus?* he thought, shaking his head as Rafael's words echoed in his mind. It was one thing pretending to be someone else, but he—Cyrus from the Low Country—as king? He lowered his head, heavy as it was with the weight of feeling like an imposter, and thought that perhaps it was some consolation that his reign was likely to be quite short.

It had been like this for hours, the same thoughts rolling through his mind, all of his old demons coming back to haunt him in what would likely be his final days, perhaps even his final hours.

The mistakes, the regrets, and everything in between. He had promised Francine safety, and yet here he was, watching on helplessly as she faced the same inevitable fate as her parents. Then there was Adaline, the mother he'd never had and now would never know. Thaddeus and Garrett, whose trust he had failed to repay at every possible opportunity. His mind wandered to Marcia and her letter and the myriad possibilities of what *might* have been. She had said she had been thinking of him, but what would she think if she saw him right now, chained and approaching death's door? He was the same helpless boy, he thought bitterly, frightened and a long way from home. Thaddeus always said that luck was a key part of any story, and it seemed that Cyrus's luck had finally run out.

Tears stung at his eyes once more, and as he lowered his head further still, the tent's mouth parted to reveal the last person he would have expected.

"Wendell?" Cyrus asked as moonlight spilled into the darkness. The bald man's head glinted unmistakeably in the glow of the single candle he carried with him, his robes rustling gently as he slipped into the tent with a finger raised to his mouth.

"Yes, Wendell," he whispered with a mixture of panic and impatience. "I'm here to get you out of here, but we need to move fast." He knelt to place the candle down and fidget with a set of keys. Cyrus's head was full of questions—he wondered if this had been Wendell's plan all along or if this was a change of heart at the last possible minute—but he remained silent, sensing that now was perhaps not the time.

"I never meant for any of this," Wendell continued unexpectedly. "Your father…" he trailed off, scratching at his temple. "We had our differences, but I should never have let this happen. It all just got out of hand, and—"

"What's done is done," Cyrus said, cutting him off firmly. Cyrus wasn't without regrets of his own, but in that moment, his only thoughts were of escaping and doing what he could to make things right. It wasn't the time for Wendell to beg for forgiveness. "We need to get back to the castle and save the others before it is too late."

Wendell nodded, the rest of his sentence having died on his tongue, and his left hand closed around a heavy metal key. He edged closer to Cyrus, a look of fear still lingering on his face as his eyes glanced quickly around them, full of concern. "I want to help," he whispered, reaching to place the key into the lock. A quick turn, and Cyrus's hands fell free.

"So help," said Cyrus, massaging sore wrists. "You can start by showing me the way out of here. He rose to his feet and offered the Master of Coin a hand of support, pulling him out of his crouching position. Wendell stood and dusted himself off, but something seemed to hold him back at the last moment.

"I knew Augustus as a baby, you know," Wendell said softly. "I saw the baby become a boy and a boy become a man. I promised myself that I would do my best to keep him safe, not through goodness or decency, not even because he was heir to the throne, but because he was Adaline's son. I tried with all my heart to keep that promise, and for many years, I did. But you know what?" Wendell looked Cyrus full in the face for the first time, their eyes meeting. Cyrus stayed silent, and Wendell said, "When I looked at Augustus, I couldn't see Adaline. He had none of your mother's kindness and all of your father's arrogance…or at least that's what

I thought it was at the time. To see that boy become king…" He shook his head. "I couldn't let it happen. I've spent the last few years wondering what happened to Augustus, how he ended up the way he did and how Adaline was somehow lost within him. But I see now…"

Wendell smiled almost wistfully, and for just a moment, the fear faded from his face. "That part of Adaline," he said, "that brilliance that makes people feel better about themselves and the world around them—it wasn't lost. It was in you."

"Wendell—"

"No," Wendell interjected, shaking his head. "It's okay. I know your mother could never love me, but the very least I can do for her is to see you returned. Fate will catch up with me soon enough, of that I'm sure. Now let's get out of here, shall we? I have an old friend with me who is excited to see you."

Cyrus wanted to ask more questions about everything the older man had said, but instead he just nodded at Wendell before following him quietly from the tent, deciding it was far more important to focus on the task at hand. A full moon shone in the night sky, but Cyrus's eyes were immediately drawn to the unconscious forms of two guards sprawled on the ground. He looked at Wendell with raised brows.

"I may be damaged, but I've not completely lost it," Wendell said with an uncharacteristic wink before passing a discarded sword to Cyrus. They moved quickly but quietly through the camp, and Cyrus's stomach dropped as he was reminded of the night in Simeon's camp that Garrett had walked unwittingly toward his own death. Wendell's words back in the tent had seemed sincere, but this was a man who had betrayed his entire family and was responsible for two of their deaths. Could Cyrus ever really trust him?

"Nearly there now," Wendell said after a few minutes, breaking their momentary silence. He gestured for Cyrus to stop as he surveyed the camp, and Cyrus dropped low before a wave of Wendell's arm finally called him forward to a band of horses gathered in a makeshift corral.

"Adagio?" Cyrus asked in disbelief, though his faithful mare's whinny was unmistakeable to him. Despite everything this disastrous evening had brought, a broad smile broke out onto Cyrus's face at the realisation that he still, at least, had Adagio. He hadn't realised how much he had missed her at his side, and he pressed his head to hers, breathing in her coat, before Adagio's hooves began to beat down with her usual impatience.

"Time to go," said Wendell, as though giving words to Adagio's very thoughts. He offered Cyrus a hand onto his mount. "Nobody knows about the door. Ride for the woods, and I will join you as soon as I can."

"Join me? But—"

"Yes, I know what you are going to say, but I left the candle back in the tent, and we might need it. I was too busy saving you, wasn't I?" He trailed off before rushing to open the gate for Adagio's exit. "Just go. I'll be fine. Oh, and Cyrus," he reached to halt Adagio by the reins, "I want you to know that I'm sorry, as inadequate as that is. I'm sorry for everything. I know that your mother will never forgive me, and truth be told, I'm not expecting any greater sympathy from you, but I just need you to know. As for that sister of yours," his lips curled into an unexpected smile, "she's a special girl, and she should never, *ever* let anyone make her feel invisible or small."

Wendell smiled weakly, and Cyrus stared back at him for a moment. The man was a lovesick traitor, yet Cyrus now saw the same thing that he'd seen in Simeon once he'd gotten to know him, and in his son, Brandon: purpose. Cyrus could see that Wendell's well of regrets was deep, that he had perhaps dug the well deeper every day in recent times, but he was still fighting to make it right, however he could.

"Good luck," said Cyrus, nodding down at Wendell and trying to match the older man's courage. Highcastle was still in peril, but all was not yet lost.

Wendell nodded wordlessly and let go of the reins, letting Adagio walk slowly through the gate. And as Cyrus looked back, he saw Wendell heading in the direction from which they had come, back toward the tent and that lone candle. The moon sat high in the sky as Adagio pushed forward, and after a few steps, she broke into a gallop onto the open plain beyond.

The evening air was mild, and Cyrus breathed deeply as it dawned on him that he was actually free, against all the odds. Dalhart Forest was already in sight, and there was nothing more to stop him from reaching the castle. He thought it was likely that Wendell would be caught by the Verderans, and in this way, justice would be served for Anselm, for Augustus, and for all the others whose suffering was yet to come. His brief sense of relief faded quickly, as he thought to the Verderan's destructive powder. He had to get back to the castle, and fast.

His face was set into a grim line as he raised Adagio's reins once more, the treeline coming into focus before him. It was only a few yards away now. He only had to make it into the forest. Back to his mother, to Francine, and to Marcia. He peered back over his shoulder, but Wendell was nowhere to be seen. Somewhere in the back of his mind, Cyrus thought that it was odd for Wendell to return for a single candlestick, and it suddenly dawned on Cyrus that the old man had no intention of returning. But why would he do that? Cyrus wondered for a moment if Wendell had gone back to betray him to the Verderans, but that would make no sense at all since Wendell was the one who had freed him in the first place. As Cyrus approached the treeline, he realised that Wendell must be up to something, trying to do what he could to give Cyrus the time to escape...

Cyrus tugged at the reins suddenly, drawing Adagio to a halt. Cyrus's breath echoing loudly around them. He wondered, could he really leave Wendell behind, even after everything that the old man had done? Perhaps Wendell could still help them to defeat the Verderans with his knowledge of the princes? He sat for a silent moment before cursing himself and shaking the thought away. The man was still a traitor, and Cyrus had to focus on those who truly deserved to be saved.

The sound of raised voices alerted Cyrus, who turned to face the Verderan camp. Perhaps they were looking for him or readying an attack on the city. Maybe Wendell had been caught already. The encampment seemed suddenly alive with activity, and Cyrus's eyes narrowed as he considered the implications.

Then came the unmistakeable sound of an explosion.

It was like thunder splitting the heavens, only louder and more ferocious. Adagio reared unexpectedly, throwing Cyrus from the saddle as the sky turned orange. His left shoulder crunched as he landed heavily, his head thudding against the hard ground as shooting pain rushed through his body, coupled with immediate dizziness. A high-pitched ringing in Cyrus's ears masked anguished cries from who knew where, while the smell of the blast powder stung at his nostrils, leaving him lightheaded and confused.

Where was he?

His only impulse was to make it back to the castle. It took a colossal effort, but he rolled onto his back, chest heaving as he gazed into the night sky, his tilted vision coming to rest on the stars twinkling in the distance. Cyrus had never felt so small, so insignificant.

The ringing in his ears cleared, giving way to the sounds of suffering all around him. Screaming, he realised, coming from the direction of Highcastle.

I have to make it back to the castle, he thought as Adagio appeared above him, looking down at him with concern in her round eyes, pawing at the ground beside him.

He staggered to his feet, one hand resting against Adagio's hindquarters as he fought to steady himself. He hardly dared look, but there was no use avoiding it, and when he eventually turned to face Highcastle, his jaw dropped with shock.

The Verderan camp was awash with flames, the hot glow illuminating Highcastle in the darkness of night. A sigh of relief escaped Cyrus with the realisation that the city was untouched, his relief tempered by the shouts and screams that continued to emanate from the enemy encampment.

A dark cloud of smoke hung ominously overhead, and Cyrus stumbled as he tried to stay upright, the smell of destruction only adding to his nausea. He thought of Wendell, and then to the carts of black powder that Rafael had shown him only hours before. It all fell into place.

It would have only needed a single candle…

Brilliant white light poured into Cyrus's eyes just as he opened them, causing him to squint. Above him, he saw after his eyes had adjusted, was a richly carved bedframe hung with the finest drapery. The room was perfectly warm, the spit and crackle of fire sounding beyond his feet, while a gentle voice whispered in hushed tones around him. The speaker was female, her words soft, distant, and shrouded in an echo.

An angel perhaps? Cyrus wondered.

He recalled falling from Adagio's back, his body buckling as it hit the ground, and it occurred to him that this comfortable room was probably a dream, or maybe even Heaven itself. He didn't dare move for fear of disturbing the dream, but his mind refused to rest. The explosion in the Verderan camp reverberated in his head, and his body felt hot at the memory, the presence of fire suddenly vicious and destructive all around him. He recalled Wendell's face, and with it, the last words that Wendell had spoken as they had parted: apologies tinged with regret and inevitably. His sacrifice had been driven by an uncharacteristic sense of morality, and in his actions, Wendell had yet given them hope.

Cyrus thought of Adagio, his faithful mount, standing over him in expectation, welcoming him back into the saddle as she always did. Where was she? Pain suddenly burned bright in his shoulder as he remembered dragging himself into a riding position before Adagio made for the woods with great urgency, carrying him away from the explosion, as though she could sense the significance of their plight.

He grimaced at the thought of Dalhart and the stone door, which Adagio would never have fit through, never mind the tunnel within. There had been no choice but to set Adagio free, her all-too-familiar reluctance no longer frustrating but instead heart-breaking. Cyrus had turned from his companion, shooing her away as he prised a gap in the rockface.

The tunnel had been dark, so dark, and there had been no source of light as he staggered back to the castle, his head spinning. His shallow breath had resounded loudly in the blackness, panicking him with the memory of the mines, every sound cowering him with the expectation that bats might screech past overhead, or that the ghost of Shep's guard, Nelson, might beat him down once more. It was the middle of the night, but the passage had been sticky hot, a thick heat like walking blindfolded though honey. He had wondered if it was not Heaven but Hell that he journeyed toward. The walls had seemed to close in around him, and he had been overwhelmed by a sense of light-headedness, a sudden weakness throughout his body that caused his legs to fold from under him.

He remembered falling to his knees, his own breaths fading to sound distant. His head never stopped spinning as he crumpled to the ground, stretched out on his back. And it was there that he had lain, helplessly alone in the darkness.

The voice in the room became clearer, and Cyrus turned to find Marcia standing at the window, her silhouette backlit by morning sunlight. Her soft, pink lips formed a smile as their eyes met. He was still dreaming, then, simply conjuring a memory of the first time that they had met. Perhaps it had all been a dream, in fact, and perhaps he had only just arrived in the castle. He wished with all his strength that Garrett would still be alive, waiting in the corridor with Thaddeus, his capricious mind only moments from an idea that would set Cyrus on the right path. He smiled at dream-Marcia once more, thinking of all the things he would do differently if given the chance. Saving Garrett would just be the start. He could make peace with Simeon, prevent the uprising, spare Colton's life, and even Flynn's, not to mention Augustus's. It was probably all just another dream, but a single tear fell from Cyrus's eye as he considered the possibilities, all the things he could do better.

"Welcome back," Marcia said, softly.

"Huh?"

"Oh, not this again," said Marcia, eyes rolling as she ended any hope of a fresh start. Cyrus knew now that this wasn't a dream. He was really in the castle, and Marcia was really here before him. "I thought one of my stories would wake you eventually," she continued. "You know all the classics, so I thought I'd regale you with something new, the story of valiant Prince Cyrus. Everyone is telling it these days."

"Valiant Prince Cyrus, eh?" he answered, quickly wiping the tear from his cheek. He wondered if the story made mention of his collapse in the tunnel, his entirely unheroic, vacant body sprawled out in the black. *That wouldn't make for a good story*, he thought. Cyrus knew better. He smiled, then grimaced at a shooting pain.

"Yes, that's quite a bump on your head," said Marcia, sensing his discomfort. "Here, put this on," and she threw a shirt onto the bed that Cyrus struggled to pull over his uncovered upper body. His shoulder was agonizingly sore, and though his head throbbed, he refused to show any further weakness in Marcia's presence.

"How did I get back here?" he asked, his memory of the previous evening having ended in the tunnel.

Marcia pursed her lips in thought. "I'm not sure, but I think Thaddeus had something to do with it. You'll have to ask him yourself," she paused, then rushed to add, "when you're ready, that is. I know that the council will want to speak to you, what with last night's explosion, and, well, everything else."

Cyrus sighed. He'd made it back to the castle one way or another, but the real danger was yet to come. "I've missed you," he ventured gently. The words surprised him, and his skin prickled with embarrassment as Marcia stared back at him expectantly. "I've missed you all, I mean. Fran, Adaline, Thaddeus, and all the others!" His attempt at recovery was even more embarrassing than his initial effort, and Marcia's smile fell in disappointment as he continued trying to wrestle the shirt over his head without moving his injured shoulder. There were a million words he wanted to say to her, but he absurdly found himself wishing he had his parchment and an inkwell so that he could write it down instead of speaking it here and now.

"They're all pleased to have you back," said Marcia flatly, her half-smile forced. "Fran hasn't been herself of late, and your mother, well, she's inconsolable since Augustus…"

She trailed off, and Cyrus heard Rafael's words about his brother's death echoing in his mind once more. Reality crashed in on him, and he wondered how he could be sitting here worrying about flirting with a girl at a time like this.

"I heard about Augustus," he said. Fearing the answer, he asked, "What happened?"

"I don't know for sure, but I think Wendell must have been conspiring with the Verderans to kill Augustus, and he succeeded. Ferdinand stabbed the king at dinner last night. It's a wonder that Adaline made it out alive. They attacked Seth as well. It didn't look good at first, but it seems he will live." She walked over to stoke the fire, flames jumping in the hearth. "What makes a man do a thing like that? How could Wendell have decided that was the right path?"

"Love," Cyrus muttered under his breath. *Or was it jealousy?*

"What?"

"Nothing," he said, shaking his head. Cyrus drew the covers away and stepped onto the cold stone floor. He thought of the many regrets Wendell had taken with him as he departed this life, and with the Verderan army poised to attack at any moment, he decided he could delay things no more, even if it felt silly to worry about a thing like love at a time like this.

"Marcia," he began with a deep intake of breath, "a lot has changed since I last saw you. I've seen awful things happen to good people, and I've learned a lot, or at least I've done my best to learn a lot. Truth be told, I don't know if we can defeat the Verderans, and I have to go and figure that out, but I cannot leave you without telling you something."

Marcia turned to face him, and she had never looked more beautiful than in that moment, the soft morning light washing over her light smattering of freckles and illuminating her green eyes. "Tell me what?" she asked, closing the space between them to take Cyrus by the hand. His heart stuttered in response.

"I just…" he mumbled, ruffling his shirt with his free hand as the warmth of the fire seemed to increase immeasurably. He did his best not to look down at their intertwined fingers and cleared his throat. "I've travelled a lot, but even in my darkest, most desperate moments, there was always something that gave me hope." He paused and ran his hand through his hair as he considered his words. This wasn't exactly as he had imagined it, not with his scalp full of dirt while sweat patches formed under his arms. "What I mean to say is, I like you, Marcia. I really like you." He took her other hand and fixed her with his eyes as the moment finally arrived. "I—"

"Cyrus, you're awake!" Adaline cried from the doorway.

Marcia's hands fell quickly, and Cyrus stepped back to smile at his mother, trying desperately not to curse her inwardly for interrupting just as he had finally gathered his nerve.

"Thank goodness, you're awake," Adaline said, rushing over to smooth Cyrus's hair, something he would normally have welcomed but that in this moment made him cringe in embarrassment. "We thought you were dead at first, and then there was the injury to your head. I thought—oh, sorry, am I interrupting something?" she asked, startled as she glanced between Cyrus and Marcia.

Marcia smiled and gave a quick, "No, your majesty," and a curtsy before backing toward the door. Cyrus had to work not to sigh as he watched her go.

It was hard to be angry with Adaline, though. Her presence was not only welcome in the sense that he had missed his mother terribly, but her arrival had probably also saved Cyrus from a great embarrassment. It was true that Marcia had been a beacon of hope during his journey away from Highcastle and back again, but perhaps it just wasn't meant to be, he told himself. What was to be gained by sharing his feelings, anyway? In the best possible case, she would return his affections, but what good would this do either of them with war at their doorstep? If anything, it would make them both more vulnerable. In the end, Cyrus decided it must be a sign of growth that he made it as far as he had, and he forced a smile as his mother pulled him close.

"I've missed you," Adaline whispered tearfully, and Cyrus felt, not for the first time, that her words were meant for another.

"I've missed you too, Mother," he said. This title when applied to the dowager queen was still new to him, but it felt natural as it fell from his mouth.

Adaline stepped back as she surveyed Cyrus. "I'm so sorry that you got dragged into all of this. You've spent your whole life in danger because of me. No—" she silenced Cyrus with a finger as he made to speak. She spoke passionately as she continued, "I can't imagine what you have been through. I wish I had a way to shut out the bad things and let you recover from all of this, but evil doesn't wait, Cyrus, and your country needs you, now more than ever. The council has called an emergency meeting, and it will raise their spirits to see you there."

Cyrus nodded, surprised by his mother's steely demeanour, despite all the tragedy that she herself had faced. "I'll be there," he said confidently, harnessing Adaline's sense of duty. His tone softened. "And my brother, where is he?"

"In the basilica," Adaline answered, her determined expression dropping if only for a moment. "There's no time to..." she trailed off before forcing a smile. "That will have to wait. All that matters is that you're king now, Cyrus. The future of Easthaven is in your hands."

⚜ ⚜ ⚜

The heavy door opened slowly, and Cyrus stepped into the Grand Hall. He was no less nervous than the first time he had attended council. Once again, all before him stood at attention, and Cyrus dragged himself to the head of the table, every step feeling like a mile. Augustus's elaborate chair resounded with the ethereal presence of the late king, and Cyrus felt guilty even sitting down in it, so he decided to remain standing.

The small group stood in place, awaiting his instruction. It was a great relief to know that Adaline was in attendance, along with Thaddeus's calming influence. The Master of Prayer, Cornelius was a somewhat less predictable attendee, but Cyrus was pleased for the breadth of expertise and opinion in a group that was completed by Broderick and two of his captains.

"Please be seated," said Cyrus, his tone equal to the sombre mood of the assembly. Adaline gave a respectful bow as she led the way, and all others followed suit, leaving Cyrus as the last man standing, an irony not lost on him as he proceeded to speak. "I have seen the Verderan camp, and we have little time to waste. I see that work has been done to strengthen the city, but our enemy fights with great weapons and even greater ambition. Thaddeus, what is our current position?"

The old man inclined his head accordingly. "We are lucky to have you with us, my king," he began, and the use of his new title made something in Cyrus's gut squirm. Thaddeus continued, "The situation is indeed a desperate one, but we are not entirely without hope. Though the Verderans arrived with around eight thousand men, we have reason to believe that last night's.... *incident*, has reduced this number quite significantly, though exact numbers are, of course, unknown."

Cyrus nodded. "You're referring to the explosion?" he asked, as the others watched on intently.

"Yes, my king," said Thaddeus. "We were hoping that you might be able to shed some light on the incident itself."

Cyrus's hand brushed against the swollen lump on the side of his head. "I can, though I take no credit for the outcome. I've heard what happened to my brother, but it was by Wendell's hand that I was freed, and it was these same hands that set the Verderan camp to flame..."

An audible gasp sounded from all in attendance. Quiet speculation began to sound between Broderick and his captains, and Thaddeus reached to place a hand upon Adaline's. The dowager queen's eyes had narrowed, and her jaw was clenched at the mention of Wendell's name.

Cyrus cleared his throat, and the room silenced once more. "The blast was created by a destructive powder that the Verderans have been trading with rebel groups in Auldhaven, right under Simeon's nose," he continued. "I believe that Wendell sacrificed himself to destroy the powder and as much of the Verderan camp as he could take with it. Whether any powder remains, I cannot say, but I don't doubt that the princes will have survived the blast, and they will want vengeance."

"Too true, my king," said Broderick, scratching at the protruding vein on his head. "We suspected that something was amiss in the Verderan camp, and it was Thaddeus's idea to utilise the tunnel as a means of inspecting the extent of the damage. This is Captain Ramsey," he added, introducing a middle-aged man with long brown hair beside him. "The captain led a small scouting party away from the castle, and that is, of course, where he found you. Captain Ramsey..."

The captain beat a closed fist against the plate armour that he wore upon his chest, the sound left to reverberate around the hall. "Yes, thank you, General," Ramsey began. "And welcome back, my king. It is an honour to serve you."

Cyrus nodded and smiled. "I owe you a debt for finding me in the tunnel," he said.

Ramsey nodded appreciatively. "Though significant damage was sustained in the blast," the captain proceeded, brushing dark strands of hair from his eyes, "the Verderans still present a sizeable force, with a number of other weapons designed to break through the city walls. The smaller camps at the eastern and western gates were unaffected by the blast, and though there are no immediate signs of offensive action, our men are on high alert."

"Thank you, Captain," said Cyrus, who might have thought the enemy was simply planning to starve them out if he hadn't witnessed, first-hand, the weapons at their disposal. "And to our defences?"

"Extensive measures have been taken to reinforce the city walls," answered Broderick, before motioning to his other captain, a bald man with a neatly cropped beard. "Captain Godric has joined us briefly from the frontline. We have swords and bows upon the parapets at each of the three gates, awaiting the Verderan advance."

"Good," said Cyrus. "And how are the men?"

Godric managed a half-smile, and Cyrus noticed tired bags under the man's eyes. "As well as can be expected, my king," said the captain. "We have around two thousand men assigned to the walls, the vast majority of which were posted from the King's Guard. They are well-drilled and ready to fight for every inch of the city."

"And is this this is the extent of our number?" asked Cyrus.

Thaddeus sat forward in his seat. "Your brother felt confident in the forces already within the city. The king felt that there was no need to call for help, and there has been no word from the Low Country, the Northern Fells, or any other province, let alone the Cornessians. Here in the capital, we have a further one thousand or so conscripted civilians, men, and boys."

"Blockades have been introduced throughout the city," added Broderick. "We will use the narrow streets to our advantage against the larger number. The walls will only hold for so long. Our aim must be to inflict maximum damage on the Verderans before falling back to the sanctuary of the old town."

Adaline, who had been observing patiently, chose this moment to speak. "The walls of the old town are aged but strong. There is only one passage in and out, and that is the King's Road, connecting the castle with the basilica in the heart of the city." Cyrus knew his mother was only explaining this for his benefit, given that he hadn't grown up in Highcastle, and he felt grateful for her presence.

"Have no fear for me," said Cornelius, unexpectedly. "The good Lord will see those Verderan heathens repelled long before they reach the basilica." As he spoke, he never even lifted his eyes from the religious text sprawled on the table before him.

"We pray that it is so, Cornelius," said Thaddeus, "but we must plan for every possible outcome. In the event of a breach, our troops have been instructed to fall back and reinforce the walls of the old town. It is from here that we can make our final stand."

Cyrus finally decided to take a seat, keen as he was to avoid Augustus's ornate chair. His head was throbbing, and his left arm continued to hang limp at his side with a dull ache. "And the people?" he asked. "The elderly, the women and children, and all those unable to fight?"

"We've already begun relocating them to the old town, my king," came Thaddeus's reply. "Conditions will be somewhat crowded, but what choice do we have?"

"Hmm," Cyrus uttered thoughtfully, scratching at the stubble on his chin. "There is, of course, the castle. What is Eldred's Keep if not a tribute to our nation's freedom? I propose that the castle gates be opened to those that you mention and that the impenetrable walls of the fortress offer sanctuary to those who need it most. Ensure that this includes space for the wounded. There are banquet halls in this castle that have probably stood empty for years. Let them serve the people of Highcastle at this time of need."

"But what of the risks?" asked Cornelius, his contribution drawing contemptuous expressions from Broderick and his captains. "Evil has many faces. Are we to risk allowing another devil into the castle? It is clearly God's will that you rule this great nation, but we cannot tempt fate, lest you share your brother's misfortune."

"Then I, too, must place my safety in the hands of a higher power," Cyrus countered, already tired of Cornelius's interventions. He wondered how Augustus had tolerated the man's presence. "I refuse to allow past events to make me suspicious of our own people, especially the ones who need our help most. Besides, I will face our enemy with the men." He turned to Adaline, whose face was decorated not with fear, but with unmistakable pride. "My mother will lead those within the castle. She is a woman of great judgement, and in the event that our efforts are unsuccessful, there is nobody better to guide our people through the passage to freedom."

Cyrus rose from his seat and strolled over to take his mother's hand in confidence, speaking more quietly than before. "The magistrate in Eriwald is named Merrill. Take the people through the tunnel to him, if it comes to that. He'll know what to do."

Adaline nodded, and Cyrus returned to his place at the head of the table. He absorbed the silent attention of the room and thought to choose his next words with care. "We remain outnumbered, yet I believe that we can win this." Thaddeus gave a nod of wordless approval, and Cyrus persisted, buoyed by the unexpected maturity in his voice. "I believe that the princes, Rafael and Alonso, are divided, and that the explosion in the camp will have damaged the confidence of their troops. The Verderans value splendour and magnificence, but this is often a veil for the absence of true substance. We will defend Highcastle with deadly conviction, and when Rafael comes for the walls of *our* city, we shall see the veil fall and determine what lies beneath!"

Rapturous applause broke out around the room, and Broderick roused his captains to their feet in boisterous approval. Cyrus could hardly believe that the words had been his own, but he knew that they were delivered in earnest. He bade silence from the room as Cornelius raised his hand for another surprise contribution.

"I do not mean to interrupt your momentum, my king," said the old man, stroking his long straggly beard. "I gather that a coronation ceremony may have to wait, but what of your brother? He was a king after all, and he deserves a proper burial."

Cyrus looked to his mother, whose eyes lowered to the table.

"There's no time," said the dowager queen. "It will have to wait."

"And leave his body at the mercy of the Verderans?" asked Cyrus, shaking his head. "No, I don't think so. Godric, Ramsey, thank you for your contributions, but please return to your position and keep me informed of any updates. The rest of you, with me, and someone gather Fran. Lead us to the basilica, Cornelius. There is always time to say goodbye."

⚜ ⚜ ⚜

Adaline stood tall and unwavering as her firstborn son was lowered slowly into the ground. Augustus's casket was a simple construction, but the rich walnut panelling alluded to an understated quality that Cyrus had failed to see in his brother when he was alive. His resting place would be a vault beneath Highcastle's famed basilica. The spot was marked by an elaborate marble slab, black and glossy against the flagstones, and though it was all someway short of the grandeur that personified the young king, Cyrus imagined that his mother would take some comfort in seeing Augustus rest beside Anselm and their grandfather, King Ailwin.

Cyrus felt a chill as he looked toward the vault and realised that he would likely be the next to join them. He wondered if the same thing had occurred to Augustus when Anselm was laid to rest, though of course his brother would not have expected to be reunited with their father so soon. Then again, Cyrus thought, Augustus might have thought himself invincible, so far from the reaches of death that he would never call the basilica home.

Adaline's head rested on Thaddeus's shoulder as the casket finally fell from view. She was a remarkably strong woman, Cyrus thought, one who loved her children unfalteringly. It was still slightly startling to him that he was counted amongst her children at all. Her words about Augustus had been heartfelt during the short ceremony, and Cyrus was reminded of his own efforts to eulogise Simeon's son, Brandon. He nodded respectfully in the face of his own mother's sorrow, trying to imagine the Augustus of whom she spoke, one of bravery and honour, a natural-born leader. He tried to put the more unsavoury memories of his brother—which were basically the only ones he had—out of his mind. After all, there was no use for them now, as he stood over Augustus's casket.

It was only a small gathering, but Thaddeus was a rich source of stories and anecdotes when called upon after Adaline had spoken. As a young prince, it seemed Augustus had shown much promise. Thaddeus spoke of a keen scholar, a prodigy with the blade, until life and its many attractions caught up with him. Cornelius played his part as celebrant, and Cyrus could tell that the Master of Prayer had indeed grown close with Augustus, as Marcia had suggested in her letter.

Whatever Cyrus had thought of his brother during their short time together, it was hard to overlook the injustice of his passing. Augustus had been a young man with a lifetime ahead of him in which to learn lessons and make things right. Who could say what he would have grown to be? Perhaps he would have grown into his father's shoes, filling them to become yet another storied king of Easthaven? Cyrus's anger and frustration was tinged with sadness at the untimely loss of yet another sibling—his memory drifted against his will back to Edgar and the sacrifice he had made to get Cyrus and Fran out of Corhollow safely—and Fran squeezed his hand tightly in support as the marble slab was returned to its rightful place in the floor, bringing the service to a close. Cyrus was certain that his little sister was thinking of their lost elder brother as well in that moment.

"Time to go," Fran whispered, her small hand still enclosed within his own larger one.

A booming organ echoed discordantly around the great expanse of the central apex, and Adaline mouthed *thank you* in Cyrus's direction before making for the exit, with all others following suit. It hadn't been the most convenient of times to attend a funeral, but Cyrus's chest warmed at the thought that he might have provided his mother with a bit of comfort in being able to say goodbye to his brother.

"So," Fran whispered, glancing around conspiratorially to make sure she wasn't being overheard, "are you actually king now?" She raised her eyebrows, and Cyrus knew his sister well enough to see that she was trying to lighten the mood, trying to lighten *his* mood.

"No. I mean…not exactly," he said, scratching his head as they passed through the main doors of the basilica and out into the atrium. "Well, I suppose so, but I don't really know. I'm not sure I'm even ready, but Highcastle needs someone, and after what happened to Anselm and Augustus, I'm all that's left."

Fran stopped, her lips pursed as she rolled her eyes. "Well, thank you, your majesty. That made everything much clearer!" She poked her tongue out at Cyrus before rushing to follow her adopted brother across the open courtyard. "It's just that nothing seems to make sense anymore," she continued, grabbing Cyrus's arm as she drew level. Her voice had dropped from playful to sad, and Cyrus's suspicions that her joviality had been a façade were confirmed as he saw through her act.

"What do you mean?" he asked, wanting her to say more. The rest of their small assembly was passing out of the atrium and descending the grand staircase, taking them out of view. Everything was quiet, and he pulled his sister to one side, encouraging her to continue with her concerns.

"I'm talking about Wendell. I thought he was my friend, but…." She paused for a moment as her young mind reached for the right words. Her expression was one of deep thought, and Cyrus couldn't help thinking how much she had grown in his absence. "Was he a bad man?" she began again in a small voice. "I overheard people talking about Gus, saying that Wendell was responsible, that he was working with the Verderans." She looked up at him, her eyes round and worried.

Cyrus paused. It was a question he was still trying to comprehend himself. He wanted to help Fran understand everything he had seen and learned in the last few weeks, but he found that the words were not so easily conjured. The stories he'd heard—even the stories he had always told—spoke of heroism and villainy as though the two were black and white. Cyrus's time away, though, had taught him that it's not always so clearly cut, that there exists a space between the black and white. Wendell, he thought, remembering the Master of Coin's sacrifice the previous night, existed somewhere in that in-between.

King Cyrus, leader of people? he thought, inwardly shaking his head at the prospect. He couldn't even console his own sister; how was he supposed to guide Highcastle to victory against such long odds? He knew he had to say something to Francine, though, and in an unexpected moment of clarity, it dawned on him to speak not from the head but from the heart.

"Was Wendell a bad man?" he asked rhetorically, if only to buy himself time. "You know, Fran, I've come to think that there is no such thing as a bad person, just people who do a mixture of good and bad things." He felt a little pretentious pontificating in this way, but the words were consistent with what he had learned. Similar conversations with Thaddeus played out in his mind, and he remembered that the "right thing" was not a staunch notion, but a feeling, a gut instinct. He looked back at Fran with a small, contented smile. She really had grown up, but perhaps she wasn't the only one.

"I know what happened with Wendell and Augustus, and I know how confusing it must seem," Cyrus continued, his confidence growing with every word, "but I do know that Wendell cared about you. He thought that you were special, and for all his wrongdoings, I think I might just agree with him on that one." Cyrus gave a comforting smile and added, "If Wendell did something bad, perhaps he felt the reasons behind it were good."

Fran's expression softened as Cyrus ruffled her hair. An untold sadness lingered behind her eyes, but Cyrus felt relieved at having offered some comfort through his newfound wisdom.

"So, killing someone doesn't necessarily make you a bad person?" she asked, her eyes wide with expectancy as though searching for reassurance. "It's okay if you had reasons? If it was for the greater good?"

At this Cyrus hesitated, his brow furrowing. Fran's questions were curious, and his words seemed to offer little more than scraps in satisfying her hunger for answers. "I don't know that I can answer that one. I don't think one answer could possibly apply to all circumstances…but you're a little young for killing yet, aren't you?" He smiled at his own attempt to lighten the mood, his efforts earning little more than a twitch in Fran's cheeks, before he continued, "Now, I don't know what's upsetting you, but try not to worry. I know I'm scared of the Verderans and the war that we're about to face, but you know what?" he used a finger to raise his sister's chin. "You cannot be a slave to your fears. You have to face them head on."

"Even if I have done something terrible?" Fran asked. Her skin had gone quite pale, and her face turned serious.

"Especially then. You're too hard on yourself sometimes, Fran. You've been through a lot already, what with your parents, Osbert, Edgar, and Augustus since. I should have been here for you so that you could have come to me sooner. Know that it's not unusual to have these fears, but I'm back now, and I will always be here for you, all right?"

"Face my fears, you say?"

"Yes, that's right."

A moment of silence passed before Fran's lips curled into a reluctant smile. "Okay," she said, linking her arm with Cyrus's as she motioned toward the grand staircase.

They took no more than a few steps before the two of them fell to a crouch at a loud noise nearby, with Cyrus stooped over to cover his sister, one arm about her shoulders. The first projectile crashed into a building near them, throwing a cloud of dust into the sky above the basilica.

Cyrus swallowed deeply, his first thought to get Fran to safety.

The battle for Highcastle had begun.

Cyrus dashed into the courtyard of Eldred's Keep, his polished silver breastplate sparkling in the sunlight. "Round up the last of the women and children!" he yelled at one of Broderick's captains. He turned to the general, who stood ready to lead a division of the King's Guard. "Broderick, with me!"

The streets were frenzied, and Cyrus felt the full weight of responsibility as he made his way toward the main gate at the north of the city, with Broderick and the men following closely behind. All around him, people were running and screaming, and as another giant rock fell from the sky to decimate the city before him, Cyrus knew that nowhere was truly safe from the chaos.

After a few quick-footed moments, Cyrus arrived at the gates of the old town, where men lined the walls with bows. He slowed to acknowledge Captain Ramsey addressing rows of reserve troops, numbering perhaps five hundred, all stood in tight formation at the foot of the walls.

"For the king!" said the captain, and the gathered troops replied in kind. Their voices boomed with confidence, but Cyrus still saw the fear in their eyes. This was the civilian contingent, of that there could be no mistake. Cyrus saw a collection of old men with shaking hands and young boys with trembling lower lips. His stomach fell at the sight of them, but he refused to let his face betray the portrait of confidence he had painted.

Cyrus raised his sword and smiled. "For your homes, your families, and for Highcastle!" and then he turned to continue through the gates, following the wide path of the King's Road, a roar of approval sounding in his wake.

"Get to the castle!" he called to a young mother and her daughter as he ran past. The girl had corkscrew curls that reminded him of Francine's, and he sighed with relief knowing that his sister was already safe within the walls of Eldred's Keep.

They broke away from the main path as the shadow of the basilica loomed over them. The narrow streets beyond were choked with blockades formed from household objects, and though it was heart-warming to see the people of the city working together, Cyrus thought of the destruction of Rafael's camp after Wendell had caused the explosion, and he found himself fearful for those in the city who were strangers to the horrors of war. He supposed it hadn't been so long ago that Cyrus himself had fallen into this category, and his unease grew with the realisation that he was now the one responsible for leading the defence.

He remembered Colton describing Ravensward as a labyrinth, but Cyrus thought now that Highcastle really was a maze. He did his level best to give the impression that he knew where he was going as they broke into a stretch of tightly huddled houses.

"Have their heads, your majesty!" came a timely call, breaking into Cyrus's thoughts. An old man with an antique sword stood defending the door to his house, while his grey-haired wife lingered in the shadows with little other than a wooden rolling pin for protection. Cyrus wondered if they thought he was Augustus, whether the people even knew that Augustus was gone yet. Would word have spread? Did it even matter?

In the end, Cyrus thought, it didn't matter who sat on the throne or that they were outnumbered and overpowered; this was their home, his home, and Cyrus recalled his own words to Mathilde during her visit to the castle only months before: *A warrior is most dangerous when fighting with purpose.* The man with the antique sword and his wife with the rolling pin had purpose, no matter who the king was, and so did Cyrus. He growled as he raised his sword in the air before gesturing his men onward toward the sounds of violence, the first signs of the decimation caused by the Verderan catapults becoming clearer with every stride.

Their urgent footsteps clattered through winding passageways as expectant faces appeared in the windows of the shops and houses that yet remained. Voices sounded out, calling women, children, and the elderly into the embrace of the castle, and as Cyrus edged closer to the city walls, an ever-increasing wave of fearful city-folk began to rush at them from the opposite direction, desperate to escape the madness. It was a battle of its own to break through the current of the crowds, yet the ramparts of the city walls soon came into view, and Cyrus called for his soldiers to join their fellow countrymen, his voice competing with the cries of their unseen enemies, who were already attempting to destroy the gates and scale the walls.

"King Cyrus!" said Captain Godric, rushing to meet Cyrus and Broderick. His bald head glistened with sweat, and the look in his eyes was no longer tired but purposeful. "Our archers have done a fine job holding them off, but we can't keep this up much longer." He turned back as a makeshift section of wooden palisade began to smoke with burgeoning flames as if to illustrate his point.

"Somebody dowse that fire!" yelled Broderick with authority and a quickness of thought that Cyrus was relieved to have at his side.

Godric continued, "Our picket slowed them and will continue to make things difficult for their cavalry, but they are already beginning to reach the wall in great numbers, and they *will* break through eventually."

Broderick put a heavy hand on Cyrus's shoulder. "You're all that we have left, my king. Take some of the men and see yourself to safety. There is no need for you to face this."

Cyrus nodded, mirroring Broderick's gesture with an arm of his own. "This is my kingdom," he said, his chest swelling as the truth of his own words hit him, "and for that reason alone, there is every need." He let his hand drop before rushing to climb one of the turrets that led out onto the parapet, with Broderick in close pursuit. "Do not let them scale the palisade," Cyrus called back to his general.

Cyrus stepped among his men, a team of bowmen firing death upon their assailants. The Verderan army descended upon the city like red wine spilled over a tablecloth, tainting all in its path. Cyrus could see no end to their numbers, and the snarling fury of every individual seemed to stare back at him, threatening all that he held dear.

"To the right!" Cyrus called to the archers, pointing to where the Verderans shielded the approach of ladders, designed to scale the city walls. Beyond this, there seemed no method to the Verderan madness. There was no sign of Rafael or Alonso yet, but their men simply broke upon the gate and the walls like a wave. The roar of catapult fire continued to sound out as enormous rocks whistled past overhead, smashing the city to pieces behind them.

"Take them down!" Cyrus cried, and a young archer took aim before sending an arrow into the heart of one of the Verderan ladder men, the wooden structure falling to rest on top of the bearded man who had been carrying it.

"Fine work!" Cyrus shouted in jubilation, and though the young archer turned, his face was not one of triumph but fear. Blood bubbled between his lips, and Cyrus reacted quickly to catch his compatriot as his body began to convulse, an angry-looking arrow lodged in his neck. Cyrus looked away from the archer's face to see more arrows sailing through the air in malice.

"The western gate!" said Broderick, and Cyrus lowered the young archer onto his back before closing the man's eyes for a final time. He ducked an arrow as he rushed to the ledge once more, and from this viewpoint, he witnessed the Verderans preparing an enormous battering ram for an attack on the doors at the northwest of the city.

"Hold them back!" he cried to those archers who remained. Their numbers were dwindling, and the turret was becoming crowded with the bodies of the dead. Below them, swarms of Verderans continued to attempt to scale the walls or destroy the city gates by force or with fire. Ladders were upright as far as the eye could see, and Cyrus glanced back into the city, where Godric was arranging his troops to face the enemy up-close. Men with swords, halberds, and pikes stood ready to defend the city as their enemy began to breach sections of the walls. There was no time to waste, he knew, and Cyrus descended the turret with the smell of fire increasingly thick in the air.

"You must return to the castle," said Broderick breathlessly, racing to keep up. His eyes were wide with fear and desperation. "It's not safe for you here, my king. The Verderans will soon fall upon the city, and I cannot see you lost so needlessly."

Cyrus felt his fist clench. "I appreciate the concern, Broderick, but that is not your decision to make. I have every faith that, with your help, Godric can make the Verderans pay dearly for the north of the city. That is why I need you to stay here and lead the line, Broderick," Cyrus continued passionately. "But none of this will matter if we surrender the western gate so cheaply."

"But my king!"

"No, Broderick," snapped Cyrus, leaving little room for negotiation. "I must ensure that the western gate holds for as long as possible. The Verderans still have the significant advantage of numbers, and we will need to deliver considerable damage from our defensive position if we are to survive the day with any hope of victory. Summon my division, Broderick," he said, his voice turning from explanatory to demanding. "That's an order."

⚜ ⚜ ⚜

It was only matter of moments before Cyrus was back in the narrow streets. His company numbered around one hundred, and

Cyrus lead the way as the men followed closely behind. The city seemed empty now but for soldiers, and though Cyrus could see the tip of the western gate above a vista of rooftops and smoking chimneys, the maze of narrow streets, jumbled houses, and improvised barricades ensured that his passage was as slow as it was frustrating.

Cyrus groaned as he and his men pushed a cart out of the way in an alley full of drying clothes strung between houses, now coated in dusty debris. Seeing this made Cyrus realise just how quickly the situation had developed; just that morning, people had hung this washing with no idea of what was to come. Cyrus cast his eyes around as he struggled to make his way through. Possessions were strewn across the streets in either an act of defiance or of panic, and he hoped that the rightful owners would return to reclaim them before the day was out.

He breathed heavily as the cart finally rolled forward to create a path, and he took a moment to survey the extent of the damage that had already befallen them. The western quarter was known for being a lively social centre. He was not far from the market, and he was in view of an open-air platform that would normally play host to groups of travelling entertainers, though the stage had been decimated during the onslaught. To his right stood a tavern, and his attention was briefly snatched by the lonely creaking of the sign above the door. The sign read, "The Day's End," and Cyrus shook his head at the gaping hole where a door had once rested. "The End of Days" seemed more appropriate in that moment.

Cyrus was about to continue on when a cacophony of high-pitched cries sounded from back the way he had come. It was the unmistakable sound of anguished screams, and he turned to see a gap in the city walls where he had stood with the archers only minutes before. It could have been him but for the grace of God or good fortune, he thought, his mouth going dry. The huge rock from the Verderan catapult appeared to have destroyed all in its path, and Cyrus could only hope for Broderick's safety as Godric's voice echoed in the distance, urging his men to rush and plug the gap.

Heavy stone boulders flew overhead, and a thick grey smog was beginning to settle over the city. Cyrus ran through the streets, zigzagging around chunks of broken buildings, and he was in sight of the western gate when a barely audible voice called to him through a pile of chalky rubble.

"Help!" came the cry, and Cyrus turned back, looking around until his eyes landed on a man at last, nearly hidden in the ruin. The man had greying hair, and Cyrus guessed that he would have a warm smile under different circumstances, though his face was currently covered in hot, sticky blood. The side of his house had been crushed by the Verderan catapults, and the lower half of the man's body was buried by the remnants of the missing wall.

"Hang on," said Cyrus, rushing to the man's aid. The brickwork had been blown apart on impact, and Cyrus had little choice but to dig frantically with his bare hands, his injured shoulder burning in agony as he removed each individual stone from the man's body. The bricks were sharp and heavy, and Cyrus's hands throbbed with the effort, but he refused to stop as the old man sneered and wheezed in pain.

"Nearly there," Cyrus growled through gritted teeth as a boot appeared among the wreckage. The boot led to a leg, the leg to a torso, and a smile of relief appeared on Cyrus's face as he sensed a small victory nearing. He would see this man free and have him live in spite of the Verderan princes' best efforts. Each brick was its own battle, but he was winning, and maybe—he thought, a surge of hope filling him—they would yet win this war. Bit by bit, he released the old man from his living grave, but as Cyrus reached to clear the man's right side, he noticed that the bricks were slick in his hand, and his palms were red with blood.

"Hang in there!" he yelled desperately, doubling his efforts in horror. As the last of the bricks tumbled away, though, they revealed a splintered wooden beam buried deep in the man's side. Cyrus's heart dropped. "Stay with me," he said, reaching to turn the man's face toward his own, but no answer was forthcoming. The man was already gone.

Cyrus swallowed as he closed yet another set of dead eyes, and then he turned to find his division of the King's Guard standing behind him in wide-eyed silence.

"To the western gate," Cyrus said sadly, rising to his feet.

The foremost of his company stepped forward. "You heard the king," he said turning his ash-stained face to rouse the others. "The Verderans will come no further. Forward to the western gate!"

⚜ ⚜ ⚜

They arrived just in time to see the western gate fall. Archers fired on the enemy or dropped hot oil and water upon them from the turret above. The gate crackled with a raging fire, and the noise was deafening as the head of the battering ram smashed through the reinforced doors, allowing the Verderan soldiers through.

"Hold them back!" cried Cyrus, rushing headlong into the melee. It felt like a scene of absolute mayhem to Cyrus, but he was pleasantly surprised to see that Broderick's captains had the troops well-organised. They moved on the enemy with an imposing shield wall, striking the Verderans down as soon as they appeared through the hole in the gate that the battering ram had caused. For a moment, it seemed victory might be simple, if they could only keep this up. Then, the battering ram smashed through the gate, collapsing the structure entirely. Daylight appeared before them, revealing hordes of bloodthirsty Verderan warriors.

Horns echoed in the air, drowned out by the maddened cry of the advancing army. Cyrus called for his men to hold the line, but the sheer ferocity of the oncoming Verderans caused the shield wall to buckle, and the invaders were soon among them in earnest. There was barely enough room to raise a sword let alone swing one, yet Cyrus and his company pushed forward, swords and shields ringing out as they fought to push their aggressors back.

"King Cyrus, look out!" came a cry, and Cyrus turned to see the ash-stained soldier take a blade that had been destined for his back. The Verderan warrior smiled as he pulled the sword from the man's chest, and Cyrus launched forward before he could even think, stabbing relentlessly until the Verderan's smile faded as he fell to his knees, blood spilling from a deep wound in his gut. Cyrus pulled his blade from the man's body and stood up, looking down at him in disgust, before turning his attention back to the battle at hand.

Men were crying and dying all around him, but Cyrus continued to push toward the gate, fighting on instinct alone. The ground was stained red, and bodies were steadily gathering underfoot. A large Verderan with no teeth swung an axe in his direction, and Cyrus was fortunate to lose his footing on a discarded shield, inadvertently dodging the blow before he rose to drive his sword into the man's thick neck. He felt lost in an overwhelming sea of enemies, but it seemed that Easthaven's defences might just be holding. Cyrus lost count of the lives he had taken as another Verderan fell at his feet, wide-eyed, as though he had never considered death a possibility.

A deafening blast suddenly pierced the air, and Cyrus could do little more than step back with his forearm above his head as meagre protection as a nearby section of wall exploded before his eyes, sending a shower of broken rock into the crowd of fighting soldiers. Cyrus was momentarily disorientated. A high-pitched ringing sounded in his ears, and his nose burned with the unmistakeable smell of the blast powder as the wall crumbled and more of the Verderans poured in.

The break in the fighting was some respite, but short-lived. Cyrus was thrown onto his back as a bald man with a bloodied nose stabbed wildly down with his sword, missing Cyrus narrowly as he rolled away to take cover among the vacant faces and broken bodies of the dead. The sights and smells were nauseating, but Cyrus crawled through the carnage to reclaim his sword, and though he climbed to his feet to meet his attacker once more, the man's head lolled to one side as a heavy sword threatened to part it from his shoulders.

Broderick appeared as Cyrus's attacker fell to the ground with blood gushing from his neck. "The main gate is lost, my king," Broderick cried. "The east will soon fall to the Verderans. You must return to the castle before it is too late!"

Broderick twisted to cut down yet another foe with his sword, and Cyrus watched as hundreds of Verderans marched into the city, either through the gateway or over the wreckage of the city walls. Highcastle's soldiers had made a brave effort, but the city's outer defences had been shattered, the remaining men acting as little more than target practice for the encroaching army.

"Fall back!" Cyrus shouted, not with the voice of a boy, nor a prince, but as King of Easthaven, with all the responsibility that the title carried with it. "Fall back to the castle!" he repeated, holding his ground beside Broderick as the shield wall reorganised around them and men turned to flee. He held as long as he could, and as his own archers pinned the Verderans with a barrage of arrows, Broderick turned to him.

"You must go now, King Cyrus. You must."

The general's face was hard and sure, and Cyrus could tell the time for argument was over. Cyrus set his jaw and nodded once, looking out for a lingering second at the chaos around him.

"Go," Broderick growled again, turning from Cyrus to get back to battle. Reluctantly, Cyrus turned from the general and back toward the sanctuary of the old town.

He ran through the streets with the remainder of his own small company in hot pursuit, ready to shield him from any surprise attacks. Buildings were in pieces all around them, and soldiers of Easthaven were hidden among the rubble with blades primed and arrows nocked in anticipation of the Verderan advance. Abandoned food carts and other homemade blockades were no longer a hindrance but an important line of defence against their unwelcome guests, and Cyrus navigated his way back to the King's Road. When he arrived at the inner walls, he was reunited with Captain Ramsey.

"Our enemy is coming," said Cyrus as more and more soldiers poured back into the old town. "Prepare to close the gates and await my signal. It ends here."

⚜ ⚜ ⚜

The inside of Eldred's Keep was no less hectic than the rest of the city, and Cyrus fought his way through those seeking refuge as he made for the parapet. The first part of his plan had worked: the most vulnerable in the city were safe. Unfortunately, they were now trapped within the castle walls, and the Verderan princes had shown little respect for Easthaven's architecture thus far.

He broke out onto the ramparts to find Thaddeus. "What's going on?" Cyrus asked, joining him to look upon the capital. To a certain extent, it was obvious, and Cyrus watched as the Verderans swarmed through the city. They faced pockets of resistance along the way, but they kept breaking through, moving ever forward, while Cyrus's own forces gave ground.

"There is nowhere left to hide," said Thaddeus sadly. "Our walls are strong, but the odds remain against us." He paused and looked up at a grey sky. Cyrus followed his gaze and realised he couldn't tell where the smoke from the battle ended and the overcast sky began.

"Sound the retreat," called Cyrus, and his message was passed through a line of captains until horns began to echo around the city, spreading the king's word. Cyrus's remaining forces abandoned their positions for the salvation of the old town.

"There was much about your brother that I didn't care for, not least his sudden fascination with religion," said Thaddeus, "but we could certainly do with a miracle right now!" He turned to Cyrus and sighed deeply as he delivered a sad smile. "It was a pleasure to serve you, my king."

At this, Cyrus reached out and pulled Thaddeus close. Every man who'd tried to be a guiding figure to Cyrus had fallen, and Cyrus couldn't bear to think that Thaddeus might follow. The man's words only served to stoke the fire that burned within him.

When they broke apart, Cyrus cried, "Close the gates," looking back across the decimated shell of the capital. But as his eyes fell upon those still swarming into the city, he noticed the arrival of a new force appearing in the distance. "More Verderans?" he asked in an exasperated tone as Thaddeus returned to his side with a spyglass trained on the distance.

Cyrus was surprised to see a broad grin breaking out on Thaddeus's face.

"That's no Verderan flag," the old man said wryly. "It seems our miracle has arrived after all. Your good friend, Queen Mathilde, yet yearns for war!"

"The Cornessians are here?" asked Cyrus, reaching to grab the spyglass unsuccessfully, blocked by Thaddeus's outstretched hand as the older man continued to peer into the distance.

"They are indeed," answered Thaddeus. "Mathilde rides at the spearhead…but wait, she appears to have a man at her side?"

Cyrus squinted as though he might be able to see even without the use of Thaddeus's spyglass. It was no use. "The queen's shield, Lucien?" he asked, referring to the giant of a man that he had somehow bested on Mathilde's last visit to the capital.

"I think I'd recognise Lucien!" Thaddeus said, shaking his head. He paused, and Cyrus saw the lines tighten around the old man's eyes as he strained to see. "Well, you certainly know how to pick them," he continued with a chuckle. "It appears your man, Merrill, has even more fight in him than we first thought. Look…" Thaddeus finally relented, passing the spyglass to Cyrus. "To the left of the queen…it's the armies of the Low Country!"

A broad smile broke out on Cyrus's face as he watched the new arrivals ride purposefully toward the city. Down below, the gates to the old town were now closed, and the forces of Highcastle had reformed in impressive lines at the walls, while Cyrus's smaller retinue manned the courtyard of Eldred's Keep in a similar fashion. Mathilde's troops were already beginning to arrive at the edge of the city, and the Verderan advance had been halted as Rafael's men, tired from their efforts so far, turned to meet the Cornessians in open battle.

"Change of plan," called Cyrus, summoning a nearby captain. "I will not allow Mathilde to fight this battle alone. Send a message to prepare our armies to march out and meet the Verderans. We will join our allies and press the enemy in a pincer movement."

The captain nodded and moved to spread Cyrus's orders. Voices and commands sounded out around them as rows of troops fell into formation. Cyrus watched as his words took effect, and Thaddeus stood watching Cyrus with a smile.

"You've the look of a king, you know?" he said, reaching to place a hand on Cyrus's shoulder. "We could never have known it would come to this when we began training you all those months ago, but I think it's safe to say that Garrett would be very proud of you."

Thaddeus's words were unexpected, but Cyrus wore them like suit of impenetrable armour. He cleared his throat, which had grown tight at the mention of Garrett. "Save your words, old man," Cyrus answered playfully. "You can finish your sentiment over dinner this evening while we celebrate a victory."

The two of them laughed, and Cyrus gave Thaddeus a warm handshake before turning to join his troops. The sounds of the battle between the Verderans and the joint forces of the Cornessian and Low Country armies were already raging in this distance, and Cyrus was keen to march his men into the city, making only a handful of strides before a set of doors crashed open and Adaline rushed out onto the ramparts looking panic-stricken.

"Cyrus, my boy!" she cried upon seeing him. She closed the space between them and threw her hands around his shoulders. "I'm so glad I found you."

"It's all right, Mother," Cyrus answered softly. "The Cornessians are here. Everything is going to be all right. We are heading out to aid their forces now."

The dowager queen paused for a moment. She had arrived with little of her normal composure, and she began to chew at a fingernail nervously. Cyrus's stomach fell as he realised something else was amiss. "It's not that," Adaline said, her voice shaking gently with every word. "You have to understand…she said she needed to confront her fears." She gave a long breath to steady herself before continuing. "I thought she just needed to return to where she killed him, to gain some closure, but…"

"Mother, what are you saying?" Cyrus said, a cold wave of panic rushing over him as he grabbed his mother by the shoulders as if to shake the answers out of her. "Who needed to confront their fears? What do you mean?"

The pause that followed was only a couple of beats, but it felt to Cyrus as though it lasted an age. Then Adaline said two words that Cyrus had dreaded but never truly expected to hear. "Your sister," said Adaline, and Cyrus's mouth went immediately dry. His hands dropped from his mother's shoulder.

Adaline continued, her voice faltering, "There was an—an incident while you were away. An assassin came for me in my quarters, and Francine…well, Francine killed him. You know she had been learning to wield a sword. She saved my life, but she hasn't been the same since. She said she was going to tell you…"

Cyrus wracked his brain to remember the specifics of his last discussion with Fran. *I will always be here for you,* he had said. Fine words, noble words, but he realised now with a horrible lurch in his chest that she hadn't needed his assurances; she'd needed him to listen. He hadn't asked her what she was talking about, hadn't gotten into the specifics with her. Instead, he had given her vague advice, assuming she would be fine.

"Where is she now?" he demanded.

"We don't know," cried Adaline. "We've checked all over the castle, but nobody has seen her. I've been so busy organising things here that she slipped away without anyone noticing. Cyrus, you must understand—"

"Enough!" Cyrus said, turning away from his mother. He walked to rest his forearms on the crenelated walls of the parapet, trying to take a couple of deep breaths. "If she's not here, then she's out there," he said, nodding his head toward the city, "and I cannot lose her, not now. Thaddeus, take the queen and secure those within the castle. Adaline…" He shook his head. "Let's hope that I can find her, or you'll be adding another name to your list of regrets."

He turned hastily and heard Thaddeus consoling his mother as Cyrus thought bitterly of new regrets of his own. His heart was thumping in his chest, and his face was set in a scowl that never wavered as he emerged into the courtyard to stand at the head of his troops.

"To the gates!" he cried, wasting no time in leading the men away from the castle. They followed the familiar route of the King's Road until the remaining forces of Highcastle came into view. It was here that Cyrus brought his men to a halt and made to meet Broderick and his captains at the gates.

"Your men are ready, my king," said the general. "The Verderans had made inroads into the city, but Mathilde's arrival has slowed their advance. The main Verderan force has turned to meet the attack, but the winding streets of the capital could yet conceal any that remain. We should proceed with caution. What is your plan?"

"Thank you, Broderick." Cyrus gave a nod to Captains Ramsey and Godric, pleased to see that both had survived the battle so far. Ramsey's long dark hair was plastered to his forehead with sweat, while Godric had a cut on his cheek and blood in the beard upon his chin. Godric, in particular, looked exhausted.

"Assemble three divisions, General," Cyrus continued, "ensuring that enough men are left to man the walls. Broderick, you will take your men to clear the streets and secure the east of the city. I need someone to do the same in the west—"

"I'll do it," said Godric, but Cyrus shook his head and placed a hand on the captain's shoulder.

"Not this time," said Cyrus. "You've earned a rest."

Ramsey never hesitated as he stepped forward to say, "Send me, my king."

Cyrus gave a reluctant nod. "Scour the west of the city and ensure that the streets are clear. There's a chance that my sister might be out there, so tread carefully. I will march my men to what's left of the basilica and drive the Verderans back from the heart of the city."

"Say a prayer for us all while you're there, won't you?" said Broderick in jest, and Ramsey smirked as he moved to join the general in assembling the men. Godric fell away to take his place with those left to man the walls, and Cyrus cleared his throat, knowing that he must momentarily put Fran from his mind as he addressed those who would be sent to reclaim the city. They stood before him, perhaps a thousand in number, purposeful and ready.

"Today is the day of your destiny!" he thundered, the might of his presence rivalling Augustus at his very best. "This war is not of our choosing, yet we are on this path, and we must see it through." He stopped to draw his sword and observe the rows of men before him through narrowed eyes. "This is our home, our city, and we will not run from our enemies anymore. These men wish to take your lives and our freedoms, but we will not allow it. Our brothers and sisters from the Low Country have travelled to aid our cause. The great warrior queen, Mathilde, has joined them with her own Cornessian army. Our allies believe that the day can yet be won," he said, with a new air of optimism and determination apparent on the faces of those gathered. "*I* believe that the day can yet be won. But will you march with me?" he asked, his voice booming against the stone walls. "Will you repay this faith with ferocity? Fight with me, and together we will see our enemies fall!"

A passionate cheer filled the air, and Cyrus raised his sword toward the sky before turning as the gates creaked open to offer a path back into the city. He began forward, thoughts of Fran still forefront in his mind. He knew that, no matter the outcome of this battle, he would never be able to forgive himself if anything happened to his sister.

Archers watched on from the parapet as Cyrus's armies divided to descend upon the city.

"For Highcastle!" screamed Godric from his spot back on the wall, and the gate slammed shut.

⚜ ⚜ ⚜

Cyrus realised that the catapults had stopped firing, but the city was already in pieces, and smoke continued to sit heavily in the air as he followed the King's Road toward the basilica. He had no idea where he would find Fran, and it was painfully clear how little time he had actually spent with her in the city, his only memory that of their regretful conversation in the courtyard after Augustus's funeral.

"Leave no inch of the city uncovered!" he called to his men, reminding himself that they were seeking out hidden Verderans, not his sister. The soldiers accordingly filtered into every building and alleyway, though the Verderans were still nowhere to be seen. Sounds of conflict carried on the air, coming from somewhere in the distance, but their immediate surroundings were eerily quiet as Cyrus's men edged through the city toward the grand staircase of the basilica. Cyrus's nerves were on edge at even the slightest movements, and his eyes flicked between the shops and houses that lined the road as he proceeded cautiously, his blade extended before him.

"Over here!" came a sudden call, and a number of Cyrus's soldiers rushed to cover their king as they made to inspect the house from which the voice had sounded.

"You may not want to see this, my king," said the same man as before. And though Cyrus had been cautioned, he pushed past his guards and through a wooden doorway to find a young girl with corkscrew hair lying motionless on the floor.

"Fran!" he cried without thinking. His whole body was consumed with cold dread, and he pushed someone's arm away as he dropped to his knees at the girl's side, nearly breaking into a sob at the familiarity of the girl's lifeless expression. It wasn't Fran, he realised, but the girl who he had seen at the very start of the battle, her outstretched fingers reaching toward her mother, who was laid out in similar fashion on the crimson-covered floor. He felt instantly guilty for the instinctive relief he felt at realising the girl was not Fran, and then he felt sick with remorse.

He had told them to go to the safety of the castle. He had done all he could to save them, hadn't he? Cyrus felt the all-too-familiar depths of despair calling to him, but he knew he had to go on, both to search for his sister and to fight the battle at hand.

"Cover them," he ordered, summoning guards to bring blankets from a nearby bed. This was a senseless waste of life, he thought, and though he held little faith in religion, Cyrus said a short prayer before turning to continue on his way.

"Monsters!" spat one of the soldiers in disgust as the group stepped back into daylight. He looked to Cyrus, who nodded silently in agreement, and though he held no issue with the man's sentiment, he knew the field of battle to offer a meagre harvest where valour was concerned. The faces of the dead now lingered in Cyrus's mind, and the mood among his troops seemed to have darkened with their grim discovery. As he looked around, Cyrus noticed that their numbers had thinned, and though they were well-armed, he began to feel vulnerable and exposed, their group tightly packed together as they approached the grand staircase that led to the basilica.

"Eyes wide," said Cyrus, giving voice to his concern. But he had barely finished his warning when an arrow landed in the chest of the man beside him, and Verderan warriors appeared atop the staircase, rushing from the atrium to meet them.

Cyrus gripped his sword tightly as cries of, "To the king!" echoed around him. The Verderans held the advantage of the higher ground, and though numbers seemed to be even, their archers continued to pick Cyrus's men off without reply.

It all happened in an instant: Cyrus raised his sword as a Verderan soldier with a lazy eye crashed down on him. The man's strike had been clumsy but powerful, and despite Cyrus's successful block, he lost his footing to fall back down the stairs and onto the cobblestones below, his sword flying from his hand in the process. Cyrus's injured shoulder reverberated with the shock of the attack, and though disorientated, he rolled away as an arrow bounced from the ground beside him. He had no idea where his sword had gone, and as he scuttled on all fours to find it, a heavy boot crunched into his torso, throwing him onto his back.

"Time to die, young king," said the Verderan. His words allowed Cyrus time to swing a leg, dropping his assailant onto the ground beside him. Though Cyrus hadn't intended it, the man's head cracked on impact with the bottom step of the basilica's staircase, and a pool of blood was already forming when Cyrus snatched his sword to return to his feet.

Battle continued before him, and as he called for assistance, he noticed a number of bodies strewn across the street, arrows sticking out of them. He had walked his men into yet another trap, he realised, the hot feeling of bile creeping up his throat. Just when it seemed that things couldn't get any worse, Rafael appeared at the top of the staircase with yet more men at his side and Fran clutched in his arms, wriggling desperately to free herself. Rafael's smirk was unbearable as he looked down the staircase toward Cyrus.

"Fran!" Cyrus cried in desperation.

Two Verderan soldiers rushed to meet him, but he ducked the first, impaling the second before one of the King's Guard stepped in to end the danger. There was no time to waste, and Cyrus rushed forward as the Verderans shielded their king into the safety of the basilica's atrium. It seemed that the momentum had started to shift. Verderan arrows were falling with lesser frequency, and Cyrus dodged as one of the archers fell from a wall with an axe buried deep in his shoulder. Despite calls to wait for reinforcements, Cyrus bounded up the stairs, teeth gritted as he raced to find his sister. He couldn't stand to think of her in Rafael's arms. There wasn't an army in the world that would have stopped him, but he was slowed by the sight of Rafael's forces, rows of Verderan warriors who stood waiting in the atrium. Cyrus took in the sight of Cornelius, Augustus's much-favoured Master of Prayer, dead on the floor.

"King Cyrus," said Rafael with a smile, his tone dripping with patronisation. "We must stop bumping into each other like this, especially when I have company. Oh, I'm sorry," he rolled his eyes dramatically as he tightened his grip around Fran. "You two have already met, haven't you? This is becoming something like a family reunion."

The fear on Francine's face was like a knife to Cyrus's heart, and he felt the sting of every kick and fall the day had brought him, his pain finally catching up with him as he stared into Fran's wide eyes.

"Don't be stupid, Rafael," Cyrus said breathlessly, his voice not unlike someone who was trying to calm a wild animal. "She's just a girl. There's no need to bring her into this. Besides, you're trapped, and your armies will soon fall to the Cornessians. Why don't you just let her go?"

He crouched, lowering his blade to the floor as the last of his men reached the top of the stairs to stand at his back. It was then that Cyrus noticed Alonso among the Verderan number, and Cyrus chanced a hopeful glance, but the prince turned away, wordless. It seemed that the brothers were united after all.

"Let her go, and we'll let you walk out of here and take your armies with you," said Cyrus. "It's time to go home, Rafael. We've all seen enough bloodshed for one day."

Rafael chuckled, his laughter spreading through the Verderans like a fire in the woods. "Another problem solved with words, eh?" he asked, turning to Alonso, whose face remained expressionless. "Your men look tired and defeated, King Cyrus. For all your heroics, you're outnumbered. I could kill you here and now, and even if we were to leave the city, there are many places to hide, many ways to escape. No..." he continued with a dramatic shake of the head, "I think I'll kill the girl and then have my men kill you for sport. You once threatened me in my palace in Casarossa. Well, the tides have indeed turned, King Cyrus, and they are about to wash the last of your family away. Kill them all!" The last three words came out harsh and clear, an order to Rafael's own men.

Fran cried out as the Verderan forces edged menacingly toward the remainder of Cyrus's company. The numbers were perhaps two to one in favour of the Verderans, and though Cyrus's guards were armed and ready, his own sword was still on the floor. He had survived so many times before, but this time it felt like death was surely inevitable. He looked at Fran a final time, a tear escaping his eye as he accepted their fate. There was no fighting his way out of this one, he thought, tempted to close his eyes but forcing himself to keep them open, to stare at his sister. He thought bizarrely of all those stories he had told her, all those tales of heroes and villains, and he wondered where he would fit into those histories now. At this thought, his heart jolted, that fierce rush of blood that comes with one last idea.

"Wait!" Cyrus cried, raising his hands to stall the oncoming Verderans. "Is this how you want to be remembered? Do you want the histories to call you a king who murdered his own father to take his throne, one who secured his legacy by killing unarmed men and children?"

He paused as Rafael's eyes narrowed, his grip tightening around Fran once more. Cyrus noticed the Verderan soldiers exchanging confused looks with each other, and he wondered if any of them were aware as to how Ferdinand's death had truly come about.

"I assume you must have storytellers in Verdera, just like we do here. I doubt they'd reflect kindly upon a man like that. You know how this works, Rafael. You must have heard a story or two in your lifetime. If you want my throne, you'll have to take it from me yourself!"

Rafael smiled, and as Cyrus glared back at his enemy, he knew that his arrow of truth had reached its intended target. Rafael was ruthless and ambitious, but at his core, he was vain, and there was no way he would allow Cyrus to blemish his moment, his crowning victory.

"All right, King Cyrus," said Rafael, throwing Fran to the floor before him. "If it means that much to you, I would be happy to see you die at the end of my sword. I'll even be good enough to let your sister watch. Alonso, take the girl…" He drew his sword as his brother nodded, reaching to help Fran from the floor. Cyrus noticed her knees were scraped up, but she seemed otherwise uninjured. A small mercy.

Rafael said, "I suggest you gather your sword, King Cyrus," as though speaking to a child. Then, almost as an afterthought, he added, "Oh, and see that your men lower theirs."

After a slight pause, Rafael lunged forward. He was every bit as elegant as Cyrus had imagined he would be, and his thin rapier of a sword seemed to buzz through the air with all the unpredictability of an angry wasp on a warm day.

"Too slow, King Cyrus," he taunted, laughing as he twisted away, lithe as a dancer. His footwork was light and fluid, and Cyrus took a moment to appreciate his rival before leaping in with an attack of his own. Their swords met with a clang, and the shrill sound echoed around the atrium as both sets of men watched on. The momentum swung back and forth, attack after attack raining in, but after minutes of vicious exchanges, there was still nothing to separate the two.

"Not bad, I'll give you that," said Rafael, his breath heavy as he folded forward for a moment's rest. The respect between them was deadly, and Cyrus knew that his first mistake would be his last. Truth be told, he had given everything, and as he took a moment for his own recovery, he wracked his brains for any forgotten wisdom, anything Thaddeus and Garrett might have taught him that could help him to victory. His energy was almost completely depleted at this point, and after a moment of consideration, he concluded his pot of wisdom was equally drained. Cyrus and Rafael were excellently matched, as though Rafael had been mentored by Thaddeus too. There was no identifiable pattern to his attacks, which were well-balanced and true, complemented by his quick feet. Put simply, Rafael fought like a king. And, as Cyrus raised to anticipate the next exchange, it occurred to him that this very fact could provide the solution he so desperately sought.

He gave Rafael no warning as he charged him down, drawing the energy from—well, he wasn't sure where. This was not the done thing, of course, and it definitely wasn't something Thaddeus would have taught him, but the time for gallantry was long behind them. Cyrus's attacks were not considered but rather instinctive. His movements became less stable but more unpredictable. His onslaught was like a whirlwind, and though Rafael was every bit equal to the task, Cyrus noticed beads of sweat on the other king's forehead, an expression he had not previously seen: fear.

"You cannot beat me!" yelled Rafael, attempting to cover his shocked expression with bravado. As their blades ground together and their faces drew close, Cyrus tuned out Rafael altogether and thought back to the contest with his brother, Edgar, at the Spring Festival, and he slammed his fist into Rafael's face, breaking the king's nose on impact.

"What is this trickery?" cried the Verderan king, who was cowering to cover the rush of blood flowing out of his nose.

"Just a little something I learned in the villages," said Cyrus. He noticed Fran smiling wryly from her spot beside Alonso, who, Cyrus had just realised, wasn't restraining his sister at all. "Do say if things are getting a little too rough for you, your highness," he added with an ironic bow.

At this, Rafael's cheeks reddened, and he launched back into action. His swordplay remained flawless, but Cyrus continued to bully his adversary, stomping, tearing, and punching at every opportunity until Rafael eventually dropped his sword and gestured for Cyrus to do the same. The Verderan raised his fists.

It was to be settled hand-to-hand, then.

Though Cyrus felt he had the upper hand, his bullying strategy had drained the very last of his energy, his reactions lethargic as Rafael rushed forward, tackling him to the ground. He was just so tired. Tired of this foolish Verderan with his ridiculous little beard. Tired of having to fight to survive. And tired of being thrown onto the flagstones, his body aching as though about to break.

He took a gulp of air and extended his arm in a final attempt to fight Rafael away, but as the man's weight came fully down upon him, Cyrus felt a tear that coursed through his body, and his injured shoulder finally gave way.

The scream escaped him before he could even attempt to stop it, such was the agony. Tears welled in his eyes, and he wanted nothing more than to lie back and cry, but Rafael would not allow it, driving fist after fist into Cyrus's face, coherent thought becoming more and more distant as his head bounced against the stone floor.

"Just a little something you learned in the villages, eh?" Rafael spat as he straddled Cyrus, grabbing a handful of hair to lift his head away from the ground. "Well, let me teach you a new lesson," he snarled, their noses almost touching, "the very last you will ever learn."

This would be the end, then. Cyrus braced himself for the inevitable. He closed his eyes, anticipating death, but the next sound was not that of his head being dashed upon the stones but instead a sickening thud followed by the gradual loosening of Rafael's grip. He heard another anguished cry, but this time it was not his own. As Cyrus's head hit the ground, his vision cleared to find Rafael above him, clasping at an arrow through his middle, his face stricken and already going pale.

"Alonso, kill them!" cried the king, his words desperate and strained.

Cyrus's head was still spinning from the onslaught he had absorbed, but he twisted to throw Rafael to the ground beside him. As he turned back to face his own handful of men, he found none other than Mathilde's chosen shield, Lucien, rushing to lift him to his feet, his movement so effortless that Cyrus might not have weighed anything.

"Mathilde!" said Cyrus weakly as the Cornessian queen came into view. The King's Guard were hidden by rows of Cornessian archers, and the queen managed a quick smile as Cyrus stumbled back to join them.

"You know what they say," said Mathilde playfully. "Behind every good man is a great woman with a big sword and few dozen archers." She grinned and placed a hand on Cyrus's shoulder. He knew she was trying to reassure him, but he had to work very hard not to wince as she lightly touched his injury. He couldn't deny a feeling of shame at the dishonourable nature of his victory, and worse still, the realisation that this was the second time that Mathilde had put herself and her people at risk to save him.

His thoughts were interrupted as the queen's eyes narrowed and her jaw set in a hard line. "So, what's it going to be, Prince Alonso?" she asked, all jest removed from her tone. "Your men are fleeing. Your brother is dying. What say you take your men back to Casarossa, and we finish this conversation another day?"

"Don't listen to the Cornessian bitch!" Rafael gurgled from his place on the floor. "Kill the girl and take the city. Avenge me, you cowards…" His voice was too weak to go on.

All eyes turned on Prince Alonso, who stood thoughtfully for a moment before walking Fran forward with his sword at her throat, its blade stark against her pale skin. "It seems that there is but one choice, then," Alonso said, arriving at his brother's side. "Just one more life, and the day is done."

Cyrus trembled as his eyes met with his sister's. Fran, brave as always, her face expressionless as she faced her own fate with her head held high.

"There will be vengeance," Alonso continued with purpose. "Not for you, brother, but for our father."

Fran fell forward as Alonso pushed her towards Cyrus, who rushed to catch her before his mind had even caught up to what was happening. Alonso crouched down to drive his sword into Rafael's chest just a few inches above the arrow that had already run him through, and the Verderan soldiers gasped as they watched their king wheeze a final breath. After a moment, their eyes left Rafael's lifeless form and turned instead to Alonso.

"My brother was a treacherous fool who killed our father, King Ferdinand, after imprisoning him for months. I do not claim to be innocent in this," said King Alonso solemnly, "but I do intend to make things right. Sound the retreat," and by the time he rose to his feet once more, the sound of horns was already echoing around the city. "We're done here," Alonso continued, and Mathilde signalled her troops to part as the new Verderan king passed through them, his men following unquestioningly until they were out of sight.

Frenzied blood was still pumping through Cyrus's veins, and though his arm hung limp at his side, he gave no thought to the pain as Fran rushed to embrace him.

"It's over," he said, pulling her close.

And just by saying the words, he felt a weight lift from his shoulders. They were safe, they were together, and with Mathilde smiling on, they were finally in the company of friends.

A good day is a good day's work. That's what Osbert had always told Cyrus, anyway. He would stride into their house in Corhollow, take off his coat, and ruffle Cyrus's hair before sitting by the fire with little Fran on his knee. His energy had been endless, and if he'd ever had a bad day, his children would never have known it. He could spend the whole day caring for people and then come home and care for three more, even if Edgar, always impressively older and independent, seemed to get by perfectly well on his own most of the time.

A good day's work, thought Cyrus, his eyes fixed upon Isidore's Chair above him as he stood alone in the throne room. They had ended the Verderan siege, hadn't they? Rafael was dead, and with him his tyrannical pursuit of kingdoms that didn't belong to him. Anselm's ambitions had finally been realised, and the time for peace was upon them.

So where was Cyrus's energy, his sense of satisfaction?

He edged slowly towards the throne, his footsteps reverberating around him as if to illustrate his own smallness, his own insignificance. The chair itself was raised high above the room. Cyrus had once thought this to be a sign of elevation and power, but he now saw the truth of the matter. To sit on the throne is to accept a level of responsibility that cannot be shared, a solitary endeavour. The throne's elevation spoke as much of loneliness and isolation as it did of power.

"Your father used to do exactly the same thing," came a soft voice. Cyrus turned to see Adaline approaching slowly, almost cautiously, though with a small smile playing at her lips, her face almost wistful with the memory. "It can't be easy," she continued gently, "the weight of expectation forever upon you. I think it would drive me to madness." She paused. "It might even drive me to say things I didn't mean to those I loved."

Cyrus let his head drop, the implication in her words obvious. She was trying to give him a way out of apologising, but he knew better than that. "Mother, I'm sorry," he said simply, feeling something like a little boy.

"There is no need to apologise," she said, and her mouth twisted to one side as she fixed him with a knowing expression. The air between them felt light, and he realised she really wasn't holding his harsh words about her responsibility in Fran going missing against him. "We'll laugh, we'll cry, and sometimes, we will even disappoint each other. It's what family does best. But we will also move past it."

"But, Mother…"

"It's all right," Adaline said, closing the gap to take him by the hand. "I'm sorry. I shouldn't have let Fran from my sight, but she's growing up fast, and that girl is capable of remarkable things." She paused as tears glinted in her eyes but did not fall. "We will have our ups and downs, Cyrus, but we will come through it all if we stick together. I am here for you, and so are your people. All they will ask is to see that you are there for them too. You have already started to show them that, but it's an obligation that lasts a lifetime."

She let go of Cyrus's hand as she walked into the shadow of Isidore's Chair, gesturing for him to sit down on the throne. Wordlessly, he obeyed, taking the seat that had been his brother's, his father's, men he hadn't known well enough but was still linked to by the very blood in his veins.

"Be open and honest, and care for your people," Adaline said, looking up at him in his rightful place. "That's what makes a truly great king. That's what will make *you* a great king, above all else. It's what has already started you on your way to greatness."

Cyrus's lips trembled at the conviction behind his mother's words. He knew now, as his father had before him, that the united stand where the divided fall. He sat up straighter in Isidore's Chair, feeling as though Anselm might be standing just behind him, a strong hand placed on his son's shoulder.

He looked down at his mother, and, needing one last bit of reassurance said, "Everything really is going to be all right, isn't it?"

"Even better," said Adaline, nodding, "you're going to change the world."

⚜ ⚜ ⚜

"Merrill of Eriwald, my king," said an armed guard as he stepped aside to let the unassuming magistrate enter the royal chambers. Cyrus rose from his seat by the empty hearth—it was too warm for a fire—and his smile was wide as he extended an arm to welcome his old friend.

"Forget 'Merrill of Eriwald!' It's 'Merrill the Magnificent,' if you believe the stories!" joked Cyrus. "It's nice of you to announce your arrival this time instead of giving us all the surprise of our lives, or are you some kind of guardian that I need only wish for in times of peril?"

Merrill's cheeks flushed at the compliment, and Cyrus laughed, patting the magistrate's shoulder as the new arrival hung his head with embarrassment. "It was the very least I could do," said Merrill, removing his tricorn hat to sit at Cyrus's side. "After everything you've done for us, for me."

"Oh, you're too modest," said Cyrus, though his eyes were momentarily distracted as Marcia swept into the room carrying two large glasses of wine. He turned back to the magistrate. "You saved us all, Merrill—you and Mathilde. I'd say that's magnificent by anyone's standards. Now, are you going to tell me how exactly you managed to pull that off?"

"Well, that is an easy one. Thank you," Merrill added, smiling at Marcia as he took one of the glasses from her. "There was a letter from a girl within the castle. I believe her name was Marcia." He waited as Marcia handed Cyrus the remaining glass, her face set with a knowing smile. He continued, "She said she was a friend of yours and that the capital was in danger. Naturally, I was concerned, but when we realised that the armies of the Low Country wouldn't be enough, I sent word of my own to Queen Mathilde."

Cyrus reached across as he listened, and the two of them clinked glasses before Merrill swilled a first mouthful, his sounds of appreciation sufficient to set Marcia on her way.

"You had told me I should call on Mathilde in a time of need, but it seems our friend Marcia had beaten me to it. I don't know who she is, but I would keep her close. She's a handy person to have around the place, that's for sure. Quick and clever."

Cyrus nodded, turning in his chair to glimpse a flash of Marcia's dress as she vanished into the hallway. "She really is quite remarkable," he agreed, taking a swig from his own glass. "So, tell me, what news of Eriwald?"

⚜ ⚜ ⚜

She really was quite remarkable, thought Cyrus a while later, though in truth he'd thought of little else since she'd brought the wine to his chambers. The conversation with Merrill was warm and lively, but news of traders and taxation held little interest when compared with his own consuming thoughts of Marcia, and Cyrus was guilty of nodding and muttering absently as his mind wandered elsewhere. The days since the battle had been busy with meetings and planning for his own coronation, but the truth remained: Marcia *was* a remarkable woman, and it was time he finally told her.

But where was she? After his long chat with Merrill, Cyrus dashed around the castle, his head spinning with nervous excitement, feeling less like a king and more like a teenage boy. Maids and squires smiled at him as he practically danced through the corridors of Eldred's Keep, and though he was prone to doubting himself, especially where girls were concerned, Cyrus had come to think that perhaps this really was meant to be. After everything he had survived, this was just another challenge, one with perhaps the biggest reward of all.

"Have you seen Marcia?" he asked a gaggle of laundresses, and their heads shook in unison before the unmistakeable sound of giggles followed him as he left them in his wake.

One after another, he asked everyone around the castle. What had started as excitement soon turned to desperation and then to embarrassment as he began to wonder whether Marcia was, in fact, avoiding him. The search took him all over Eldred's Keep, and with time passing and hope slipping away, he rounded a corner to find Fran.

"Lost your girlfriend, have you?" she asked with a grin.

Cyrus grimaced at the question. It was great to see his sister recovering from her recent ordeals, but that was a little harder to appreciate during this particular moment.

"Only, I've been watching you chase her around the castle all afternoon," Fran continued playfully. "Silly, really, when the answer is so obvious."

"Obvious?" asked Cyrus, his eyes narrowed in thought.

"Yes, obvious," said Francine, and there was time for a frown of her own. "I know you took a knock on the head, Cyrus, but think about it. She's Adaline's lady-in-waiting, so…"

"She's in Adaline's quarters!" snapped Cyrus, internally kicking himself. "Thanks, Fran," he continued, pulling her into a suffocating embrace that he thought Aunt Aggie would have been proud of had she lived to see it. He straightened up and tried to make his voice sound serious as he continued, "I just need to see her is all. You know, official business."

"Hmm," answered Fran, and her eyebrows raised in unison. "And do you usually intend to kiss people during your 'official business' with them? I'll be sure to let Thaddeus and Broderick know. They deserve a warning at least, if this is going to become standard practise."

"What?" Cyrus asked, his neck suddenly feeling very hot.

Fran laughed as she shook her head. "Good luck, Cyrus," she said, with no effort at containing her amusement. As Cyrus turned to make his way back through the castle, he heard exaggerated kissing noises echoing out behind him. He wanted to scowl at his sister's cheek, but he couldn't seem to find a way to remove the grin from his face.

⚜ ⚜ ⚜

He probably deserved the ridicule, all told. But in Cyrus's defence, it was his heart, not his head, that was doing the thinking. He could already hear Marcia humming as he approached his mother's chambers, and he felt the pace of his heart double, a sheen of sweat forming on his brow.

Enough was enough. He liked her, she liked him—or at least he was pretty sure she did. It was simple. Just a few little words and the final piece of the puzzle would finally fall into place. He had his kingdom, but what was a king if not the husband to a queen?

He hesitated with the realisation that he was getting way ahead of himself. He shook his head as though to clear away thoughts of marriage, his future queen, and the lot. He needed to take it one step at a time and deal with the matter at hand. Whatever the outcome, he had learned to trust his heart and follow his dreams. He straightened his elaborate red jacket with gold trim that he had "borrowed" from Augustus's wardrobe and stepped forward to peer into Adaline's chambers.

And there she was.

Her voice was every bit as beautiful and elegant as her handwriting: effortless, yet full of unexpected flourishes. He breathed deeply as he watched her glide around the room, arranging this, moving that, somehow managing to make everything look so...wonderful.

Cyrus tried to tamp down the panic rising inside of him. It was the day of battle all over again, yet this time, he was the invader, fighting to break down the walls of Marcia's heart. It was now or never, he knew, and he placed his hand to the door as Marcia began to arrange the bedsheets unknowingly. This was his moment, and nothing could stop him now—

"King Cyrus!" came the call. Cyrus clenched his eyes shut, resting his forehead lightly on the door.

He turned toward the man who had spoken. It took Cyrus a moment, but he recognised the man as Captain Godric, and he appeared to be every bit as flustered as Cyrus himself felt. "You have to come quickly," the captain continued breathlessly. "There are riders approaching."

It was everything Cyrus could do not to sigh aloud. Couldn't he have just a moment of peace? A moment later, Marcia appeared in the doorway. "Is everything all right?" she asked, seemingly surprised to see Cyrus standing in the hallway.

"Everything is just perfect," said Cyrus flatly, forcing a painful smile. But his grip was still tight on the doorhandle, and Marcia looked at him curiously, as though she knew better than to believe him.

⚜ ⚜ ⚜

"What now?" asked Cyrus, sounding distinctly grumpy as he marched towards a vantage point upon the walls of the castle. He peered out. His arm might have been injured, but there was no problem with his eyesight.

"Auldhaven?" he mused at Thaddeus, who had joined him. Cyrus's eyes narrowed in confusion as the old man strained to observe green flags appearing in the distance, pulling out his spyglass to confirm Cyrus's suspicions.

"It certainly seems so," came his response. The spyglass dropped, and Cyrus noted the old man's expression of concern as Thaddeus turned to face him. "Soldiers," he began ominously. "No sign of Simeon, but Lambert is leading them. I suggest we summon the King's Guard and ride out to parley."

Simeon's absence was no surprise to Cyrus, but Lambert's presence was as unexpected as it was unsettling. Cyrus's body still ached from battle, and he rested his head in his free hand.

"The men are helping with repairs around the city," he said wearily. "I know Lambert. Fetch me a horse, and I will ride out to meet him."

He stopped to look at Thaddeus, whose eyes were raised with apprehension.

"These are times of peace," he said with a reassuring tone. "Come with me, Thaddeus, and together we will see that they continue."

⚜ ⚜ ⚜

The streets of Highcastle were busy and bustling as Cyrus passed through them. Though the city was scarred by war, Cyrus was surprised to find buildings already under reconstruction, with piles of debris cleared to allow passage through even the narrowest of alleyways. Men, women, and children worked tirelessly but with smiles on their faces, and Cyrus witnessed acts of selflessness all around: a woman bringing lunches out to some of the workers, a young boy helping an elderly man who looked as though he'd lost his walking stick to a resting spot, and other children helping to move the rubble, one stone at a time.

"Life goes on," said Thaddeus, smiling as his horse drew level. And he wasn't wrong. With every step, people cheered and waved at their king, and Cyrus felt like more of an imposter than ever before, looking down as the true heroes applauded him, as kings so often do.

"It seems so," he said with a nod. It occurred to him then that if so much hurt and damage could be repaired, then perhaps he would yet secure long-lasting peace with Auldhaven. This was his chance to give something back to his people, to make things right for all those who had supported him. He ushered his steed forward, and to his surprise, the horse did exactly as instructed. He was disciplined, responsive, boring.

Cyrus had never expected to miss Adagio and her stubborn nature, but as he trotted away from the city on the back of this anonymous horse, he began to feel the sting of her absence more than ever before. She had been there for so many of his adventures, and despite all they had been through, she had never willingly left his side. Adagio was not a creature of myth or legend but a reliable companion and the embodiment of all those who had helped him thus far. She was another of his story's unsung heroes, and it suddenly dawned on him how exposed he felt riding into danger without her, and how lonely it would feel to ride to his coronation on the back of some other nameless beast.

His thoughts had carried him beyond the city walls. Cyrus tugged on the reins, drawing to a halt no more than ten feet from Lambert and his men. For all that had changed, the general had lost none of his confidence, and Cyrus wondered if he wouldn't feel the same if accompanied by so many heavily armed men.

"You're too late," Cyrus said, silently calculating their number at around one hundred. "The war is over, and the Verderans are on their way home already. I suggest that you do the same."

At this, Lambert only laughed. "I'm afraid I can't do that," he said firmly. "I'm relieved to hear of your success in the recent battle, but there is business between us that remains as yet…unresolved."

"I've no hunger for war," said Cyrus wearily, though his hand was drawn to the pommel of his sword.

"Oh, there's no need for that," Lambert said, chuckling to himself before a young squire made to help him from his horse. "I come with news of Simeon," he continued. "How you react to it is your own prerogative. But perhaps you would care to dismount first. That would surely make our conversation more…comfortable."

Cyrus nodded at Thaddeus, and they both stepped down from their mounts. It was an unsettling situation in which to find himself, but he was keen to hide his unease in his actions. "Speak then," he said to Lambert, eager to maintain a peaceable demeanour. He had walked into too many traps of late, and in spite of the niceties, he remained vigilant as an army watched on.

"As you wish," said Lambert flatly. "Simeon was not a well man, as you know. His condition continued to worsen after your departure from Ravensward, and despite the efforts of our best physicians and their finest remedies, the king succumbed to his final battle three nights ago."

It was one thing to know that Simeon's death was coming, but the news itself hit like another of Rafael's punches, and Cyrus found himself at a sudden loss for words. After a few seconds, he couldn't help but forget the stately façade he had been trying to maintain and asked, "So he's dead?" Surely this was a moment for celebration, one that he had planned so many times and even dreamt of? Through a strange turn of events, it had been Cyrus's own hand that had killed Simeon, and yet he found no joy in this, only the sadness of another loss and the fear of what might follow.

"He passed peacefully within his chambers in the capital," Lambert continued, pausing to compose himself, his sombreness reflected on the face of every soldier of Auldhaven. "It was Simeon's lifelong dream to unify our two countries, and while he is no longer with us, I am here to see his final wish realised. The very ambition that he never stopped working toward, even during his final hours..."

"So, you *are* here to wage war," said Thaddeus, but his assertion was met only with a sad smile.

"Oh, quite the opposite," said the general. "I served my king for many years, in war and peace, in wealth and in poverty. No matter the circumstances, I knew that whatever Simeon decided, it was in the best interest of our people."

He paused to reach into his pocket, and Cyrus felt his nerve pushed to its very limit as he tried to predict the general's next move.

"I can't say that I agreed with every decision, but in this, I see the wisdom of a man who I had grown not only to respect, but to love. A man who spent his final days working tirelessly so that our country would not fall victim to years of warmongering and revolution. A king who grew to respect and perhaps even love his greatest enemy, seeing something of himself reflected there."

He finally drew his hand from his pocket, unrolling a piece of parchment, which he handed across to Thaddeus.

"This letter is the final will and testament of King Simeon the First, a decree that in the absence of a natural heir to the throne, Auldhaven must cede to Easthaven and its king, relinquishing all power over the land and its people. We are to be as one again."

There was a moment of deafening silence as the news fell upon them. Thaddeus's eyes were scanning over the parchment at a speed Cyrus would previously have thought impossible.

"He's right," said Thaddeus, looking up with wide eyes. "It's all here in writing. It means that you are—"

"King of Auldhaven," said Lambert, dropping to one knee. His men followed suit, dropping one after the other to join their general. "And I, for one, will be honoured to serve you, my king."

⚜ ⚜ ⚜

Thaddeus said that it would take a little time for things to sink in, but for all of the luxuries at Cyrus's disposal, time did not appear to be one of them. It continued rushing forward, and after little more than a week since the Battle of Highcastle—as it was now being called—Cyrus found his coronation day upon him.

"There! You look magnificent!" said the chamberlain, stepping back to admire his work. "Well, other than the face and the arm, but my wizardry lies in needlecraft, not magic itself!"

"It's...nice," said Cyrus, peering at himself in the mirror and fidgeting in the uncomfortable ensemble that had been chosen for him. He personally thought it was a bit too decorative, more Augustus's style than his own, but his mother had been the first to remind him the importance of perception, and so the white jacket and gold, fur-trimmed robe remained.

The chamberlain admired his work once more, and though the attention was more than a little flattering, Cyrus was pleased to be left with only Thaddeus for company. He rolled his left shoulder, and though the aching pain was still present, he found that it was improving with every day. A miraculous powder had been applied to mask the bruising under his eyes, but his face remained somewhat swollen, a reminder of the punishment he had suffered at the hands of King Rafael.

"What a week, eh?" Cyrus asked, reaching for a glass of wine to steady his nerves.

Thaddeus wandered over to clink glasses with Cyrus before taking a swig of his own. "I must admit it has been one of the more, shall we say, unexpected periods of my time in service, yet things have been anything but boring from the moment you arrived in the castle."

"I suppose you're right," Cyrus said with a wistful smile. His reflection was the perfect picture of relief and regret, these conflicting emotions melding as one in his features. "I still can't believe it, you know?" he added, turning away from the mirror. "I'm just a normal boy from the villages, or at least that's what I feel like in my own head. I would never have made it without your help. Well, yours, Seth's, Garrett's, Merrill's, Mathilde's, and everyone else's. I don't know how the storytellers will tell it, but I would have been dead a hundred times over if left to my own devices."

Thaddeus nodded, "The feeling of being an imposter…" he began, and Cyrus felt taken aback as he always did by the old man's ability to see right to the heart of his own inner struggles. "Your father felt the same way, even after growing up knowing he would be king someday, and I must say that it took me many years before I came to accept my own place and responsibility in the castle. I'll tell you something though…"

He placed his wine back on the table before stepping forward to turn Cyrus toward the mirror once more.

"Your grandfather, King Ailwin, once said that leadership is about entrusting people with great responsibility and then sitting back to watch them make you proud." He paused as tears welled in his eyes. "It's for you to decide how you measure yourself, young king, but you made Garrett and me proud from the very moment that we met you, always rising to every seemingly outlandish occasion that was set for you. And you know what? When you set the right example, don't be surprised if people choose to follow it."

Cyrus breathed deeply, tears stinging at his eyes, and for just a moment, he thought he could see Garrett standing next to Thaddeus in the mirror, that foolish grin that had always appeared when he knew he was right, a grin Cyrus had come to love and that he still missed every day.

"I'll do my best," said Cyrus, clearing his throat.

"It's all any man can do," said Thaddeus, and he stepped back to leave Cyrus alone with his reflection. No longer did a boy stare back at him, but a man. A king.

"It's time!" said Adaline, and Cyrus turned to see his mother sweeping into the room. The queen was often described as a timeless beauty, but it never ceased to amaze Cyrus that Adaline appeared somehow more elegant with each passing day. Her face bore maturity and dignity, her long hair braided into a golden crown as it had been during their very first meeting.

"Well, we *were* running right on schedule," added Seth, who hobbled into the doorway on a set of walking sticks. "We're actually late now, but you have your sister to thank for that."

"Oi!" said Fran as she came into view, and Cyrus hardly recognised his sister among the extravagant fur, silk, and lace of the blue dress she was wearing. She looked, Cyrus realised, like a young woman, a young princess. The girl from Corhollow was no more, he thought for a moment, but then he found her there, in the stubborn set of Fran's jaw.

"I don't know what has gotten into you," Seth continued, "but that's the fourth dress I've seen you in today."

Fran scowled. "It's an occasion."

"Oh, so it has nothing to do with the boy you saw downstairs then?" asked Seth, flashing a smile in Cyrus's direction.

"*Official business*, perhaps?" he asked Fran knowingly, his eyebrows raised. But Fran only shook her head before turning away. "Oh, I can't wait to hear all about this," Cyrus continued, and he followed his mother as she led them away from his chambers, down through the castle, and into the courtyard below.

⚜ ⚜ ⚜

The sun sat high in the sky as Cyrus emerged to meet his royal entourage, at the forefront of which stood two proud generals. Two men of war, their differences set aside in pursuit of a brighter future.

"Broderick, Lambert," said Cyrus, inclining his head. The two men bowed, and then wide smiles appeared on their faces as they parted to showcase their men, rows of soldiers neither in red nor green but striking uniforms trimmed with white, the identity of a new nation, and with it, new dreams.

"Your moment awaits," said Adaline from behind him, her face beaming with a look of pride that Cyrus hadn't known he needed until that moment. To say that he was nervous was the understatement of a lifetime, but with these people at his side, Cyrus knew he was finally ready.

"There's just one more thing, though," said Lambert, stepping forward to announce himself.

Cyrus wondered if he might yet wake from the dream, if he might see all of this fall down around him, only to wake up in Mistcliff, another boy from a burnt village, broken and alone but for his sister.

Lambert continued, "It is one thing to have the finest tailor or the finest smith," he said, pointing at the ceremonial blade at Cyrus's side, "but a great king—a *truly* great king—deserves the very finest horse. I only hope that she will see you to even greater fortune in the years to come."

Lambert raised his sword, and the soldiers fell away to reveal a magnificent brown mare waiting at the castle gates. She was lean, muscular, and her hooves stamped with impatience. Adagio.

"Some of the men found her in Dalhart Forest," Lambert explained. "I would have recognised her anywhere, and I thought you might be missing her, my king."

Cyrus beamed at Lambert in thanks, and it was all that he could do to contain a sob of relief as he rushed to greet his companion. "Come on, old girl," he said, nuzzling into her mane as Adagio whinnied at their reunion. "It's good to see you, but it's time for us to collect our crown."

⚜ ⚜ ⚜

"All rise for Cyrus, the first King of Peacehaven!" called a voice, and two daunting yet familiar wooden doors swung open to reveal the Grand Hall of Eldred's Keep. He had known his friends and family would be here; after all, they'd been part of his escort as he had passed the lines of crowds along the King's Road on

Adagio's back. They had sat and watched him accept his crown in the basilica. But to have everyone he held dear in one place—*this* was the moment Cyrus had been waiting for.

At the coronation feast, the long tables were configured in their customary horseshoe design, but there was no division among them. Lambert and Broderick stood with arms at each other's shoulders while their captains clapped in celebration. Mathilde and Lucien exchanged a look of silent approval, a conversation without words that exists only in the truest of friendships. Next to them, Thaddeus simply nodded as though things had played out exactly as he had anticipated. They hadn't, of course, but the old man looked contented all the same.

And at the centre of the horseshoe, the middle of it all, was an empty spot just waiting for Cyrus, who stood by the door drinking in the scene before him, his crown glittering atop his blonde head.

It all felt like a wonderful and frightening dream: people from his past, present, and future assembled in a room of celebration and hope. In every gap, he saw the faces of those he had lost—family, friends, and allies—absent, yet no less a part of the moment.

"Will you sit down? Some of us are dying of thirst here!" came Roscoe's voice, but the man before Cyrus was so neat, tidy, and well-dressed in a pristine white shirt and a fitted black tunic that Cyrus could scarcely believe his eyes. The pirate had been transformed into a gentleman. At his side stood a boy, his outfit identical to Roscoe's, and though his face was unmistakable, Cyrus couldn't help but smile at the handsome young man that Patch was becoming. The boy's expression was relaxed, maybe even happy, and his hair held the early promise of fashionable curls.

Cyrus scrunched his face at Roscoe in response before making his way to the top table, where his mother and sister were waiting. Lively music broke through the applause, and Cyrus breathed a deep sigh of relief as he fell into the ornate chair that had been waiting for his arrival.

"Please be seated," he called over the hubbub, and as if by magic, an army of serving staff descended upon them, carrying with them a banquet that was unquestionably fit for a king.

⚜ ⚜ ⚜

"Delicious, wasn't it?" Cyrus reclined in his chair and rested both hands on his newly inflated stomach.

"Hmm," said Fran stoically, though this in itself was more than Cyrus had expected. The food *had* been delicious, but Fran's plate had hardly been touched, and she had been uncharacteristically distant through not only the feast but the entire day.

"He's right, you know?" said Cyrus, snatching a slice of ham from his sister's plate. When Fran looked at him quizzically, Cyrus continued, "Seth. He said you were acting funny, and I see it now. What's wrong?"

"It's nothing," said Fran, eyes rolling at her brother's interrogation. There clearly was something, though, and Cyrus frowned as Fran pulled a small mirror from her pocket, the mirror of Amabel that he had purchased for her in Casarossa. "Just leave it," she said adjusting an assortment of clips in the elaborate curls of her hair. She never gave Cyrus the slightest hint of eye contact, but the pink tinge to her cheeks brought to mind Seth's teasing prior to the coronation. After all of the ridicule she had given him over his feelings about Marcia, Cyrus thought this could be his opportunity to even yet another score.

"It's a boy, isn't it?" he said, and he nudged his sister as he followed her line of sight in the direction of Roscoe. "Isn't Roscoe a little old for you?" he joked, but when he glanced back at Fran and then back toward the pirate, he realised another—thankfully much younger—face was staring back in their direction. "Patch?" he asked with a light laugh. "Well, why didn't you just say? He's not the most talkative, but come on, I'll introduce you!"

Fran tried to escape his clutches, but Cyrus had her hand held tight, and it was clear that she was in no mind to make a scene.

"Roscoe," he called, approaching the pirate's place at the table. "So glad you could make it. Fran, this is Roscoe, and this here is Patch."

"It is good to see you again, King Cyrus," the young boy stuttered, his words rough at the edges but formal beyond Cyrus's expectations. "And you, Princess Francine. It is my pleasure."

Silence.

"Well say, hello," urged Cyrus, looking down at his sister with a nonplussed expression. But after hours of staring in Patch's direction, it seemed that Fran's interests were suddenly drawn toward the walls and doors of the Grand Hall as though she had been instructed to study them, her gaze avoiding Patch as one might avoid staring into the sun.

"I'm sorry, it seems that someone has turned a little shy," said Cyrus sensing that he was pushing his luck. If he wasn't careful, Fran would be sure to stamp on his foot soon enough, he knew. "But,

Roscoe, I heard what happened in Kingsport. It seems you gave the Verderans quite the surprise!"

Cyrus grimaced as Fran squeezed his hand as hard as she could without making it too obvious.

Roscoe laughed. "You're not wrong there. I thought about what you said in Auldhaven, and I wanted to make things right." He turned and smiled at Patch, who watched on in admiration. "Now, I don't know about destroying cities, but good old-fashioned fire will do more than enough damage to a fleet of warships. By the time they'd realised, my men were already within the city walls, and there are few that remain brave in the face of a pirate army…it certainly scares the life out of me!"

"You never cease to amaze me," said Cyrus shaking his head.

"I suspect Alonso feels the same about you," Roscoe continued. "No doubt they were looking forward to the comfort of those ships when you booted them out of Highcastle." He paused and raised a palm as he glugged from a tankard of ale. "As it is, they'll be marching the long way back to Casarossa. Let's hope their cobblers are as good as their carpenters!"

Laughter broke out among them, and it seemed that even Fran was not immune to Roscoe's indescribable charm.

"You know, I've been thinking," said Cyrus, purposefully changing his tone to a serious one. "How do you reward a man who already has all the money, ships, and good men he could ask for?" He stopped to nudge Patch playfully, the boy responding with a smile and a reverent bow. "I mean, what is the one thing an old seadog like you might want after all these years on the water? What treasure is it that you've truly been searching for all along? It surely is a puzzle…."

Cyrus clicked his tongue as the music swelled, and people began to sing and dance around them. He stroked his chin, creating the impression that he was truly puzzling over his own question. Then he raised his index finger, as though struck by an idea. "But then I remembered our conversation in Mirramar," he continued, "that day on the beach. I thought to myself, what this man needs, what he really needs is a—"

"Home," finished Roscoe soberly, and Cyrus smiled at the silent appreciation on his friend's face. To think that he had mistaken Roscoe for a devious vagabond. This good man who had struggled for so long, warring with his own nature as he tried to forge a better life. Here he stood, a man ready to lay roots, a man deserving of yet another second chance.

"Exactly," Cyrus agreed. "So, stay. Make Kingsport your home. The recent attack has shown it to be a vulnerability, but with a strong magistrate in the city, a man who knows the waters...well, there are few who could remain brave in the face of a pirate army!" He released Fran's hand to raise a tankard in Roscoe's direction. "What do you say? Help me control the waters. Help me move goods to our brothers and sisters to the west. Help me trade with our neighbours. If nothing else, it's an honest day's work," he finished with a smile.

"I'd say that sounds like a fine offer," said Roscoe, and their tankards clashed together as celebration continued all around them, their deal sealed with a drink.

"You're such a hypocrite," said Fran, a reluctant smile on her face as they returned to their seats at the top table.

"And you're a sore loser," Cyrus responded bravely.

Fran sat back and fixed him with a stare. "Do you know why I admire you?" she asked, and if it wasn't already clear to Cyrus, he now knew that the joke was over. "You've always seemed fearless, full of adventure. You see something that you want, and you make it happen." She placed her hand on top of his, and his eyes were drawn to the bracelet she had made him a lifetime ago, which still sat in its place of honour on his wrist. "You've made me want to travel the world and have adventures of my own. You've given me hopes and dreams, you've given Roscoe a home, but what is it that you want, King Cyrus?"

At this, Cyrus hesitated, and like so many times before, he wondered when his little sister had become so intuitive. "I don't know what you mean," he said, taking a swift drink, but it was his turn to avoid eye contact, and Fran was a long way from letting him off the hook.

"Do I need to drag you over there?" she asked, and Cyrus followed his sister's gaze to find Marcia pouring wine into Merrill's empty glass. Her hair was shining in the half-light of the early evening, and her smile was bright enough to light up even the grandest room.

"It's not that easy, Fran," said Cyrus, preparing his excuses. "I'm not brave, fearless, or any of those things."

"Maybe not," came Fran's answer, "but guess what? There's no time like the present. Now, I'll ask you again: do you need me to drag you over there?"

And just like that she'd managed to win again. "*Official business*?" he asked with a wry smile.

"*Official business.*"

Cyrus reached across and kissed his sister's hand. "I don't deserve you," he said, and he sprang from his seat to follow Marcia, the hem of her gown flowing along the floor behind her as she made her way to the cellars, presumably in pursuit of more wine.

"Marcia," he called, his voice echoing in the corridor. She seemed surprised to see him at first, but then a shy smile crept across her face.

"It's 'King Cyrus' these days, isn't it?" she asked in jest.

Cyrus gave a silent nod, knowing she was poking fun at him for how busy he had been since the battle and how little they had been able to speak. "I'm sorry," he said. "Things have been so busy of late. Here, let me help you…"

Marcia was clearly struggling to balance several empty wine carafes in her arms, and by the time he'd relieved her, only a matter of inches remained between them. He was pleasantly startled to find her green eyes upon him like two precious emeralds.

"I tried to come and see you," he said to a backdrop of subtle clinking, the carafes shaking ever so slightly in his nervous grasp. "I've been meaning to speak to you. There's something I need to tell you, something I've been trying to tell you for some time now."

Marcia laughed before her face settled in a thoughtful frown. "Well, I really should fill the wine, but I guess that can wait, if the king so orders it." Her smile broadened, and it occurred to Cyrus that she might just be enjoying every moment of his discomfiture. "So, here we are," she said. "Just the two of us. What was it that you wanted to say?"

So, he really was going to have to do it. This was it, at last.

"I just..." he began optimistically, hoping the words would find their own way out. "I just wanted to say that..." He was already beginning to hate himself for failing at such a simple task. Why hadn't he planned this better? He'd had all of this time. Why hadn't he thought of something clever or romantic to say?

"What I wanted to say is...." A final pause as he braced himself to say a small phrase that felt every bit as consequential as every grand speech he'd ever given.

"I just wanted to tell you that...I love you."

He let out an embarrassingly loud sigh of relief after the words came out. In the end, it hadn't been so difficult.

But if he had hoped for Marcia to fall into his arms, he had been sorely mistaken. Her laughter echoed through the corridors, and the only consolation was that there was no one else nearby to overhear.

"No, you don't, you big idiot," she joked as Cyrus's skin was already turning a hot shade of pink. "Not yet anyway," she added with a wink, "but give it time, and you just might..."

And with that, her lips met his. His eyes closed, and his arms fell completely limp, sending the carafes crashing to the floor all around them. Cyrus was someone who had entranced village crowds with his stories, who had led clamouring soldiers to victory, who had been crowned a king of two nations, and even still, this was, without a doubt, the most wonderful feeling he'd encountered thus far. Perhaps for the first time in his life, he was exactly who, and where, he had always wanted to be.

It smelled like blood.

It sounded like suffering.

It looked like death.

"He's going to die, isn't he?" Locke asked with a tremble in his voice. He winced and turned away as the surgeon replaced the bandages around his father's face. This was one of the most illustrious banquet halls in Eldred's Keep, a space normally reserved for parties and occasions; the battle of Highcastle was over, but there was no sign of celebration here.

He turned back as the surgeon gave a subtle shake of his head.

"He'll live," said Captain Godric, scratching at his bearded chin. "He's going to lose that left eye, and I doubt he'll be winning a footrace anytime soon, but your father is made of tough stuff. He'll live."

"See, I told you." Locke's eyes shifted to find his brother, Ralph, with an optimistic smile on his face. Ralph was three years

Locke's senior and looking more like their father with every day. His long, dark hair contrasted with the lighter features that Locke shared with their mother, and Locke was increasingly envious of the broad, muscular physique which hinted at his brother's approach toward manhood.

Their mother stepped forward to place a hand on Locke's shoulder, and maybe for a moment, it seemed that everything was going to be all right.

An agonizing scream soon shattered the illusion. Locke glanced beyond his mother to see rows of injured warriors lining the floors, surgeons hurrying among them.

"Try not to stare, darling," said his mother, squeezing his shoulder gently. He wanted to turn away but found his attention fixed on another of the wounded, a young man whose arm was severed at the wrist. The surgeon kneeled to pour ale into his trembling lips, and a sheen of sweat formed on the man's brow as work began to cauterize the wound. Another scream, and Locke snatched back to where his mother and brother were huddled over his father's cot bed.

"He's a hero, you know," Godric continued. "It should have been me, but your father took my place and led our armies back into the city before rounding on the Verderans. Captain Ramsey fought alongside General Broderick in battle and was struck down following direct orders from the king."

Locke's eyes widened. "King Cyrus himself?"

"The very same," said Godric with a smile. "Our forces were in retreat before the Cornessians arrived. Your father was charged with securing the west of the city, but his ferocity tore through the Verderan lines and forced them back beyond the city walls."

Ralph's hands balled into fists. "You hear that, Locke? Father was a hero. He's survived this far, and he'll be back on his feet in no time."

Locke grimaced as the surgeon wound fresh bandages around a gash in their father's thigh. "He'll need that positivity," said Godric with a sigh. "I've known Captain Ramsey for many years, and it'll take more than a few scrapes to keep him down."

"You can't possibly think that he'll return to the army?" Locke's mother asked in desperation.

Godric shrugged, before scratching the top of his bald head. "You know Ramsey better than anyone, Cecilia. Do you think he'll be able to just walk away? We both know that his soldiering days are over, but not all battles are fought with swords, remember that."

"What does he mean?" asked Locke, looking at his mother.

It was Godric who answered. "I mean that your father has suffered some terrible wounds. The scars will heal, and he will learn to adjust, but everything changed that day on the battlefield. Captain Ramsey is a proud man and a brave warrior, but we live in a time of peace once more, and your father is going to need to find some peace of his own, along with some purpose."

Locke forced back tears as his mother nodded sadly. An eruption of applause sounded down the hallway, and the surgeon startled briefly before returning to his work.

"The King's coronation party," said Godric, forcing a half-smile. "I know that King Cyrus would like to be down here with his troops, but today is a very important day for—"

"Pfft," scoffed Ralph, and the captain silenced abruptly. "Lucky him to have the choice." Locke's brother sneered. "No doubt he'll be laughing, drinking, and accepting laurels while the real heroes are down here dying. It's a joke!"

A momentary silence settled among them, and Locke's eyes widened at his brother's unexpected outburst.

"Careful, boy," said Godric with newfound firmness. "Your father was a warrior, and he knew the risks. Remember that he chose to fight for the very same king that you are now questioning." He paused to raise an eyebrow, his glare still fixed on Ralph. "Your father was a hero, but his actions will not save you if you choose to continue this treasonous scorn."

Locke swallowed hard as a timely arm appeared at Ralph's shoulder. "Just a silly misunderstanding," Locke's mother intervened. She stepped forward to wrap a hand around Godric's forearm. "He's just a boy, Godric, and emotions are running high, what with his father's injuries. You have a family, don't you?" She turned toward her eldest son with a menacing look on her face. "Ralph, apologise to the captain."

Locke held his breath as Ralph stepped forward to deliver his apology.

"Long forgotten," Godric answered flatly before Ralph could say a word.

Locke's mother let out a sigh of relief, and Ralph returned to his father's side wordlessly.

"Everything's going to be all right, isn't it?" asked Locke.

His mother smiled. "Come on, let's leave your father to rest."

Through it all, the captain never stirred. Locke didn't know what to think, but he sensed that everything was about to change.

Acknowledgements

If *The Look of a King* was the achievement of a lifelong ambition, then *No Place for Peace* is beyond my wildest dreams. It was an absolute pleasure to return to the Quadripartite and follow this colourful cast of characters on their journey. Writing has become a part of my life, but this book would not have been possible without the following:

Linda and Greg Dumbrell – for entertaining my new hobby, taking every opportunity to promote my work, and for giving *The Look of a King* a read.

Steve Cooling-Smith at Chilligraphics – for being the most patient man alive! The cover of *The Look of a King* set a high standard, and Steve worked tirelessly to ensure that *No Place for Peace* was every bit as striking. It may have taken a hundred different versions (perhaps more!), but it was all worth it in the end. You can find Steve at www.chilligraphics.com.

Breana Dumbrell at Bee, Your Editor – for patiently enduring months of talk about both books. For helping me establish a social media presence, and for an incredible editing job on *No Place for Peace*. You can find Breana at www.beeyoureditor.wordpress.com.

Finally, thank you to everyone who has read this book and *The Look of a King* before it. Special acknowledgement for the Bookstagram community, which has provided an invaluable source of support. Your messages, posts, and stories mean the world – keep it to yourself if you didn't enjoy this one though…

About the Author

Tom was born in 1987 in Chelmsford, Essex. As a boy, he fell in love with the fantasy worlds of video games and those written by the likes of J.R.R Tolkien and Philip Pullman.

Despite an early passion for storytelling, Tom obtained a BA in Tourism Management before a varied career in the travel industry, bringing to life another of his passions. When he is not working, Tom is an avid fan of his beloved Ipswich Town. He also writes and performs music and enjoys long walks with his wife and dogs.

Tom currently lives near Colchester, Essex, and *No Place for Peace* is the sequel to his debut novel *The Look of a King*. Both books were written during the coronavirus pandemic with huge influence and editing support from his wife, Breana.

Contact Tom: tomdumbrell@aol.com
Instagram: @tom_dumbrell

Suggested Reading
Joe Abercrombie – *Shattered Sea* & *First Law* Trilogies
Chris Wooding – *Tales of the Ketty Jay*
Scott Lynch – *The Gentleman Bastard Sequence*
V.E. Schwab – *The Invisible Life of Addie LaRue*

Printed in Great Britain
by Amazon

24021566R10180